'In what way [...]
Lord Aldwor [...]
requirements [...]

'The tendency to [...]
said Lady Chilha [...]
never persuade him—or Lady Aldworth—that
you were even a suitable candidate.'

'Could we not, indeed?' said Serafina, her eyes
glittering. 'I would wager, ma'am, that I could
play the role of the pretty doll Lord Aldworth
seems to require as well as anyone. Indeed, I
might even enjoy it!'

Dear Reader

As our gardens show signs of life, so we have the green shoots of excellent reading for you. Sylvia Andrew has another marvellous Regency heroine in SERAFINA, and Laura Cassidy explores the tribulations of civil war in A REMEMBERED LOVE. Laurel Ames gives us Bristol 1818 in CASTAWAY, an unusual setting for a Regency, and in THE NAKED HUNTRESS, by Shirley Parenteau, Lyris is blackmailed into marriage. Enjoy!

The Editor

Sylvia Andrew taught modern languages for years, ending up as vice-principal of a sixth-form college. She lives in Somerset with two cats, a dog, and a husband who has a very necessary sense of humour, and a stern approach to punctuation. Sylvia has one daughter living in London, and they share a lively interest in the theatre. She describes herself as an 'unrepentant romantic'.

Recent titles by the same author:

ELEANOR
SERENA
A DARLING AMAZON
PERDITA

SERAFINA

Sylvia Andrew

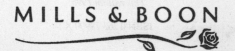

MILLS & BOON

MILLS & BOON LIMITED
ETON HOUSE, 18–24 PARADISE ROAD
RICHMOND, SURREY, TW9 1SR

MILLS & BOON, the Rose Device and LEGACY OF LOVE are trademarks of the publisher.

*First published in Great Britain 1994
by Mills & Boon Limited*

© Sylvia Andrew 1994

*Australian copyright 1994   Philippine copyright 1995
This edition 1995*

ISBN 0 263 78990 X

*Set in 10 on 12 pt Linotron Times
04-9502-82801*

*Typeset in Great Britain by Centracet, Cambridge
Printed in Great Britain by
BPC Paperbacks Ltd*

CHAPTER ONE

It HAD been a lovely afternoon. Even though summer
was quite definitely over the sun was dazzling as it shone
through the leaves of the oak tree, and Mr Hartley
Pennyworth was forced to shade his eyes when he
looked up. As he peered through the foliage he had a
tantalising glimpse of a figure perched on a branch some
way up. Its legs were stretched out along the branch,
and it was leaning comfortably against the trunk of the
tree. Hartley drew nearer. Now he could see that the
figure held a half-eaten apple in one hand and a book in
the other.

'Miss Feverel!'

The figure gave a sigh, leaned over to look down and
said, 'Gracious, it's you, Hartley! Who told you I was
here?'

'Rafe.'

Miss Feverel's frown boded ill for her youngest
brother, but Mr Pennyworth was not to be deterred.
'Miss Feverel, I have come to ask you to marry me!'

'Oh, Hartley, I thought we had settled all this! You
know I don't wish to marry you, and I am sure you
would regret it if I did. Has your mother been at you
again? It's too bad of her.'

Mr Pennyworth ignored this. He had come, in his
mother's words, to 'act like a man', to storm the citadel
and to return to Pennyworth Lodge affianced to Serafina

Feverel, and, since he was a man of few but fixed ideas, nothing was going to put him off.

'Miss Feverel——'

'And I do wish that you would not keep calling me Miss Feverel in that idiotic way. We have known each other forever, and until this summer you have always called me Serafina. Why have you suddenly decided to change?'

'Because we are no longer children,' said Mr Pennyworth in throbbing accents. 'I am a man with a man's needs, Miss Feverel, and I love you.' His tone changed and he said somewhat peevishly, 'I wish you would come down, Serafina. It is very awkward proposing to you when I can hardly see you.'

'But I don't want you to propose! I thought I had made that more than clear. Oh, very well, I suppose I'll have to come down. My afternoon's reading is quite spoiled anyway.'

Serafina threw her apple away, put her book in the capacious pocket of her old-fashioned jacket, shook herself and started to climb down. As she did so one of her boots slipped off and it fell, narrowly missing Mr Pennyworth. A man with a greater sense of humour might have been amused at the contrast between Serafina's slender, white-stockinged ankle and delicately arched foot and the heavy boot, obviously not meant for a lady. But Mr Pennyworth was devoid of a sense of humour, and, what was more, he was a man in love. He caught the foot as she descended and kissed it.

'Oh, Miss Feverel,' he cried. 'My life will be in ruins if you will not say you'll be mine.'

'Your life will more likely be ruined if I do say so. Stop talking like a Gothic romance, Hartley, and let go of my foot. I need it to stand on,' she said coldly, wrenching it away from him and jumping lightly to the ground. 'And if you do such a ridiculous thing again I shall complain to your mama.'

'She would understand. Mother knows how much I adore you. In fact it was she who told me to make my feelings plainer, and she is usually right.' He looked sorrowfully at Serafina's frowning face. 'But I think I have only made you angry.'

Serafina sighed and said, 'I am sorry to cause you pain, Hartley. But we really shouldn't suit, you know. You are too. . .too worthy a man for a harum-scarum like me. Besides, I like reading and discussion, and things like that, and you do not. You always become quite agitated when I argue with you and frequently end up in a sulk. And you don't like it when I laugh at you, either. How on earth should we get on if we were married?'

'Mother says that things would be different then. As my wife, you would naturally defer to me.'

'I see. Well, since I am most unlikely to change my ways for any husband, whatever your mama says, you must abandon the thought of marrying me and try someone else. What about Lizzie Beaminster? She would suit you so much better, and I know for a fact that she admires you.'

'She does?' Hartley was so little used to admiration from anyone but his mother that he was obviously impressed by this piece of information. Then his face clouded over and he said heavily, 'But it is you I love! I cannot sleep for thinking of you. I cannot eat for thinking of you. Mother says I am wasting away. No one else could possibly make me happy!'

'What rubbish!' said Serafina briskly, eyeing Mr Pennyworth's well-fed figure. 'Really, I haven't time or patience for any more of this nonsense—it must stop! You have been cozening your mother most shamefully, Hartley, just as you did when you were a little boy and sulked until she gave you what you wanted. Remember the fuss you made over a parrot you saw in Brighton? And then you gave it away again, not a year later. Well, I am not a parrot, and this is something that your mama cannot arrange for you. Indeed, I am surprised that she wishes to! I have no fortune, and the Feverel estate will go to Gabriel.'

'That's what she said—that we can afford to overlook your lack of dowry where others might not, and that you ought to be delighted to accept such a handsome offer. And she said that, if you didn't, she feared you would end up an over-educated old maid——' Here Mr Pennyworth, realising that this last sentence was hardly likely to advance his cause, stopped short.

'How very kind of her,' said Serafina with a glitter in her eye, 'to have such concern for my future! Do, pray, thank your mama for her solicitude.'

Mr Pennyworth looked doubtful. 'Er. . .what do you wish me to say to her, Serafina?'

'That I. . .will. . .not. . .marry. . .you. Not now. Not ever. In any circumstances! Nor do I wish to see you again before you have recovered your senses. Goodbye, Hartley.'

Mr Pennyworth flushed unbecomingly and turned away. He stopped after a few yards, however, and said, 'You're too clever for your own good, Serafina Feverel! Don't think I shall ask you again, for I shan't. My eyes are open at last. My mother was right—who wants an

opinionated bluestocking for a wife?' With this parting
shot he disappeared. Serafina watched him go without
regret. Mrs Pennyworth would doubtless be relieved to
hear that Hartley had finally given up—if indeed he had.
As a doting mother, who had never denied her son
anything in his life, Mrs Pennyworth had encouraged
him in his plans only because his heart had seemed set
on marriage to Serafina. But she would now work hard to
help him to forget. Serafina cordially wished her rapid
and complete success, and turned towards the house.

Halfway up the drive she was met by a girl accompanied by a little boy. 'Ah, Rafe! I have a bone to pick
with you. . .'

'No, honestly, Sally, I didn't mean to tell him! It
slipped out before I could stop it.'

'Are you going to marry Hartley Pennyworth?' asked
the girl.

'What do you think, Angy?'

'She's not such a clunch!' Rafe exclaimed scornfully.

'No more I am, Rafe, but if you wish to please me
you'll try for once to keep it to yourself. Gentlemen
don't like gossip about unsuccessful offers. Understand,
both of you? Promise?' Rafe solemnly drew his finger
across his throat, and Angelica, as befitted a young lady
of fifteen summers, nodded sedately. They set off again.

'Where's Michael?' Serafina asked.

'He's gone with Colonel Smithers to see the militia
exercising. Sally, where's your other boot?' asked
Angelica. They all looked down, and Serafina stared at
her feet—one in a boot and one in a white stocking—
and started to laugh. 'It's under the tree. I dropped it.
Oh, my goodness, look at my stocking!'

'I'll fetch it for you!' Rafe ran back to where the forgotten boot lay.

'Mama will scold and Hetty will complain about the holes in this stocking,' mourned Serafina as she put the boot on again.

'Mama will say that you shouldn't use Michael's old boots at all,' said Angelica. 'They're too big, and you will never learn to walk as a lady should while you continue to wear them.'

'But they're much more use for walking on rough ground and climbing trees and fences! Ladies' thin slippers are useless.'

'Ladies don't climb trees and fences, either,' said Angelica primly. 'I'm afraid Mama is quite right, Sally. You are a hoyden.'

Rafe was quick to defend his beloved elder sister. 'You're just saying that because she's better than you at climbing trees. And at riding. In fact, she's better than you at anything!'

'She is not! She's older, that's all!'

'She is so, she is so!' crowed Rafe, happy to have roused Angelica into losing a little of her dignity.

The quarrel went on until they reached the house. Serafina ignored it—she was used to these spats between her brothers and sister and they didn't mean anything. Later today, or tomorrow, or whenever it pleased them, Angelica and Rafe were quite likely to join forces against Michael or herself. Basically the family was a happy one, though, since they had all been brought up to have minds of their own, it was never dull.

Lucius Feverel, Serafina's father, was a genius. He was not only a noted scholar, he also had that rarest of

gifts—the ability to convey his own interests and enthu-
siasms to his children. Except for Gabriel, the eldest
boy, who was now up at Oxford, he taught them for the
most part himself. Mornings were devoted to formal
lessons, but his true genius revealed itself in the children's regular afternoon walk. Then the natural history,
geography or mathematics they learned in the schoolroom came to life while they splashed about in the
stream which meandered along the boundary of their
estate, roamed the woods and fields round their home,
or calculated the numbers of ears of corn in Mr Halkyn's
Five Acre field.

Among their neighbours the Feverels were regarded
as eccentric, for Lucius did not behave as other fathers
behaved. He seldom scolded or punished his family, and
he treated his daughters exactly the same as his sons,
setting them the same high standards. At twelve
Serafina had been able to read Latin and Greek with
ease. At fifteen, after the widow of a French emigré had
stayed with them for a year, she was fluent in French.
Now she had a good working knowledge of most other
European languages, too. She had been trained in the
more advanced principles of mathematics and logic, and
since Gabriel's departure to Oxford she had been the
object of her father's particular attention. He often read
out to Serafina the letters and articles he sent regularly
to various learned journals, and was disappointed if she
was not prepared to comment on them. Mr Feverel was
proud of all his children, but Serafina, the eldest, was
his special pride and joy.

Few of the neighbours, it was true, could boast that
their own offspring were as handsome as the Feverel
family. But to the outside world the five Feverel chil-

dren were an undisciplined, noisy gang—girls as well as boys. They roamed the countryside looking like blond gypsies, and on the few occasions when visitors called the children had little, if any, notion of how to behave in company. The ladies of the neighbourhood were shocked that neither of the Feverel girls had had a single lesson in deportment or dancing in her life, and they particularly deplored Serafina's lack of interest in her clothes and appearance. The gentlemen, though impressed with her beauty, quickly came to resent her readiness to give an opinion on matters which they did not consider to be suitable for a lady, and, even more, they resented her ability to express herself with clarity and logic. It had to be said, and the neighbours said it often, that Serafina, or Sally as her family called her, was an opinionated hoyden—gifted, well-read and exasperatingly lovely, but a hoyden none the less. Poor Mrs Feverel.

Mrs Feverel was a talented artist, but she was an invalid, often confined by a debilitating disease to her sofa or her bed. Her family, including her husband, all adored her. The only time the children ever saw Mr Feverel angry was when his wife had been upset, whatever the reason. They spent much of their leisure devising ways of amusing her, and the weekly playlet in which they entertained her with village news in dramatic form was the highlight of Saturday evenings. They sought small gifts for her to paint, too—a lilac-grey dove's feather from Rafe, an interesting bunch of roadside flowers from Angelica, shells, berries or leaves from Michael and Serafina. She received them all with loving gratitude.

It was not easy to keep some kind of order in this

strange household, but Mrs Feverel had decided long ago that the best discipline she could exercise was one of love. Of course she worried about them. Gabriel, the eldest boy, was very young to be on his own at Oxford, though he was doing well there. And the girls—they should be presented soon. Indeed, Serafina was already more than old enough. But Mrs Feverel shuddered to think what would happen if her daughters were launched on an unsuspecting world without a great deal of expensive preparation. And then careers for Michael and Rafe would soon have to be considered. Yes, Mr Feverel would have been astonished if he had known how much Mrs Feverel worried. He himself had a mind above economic cares.

Mrs Feverel sighed now as her elder daughter came into her room. Serafina had changed out of her shabby skirt and disreputable jacket, but she was without shoes, and one of her stockings looked decidedly the worse for wear. She looked guilty.

'What is it, Serafina?'

'I'm afraid I have spoilt my stocking, Mama.'

'The second pair this week, my daughter. How did you do it this time?'

'It really wasn't my fault! At least, I suppose it was, because I did forget my—er—shoe——'

'One of Michael's boots?'

'Well, yes. And it came off. But I would have remembered it except for the fact that I was so annoyed with Hartley Pennyworth. He found me up the oak tree, and I had to listen to a proposal from him yet again. I think I may have finally disillusioned him today. But why does he persist so, Mama?'

'He thinks himself in love with you.'

'In love! How ridiculous!'

'Hartley may not be your ideal, Serafina, but he is not ridiculous. Love is very painful, not funny at all.'

'But Mama, he has no reason to believe himself in love with me!'

Mrs Feverel laughed. 'Reason has little to do with it, child!'

'I suppose you are right.' Serafina shook her head. 'It is odd that people can suffer from such an irrational emotion. It makes life very hard for them, and I am sure it is better avoided. However much in love with me Hartley might have been, Mama, he must have known that it would be madness to *marry* me! I have no fortune, we haven't a single interest in common, and I'm not at all the amenable sort of girl he needs.'

'Perhaps he has seen that now—just like all the other young men of the neighbourhood. Perhaps you are too nice in your requirements for a husband, Serafina. Or do you intend never to marry at all?'

'Oh, I should like to marry—a man with understanding, perhaps. Someone like Papa, I suppose. An intelligent man who. . .who doesn't moon over me, but is prepared to listen to what I have to say, and treat it seriously. Someone who would share my interests and is prepared to treat me as a human being, not a cross between a mindless doll and some sort of goddess. But I would certainly not dream of marrying for anything so irrational as love! Literature is full of the most dire examples of what happens when you allow your heart to rule your head.'

Mrs Feverel looked curiously at her daughter. 'And your heart has never ruled your head?'

Serafina considered this seriously. 'I don't think so. . . Certainly nothing to cause me to behave as stupidly as Hartley. I'm not sure it ever will.' She smiled suddenly and added, 'But I love you, Mama. I might do foolish things for you.'

'I'd like you to do sensible ones, Serafina. Such as wearing your own shoes, and remembering to keep them on!'

'Well, then, I will!'

When she considered Serafina's cool assessment of her future, Mrs Feverel was inclined to believe that such a marriage would work for her. Serafina was a level-headed, intelligent girl. Her real interest had always been in matters of the head, not the heart, and an undemanding relationship with a man she respected would suit her very well. If she ever married at all. Mrs Feverel sighed. Unless she was introduced to Society quite soon, Serafina would miss her chance altogether.

A short while before, in an effort to solve this problem, Mrs Feverel had invited Serafina's godmother, who was now a childless widow, for a visit. Lady Chilham had admired Serafina's looks, and had been very impressed with the girl's devotion to her mother. The children had exerted themselves to entertain her, and their Saturday evening entertainment had been a considerable success. The great news of the week had been the curate's engagement to Miss Twitch, and the visitor had laughed as much as anyone at Serafina's portrayal of the shy little spinster—the downcast eye and modestly folded hands, hampered by her insistence on propriety, but with an ill-concealed eagerness to accept her suitor's offer. Lady Chilham had appeared to be in such good humour and so impressed with Serafina that Mrs Feverel's hopes that she would do something for her were very high.

But Lady Chilham had expressed strong disapproval of the manner in which the two girls were being educated. 'It is too much! They do not need all this Latin and Greek! And politics!' Lady Chilham's nose had wrinkled in distaste. 'Sarah, I warn you, they are both in danger of becoming unmarriageable bluestockings—Serafina in particular.'

Mr Feverel had been outraged, and he and Lady Chilham had almost quarrelled over the matter. Only the regard they both shared for Mrs Feverel had prevented an open breach. Mrs Feverel had decided to postpone any attempt to gain Lady Chilham's help until matters had calmed down a little, and had waited until the last day of her friend's visit before she'd finally spoken. Lady Chilham had proved to be so sympathetic that Mrs Feverel had revealed rather more of the family's financial worries than she had intended.

'It's the girls I worry about most, Elizabeth. Once we have paid for Gabriel at Oxford, and Michael——'

'Does Michael wish to go to Oxford, too? He seems to me to be less academic than his brother.'

'No, he wishes for a career in the army, which as you know can be ruinously expensive. And heaven knows what Rafe will want to do when he is older!'

'Well, I am glad that you have confided in me at last, Sarah. I shall do something for Serafina, of course. But in fact there is an obvious solution to your problems, if you would care to make use of it. If you were not married to a crank you would have thought of it yourself before now.'

'You have never understood Lucius, Elizabeth. He is an idealist, not a crank,' said Mrs Feverel with a smile.

'Idealism don't pay bills!' was Lady Chilham's crisp reply. 'But I believe my views on that topic are already known to you. However, it is my considered view that the family's greatest potential asset is Serafina—I say potential, you'll note. I still have to establish how much damage has already been done by her extraordinary upbringing.'

'Serafina? How?' asked Mrs Feverel, ignoring this provocation.

'The girl is lovely enough to make a wealthy match, if all went well. Indeed, she could aim very high. I have not seen such a lovely face for several seasons. Think of what a wealthy son-in-law could do for the family!'

'But——'

'And,' said Lady Chilham firmly, 'the girl deserves a better fate than wasting her beauty down here. Neither her looks nor all this education will help her when she has to choose between marrying a country bumpkin or becoming her brother's pensioner. How many offers has she had, may I ask?'

'Only one,' said Mrs Feverel. 'From someone she regards as a joke. The rest of the young men of the neighbourhood are frightened of her. She does most things as well if not better than they do. And she argues with them.'

'What did I tell you? Now, in London I am sure it would not be difficult to find a sensible man, with a reasonable fortune, whom she could respect. But she will never attract the kind of offer I have in mind until she has more worldly sense. She must learn that being clever is a handicap to a woman, not an asset. She moves gracefully enough, and her voice is attractive—I could soon put her in the way of ladylike behaviour. She could even be one of next season's successes! If you wish, I will arrange something.'

After Lady Chilham had gone Mr Feverel had been ready to pour scorn on the idea of employing Serafina's gifts in such an unworthy cause. Besides, he would miss her! But he'd been silenced when he'd seen that his wife, frightened by Lady Chilham's prophecy of Serafina's future if she remained in Sussex, and worried about the rest of her children too, had set her heart on it. Serafina herself would not have been normal if she had not been excited at the prospect of a visit to London.

A few weeks later word came from Lady Chilham. She had decided to invite Serafina for a brief visit before Christmas.

There is little by way of entertainment at this time of year, but I feel that Serafina and I could get better acquainted with each other. The season doesn't start till next May, but if I decided to present her she would have to be carefully prepared for it, beginning in about March. What she needs most, of course, is to acquire some worldly sense!

The letter continued in a very kindly tone, but it was obvious that Serafina was to be on trial before her godmother would agree to sponsor her during the next season. Mrs Feverel was nervous of her husband's reaction, but to her surprise he raised few objections, merely saying that he would miss his daughter, but that she should take what advantage she could from a visit to London. The British Museum was particularly worth a

visit. Preparations for Serafina's trip were put in hand
with a number of visits to the dressmaker and the shops
in Brighton. But she still found time to visit old haunts.

Over the hill from Feverel Place and the village of
Hardington was a mansion which had been unoccupied
for some time. Blanchards had once been a handsome
estate—a beautiful house, built in the reign of Queen
Anne, surrounded by well-kept grounds and gardens.
But during the past thirty years it had been sadly
neglected. The house was somewhat isolated, and old
Mrs Dacre, who had been a recluse, had leased out most
of the land many years before. After she died
Blanchards remained unoccupied. Now it lay forgotten
and deserted, slowly falling into ruin. Mrs Dacre had
been a connection of the Aldworth family, and her
estate had been left to them. For a while it had been
hoped that Lord Aldworth would restore the house and
make it habitable again, but then tragedy had struck the
Aldworth family twice in quick succession. First old
Lord Aldworth had died, then Gervase, his son, had
succumbed to an illness quite soon afterwards. Charles,
the younger son, had succeeded his brother to the title,
but he was a diplomat and spent most of his time
abroad. None of the Aldworths bothered with
Blanchards, and Sam Eckford, the caretaker, remained
its sole employee.

For two of the Feverels at least, this continuing
neglect of Blanchards had come as a relief. Sam Eckford
was idle, and in any case had little reason to worry
overmuch about his masters. He was seldom to be seen
anywhere near the house, contenting himself with a
brief tour round the outside each morning and remain-
ing in the lodge the rest of the time. He never went near

the gardens. This meant that the Feverel children could roam there more or less at will whenever they were free.

Serafina and Michael had discovered the walled garden behind the house some time before. The overgrown tangle of currant bushes and raspberry canes testified to the years of neglect, but earlier in the summer they had found some fruit. Best of all, an old vine still flourished in the greenhouse set against the ancient south-facing wall—the sole survivor of a once luxuriant collection of exotic fruit trees. The children had tended this vine all summer, and were now reaping the results of their labours. Mrs Feverel had already received several baskets filled with bunches of sweet-tasting grapes.

A short time after the arrival of Lady Chilham's letter Serafina and Michael were in the greenhouse at Blanchards. Serafina was once again wearing her shabby skirt and disreputable jacket, together with a woolly cap and Michael's boots. After all, it was only sensible to wear boots for clambering over stone walls! The slight breeze coming in through the panes of broken glass overhead set the vine leaves dancing, scattering the sunlight among the vividly coloured leaves. Serafina paused to admire the rich display of green and gold, red and purple. Her mother would enjoy painting those leaves. . . The best ones were at the top near the roof. So were the best grapes! Serafina tucked her hair more firmly into her red woolly cap, hitched her skirt above her knees and, ignoring Michael's warnings, clambered up between the wall and the thick stem of the vine till she could perch on the cross-bar which supported the roof. In fact, the cross-bar was probably holding the whole rickety structure together. The autumn sun was warm and strong, and she found it stifling up there. Taking off her jacket, she draped it over the bar. There were more grapes here than she had thought. . .

'Sally! Come on! We shall be late!'

Serafina hastily cut one more bunch and scrambled down. She squeezed out through the door, which was still locked, even though all of its glass and most of its wooden panels had long since disappeared, and joined Michael, who was waiting impatiently outside.

'We'll soon have to think of something else for Mama, Michael,' she said. 'The grapes are very nearly finished.'

'Never mind that now! You know how disappointed Pa will be if we're not there for our walk. Come, I'll go over the wall first, then I'll take the basket from you.'

'If he wants us to be on time he shouldn't keep us late at morning lessons,' panted Serafina as she hitched up her skirts and scrambled up the tree after her brother.

'It's your fault. You shouldn't have asked him about that last bit of Xenophon.'

Serafina didn't reply—she was saving her breath for the run home. But as she perched on the top of the wall before jumping down she suddenly realised that she had left her jacket in the greenhouse.

'You'll have to go on, Michael. I'll get my jacket and join you as soon as I can. You'll have to try to explain to Pa. . . Here, take the grapes!'

Michael set off at a run, and Serafina returned to the greenhouse. She clambered up the vine once again, collected her jacket, put it on, and prepared to climb down again. But then she froze as she heard the sound of voices. . . Cautiously she peered down, but could see nothing between the broad leaves. The voices came nearer and she heard the sound of a key turning in the rusty lock of the greenhouse. Two people came in. One was Sam Eckford—he never came near the place, what was he doing here? The other's voice was deeper and immensely authoritative.

'This will all have to come down, Eckford.' It's dangerous. I'm surprised this vine has survived for so long. Have you been looking after it? You'd have done better to repair some of the boards, or even to remove the whole thing.' The speaker moved forward and Serafina had a tantalising glimpse of him. Tall, athletic figure, black hair—he was the handsomest man she had ever seen, and obviously both rich and fashionable. His travelling-cloak was open, and she had the impression of a snowy cravat and fawn-coloured pantaloons. He had obviously come some distance, and she wondered briefly how he managed to look so immaculately clean!

'No, no, your lordship! I was never told to look after anything but the house. And that was bad enough. It needs a lot doing to it, begging your lordship's pardon.'

'Yes, yes. We'll have to get an army of workers in if it is to be habitable before Christmas—which is what I want. Get this lot pulled down before I come again, will you?' They were turning away, but the gentleman suddenly stopped. 'What the devil. . .?' Before Serafina realised what was happening a lean hand had stretched up and grasped her ankle. 'What are you doing here? Come down at once!'

Serafina held on to her perch for dear life and kicked hard. It was quite effective, for Michael's old boots were heavy.

'Ouch! Why, you——'

Sam, seeing his master attacked, cried, 'Come down, you little varmint!' and started to pull at the vine.

'No, don't do that, Eckford! You'll have the place down——'

But it was too late. The structure gave a groan and slowly disintegrated. Man and master were buried under the old vine as Serafina slid helplessly along the pole to land gently on the ground outside some feet away. Horrified, she turned to see the damage. What glass remained had fortunately stayed in place so the two men were in no real danger, but they were trapped under the vine and its supports. She hesitated and went back to the ruins of the greenhouse.

'Are. . .are you all right?' she said.

'Good God, it's a girl!' An irate face peered out between the branches—furious grey eyes and cheeks flushed with anger. His hair was dishevelled and his cravat filthy with cobwebs and dust. But he was still very handsome. However, Serafina dared not linger to admire him—the gentleman was starting to push his way out of the tangle of leaves, branches and wooden supports. Ignoring his shout of, 'Wait, you!', she ran to the tree by the wall, threw herself over and fled for dear life up the hill. When she reached the shelter of some trees she paused and looked back. To her relief they had obviously decided against pursuit. She limped home, but was not sorry to discover that the walking party had set off without her. She felt she needed time to pull herself together!

Later that afternoon when Serafina, having washed the dirt and dust from her own person, was sitting demurely with her mother, the children came rushing in to report on the walk.

'You missed a lot of fun, Sally,' said Rafe. 'We marched and marched till we could see the sea—just like the Greeks.'

'Greeks?' Mrs Feverel looked puzzled.

'Xenophon,' explained Angelica. 'And his army of ten thousand. They marched through Persia to the sea. We read about it this morning.'

'Hundreds of miles, Mama!' said Rafe, his eyes shining. 'They were real heroes. And when they saw the sea they shouted, "*Thalassa, thalassa*!". And so did we. "*Thalassa*!" Mrs Pennyworth was very surprised. I don't think she liked it.'

'Oh, goodness, was she there?' asked Serafina.

'She was out for a drive with Hartley. Lizzie Beaminster was in the carriage with them.'

'Never mind that,' said Michael. 'Mama—guess what? Lord Aldworth is coming down himself any day now to see Blanchards. Miss Twitch told us. Perhaps he's going to let it? What do you think, Mama? Will he call on us when he's here?'

'I shouldn't imagine so, Michael,' said Mrs Feverel, to Serafina's profound relief. 'Not this time, anyway.' She turned to her daughter. 'So, Serafina—your grape-gathering days are over. I'm not altogether sorry, for I had an uneasy conscience about your taking them, even though no one else appeared to want them. But I shall miss my delicious dessert. I wonder if Lord Aldworth will cultivate the vine? Perhaps he would even let you have some?'

'I doubt it, Mama,' murmured Serafina.

There was something in Serafina's voice, something in the blindingly innocent expression on her face that caused Mrs Feverel to look sharply at her daughter.

What had Serafina been up to? Mrs Feverel, as so often in the past, decided it was better not to ask.

Nothing more was heard of Lord Aldworth. Apparently he had merely called in at Blanchards on his way from Newhaven. He stayed there only one night, and left for London and his own estate in Berkshire the next morning.

Serafina had been relieved not to run the risk of meeting him again. But she was annoyed to find that his handsome face had a totally irrational tendency to haunt her dreams.

CHAPTER TWO

LORD ALDWORTH reined in his horse and contemplated the view. The morning sun slanted across the countryside, creating a patchwork of light and shade in the broad valley and bathing the hills opposite in its glow. Below, the river glinted in the light as it wound its lazy way to London and the sea, and across the valley in the hollows not yet reached by the sun fingers of September mist curled round the trees and hedges, and covered the fields with an insubstantial veil. Huge beech trees on the hills above shone green and gold in the sunlight. Lord Aldworth took in a deep breath of scented downland air, and let it out in a sigh. To his mind there was no lovelier place than this in the whole of Europe, but he could not wait to leave it. Though he had been back in Berkshire for only three weeks, the situation was already almost intolerable—another week of living at Aldworth with his sister-in-law, his stepmother, not to mention his three stepsisters. . . He grimaced. It was unthinkable.

There was one person who would not be pleased when he told her he was going back to Vienna. He could already imagine what his grandmother would say, and it would not be agreeable. But there was no point in postponing the interview—he would see her tonight. One more gallop then he would return to the house which was now his—damn it!—and work his way through the mountain of chores to be completed before he could leave England with an easy conscience. A comparatively easy conscience. Lord Aldworth was not a man to disguise the truth from himself. He was deserting his proper post, and he knew it.

The sun was still shining as Lord Aldworth approached the Dower House that evening, but its rays were not permitted to enter the drawing-room, where his grandmother, the Dowager Lady Aldworth, waited to receive him. As a thrifty Frenchwoman she took measures to avoid the damage done to curtains and carpets by unshaded sunlight. Complexions, too, were better preserved without it and, even though she was nearly eighty, the Dowager thought of such things. However, a frown marred her carefully preserved features as she listened to what her grandson was saying a few minutes later. They were speaking in French, for Lady Aldworth was the daughter of a French aristocrat. She always used English with the rest of her family, but Charles, she was used to say, was one of the few Englishmen whose French accent she could tolerate, and she usually took pleasure in conversing with him in her native tongue. Not this evening.

'I have never interfered before, Charles; you cannot accuse me of that. You have done exactly as you please ever since you left Oxford. I have to admit that your public career has been exemplary, but your private life is another matter.' She paused, then added scrupulously, 'Though I suppose you have a perfect right to as many mistresses as you choose. You are, after all, a bachelor and in the prime of manhood.'

'I am grateful for your broad-minded attitude, ma'am, but I have to confess that I never have more than one mistress at a time. It can lead to confusion,' he assured her with a grin.

The Dowager was not to be diverted.

'But things have changed now,' she went on repressively. 'You are no longer Charles Dacre, a charming bachelor diplomat. You are the fifteenth Baron Aldworth, with a title and large estates to care for. When your idiot of a brother succumbed to a trifling illness without first having the good sense to get an heir, he left a nice mess for us all. As if your stepmother and three stepsisters were not enough, we now have another widowed Lady Aldworth——'

'Not to mention yourself, ma'am,' interrupted Lord Aldworth with a graceful bow.

'Impudence!'

'And,' he went on, 'dare I point out to you that Gervase had hardly been married six months when he died? It would surely have been precipitate if his wife had borne a child much before their first anniversary— and Gervase was never that in his life, as we both know.'

'He was an incompetent shuffler,' said Lady Aldworth, not mincing matters. 'The point is, Charles, that he didn't take a wife till he was well over thirty! He would have had plenty of time to get all the brats the title needed if he had bestirred himself. Why, your father was only twenty-two when Gervase was born. As for the shrew Gervase married. . .'

'Well, there I have to agree with you. I think I too would feel disinclined to survive if I were obliged to endure her company for long. She has a voice like a screech-owl.'

'Well, what are you proposing to do about it?'

'About my sister-in-law? What can I do but leave her where she is? And avoid listening to her.'

'No, that's not what I meant at all, and you know it! You're already close to thirty yourself. I want to know what you are proposing to do about an heir!'

Lord Aldworth shut the snuff-box he had been admiring with a snap, and turned to face his grandmother. 'I know you do, ma'am. You have, after all, been saying so ever since I returned from Vienna. And I will say again, I have no wish to change my present way of life. What is the reason for all the anxious haste? You can hardly say I am halfway to my dotage, and I feel no diminution of my. . .'

'Of your virility. I do not mince words, me! I must confess you don't look as if you do, either!' She eyed her grandson with grudging admiration. He always dressed fashionably, though not extravagantly, and here in the country his superbly cut dark green riding-coat and close fitting pantaloons did nothing to disguise the set of his powerful shoulders and the athletic grace of his build. For all the care taken with the folds of his immaculately starched cravat, the unconscious elegance of his hand on the mantelpiece, the lazy negligence of his pose, there was nothing effete about Charles Dacre. From his crisp black hair down to his gleaming top-boots he was all confident male.

The Dowager pulled herself together, and said with a return to her former tone, 'You owe it to the family, Charles. Good God, what is wrong with your generation? Your father did his duty—two sons while he was still in his twenties—and now it is up to you to do yours. Accidents can happen to the healthiest among us, and you cannot say that jauntering about the Continent is the safest way to live. From what I've heard there could well be a few husbands who wouldn't mind seeing you off, too.'

'Let them try,' her grandson said indifferently. 'I never took anything that was not freely given, Grand-mère!'

'As if that were anything to the purpose! And now this South American business——'

'What South American business? What do you mean?'

'You needn't pretend, Charles. I am not yet in my dotage either, and I hear a thing or two. Don't worry, I know you have your duty, and, though I could wish you were not involved, I'm not going to tease you into giving it up before it's finished. But you cannot claim it isn't dangerous.'

'I can—it is mere routine. But it worries me that you know anything about it. How many others do?'

'None! My source is discreet, and so am I. We shall forget it, if that is what you wish. But—why not marry first?' When he shook his head in a gesture of repudiation she asked, 'Why do you dislike the idea of marriage so much? Have you never even contemplated it?'

'Frequently,' he said with a short laugh. 'And always with horror! What, abandon the very civilised pleasures I enjoy at present—the challenge of pursuit, the delights of a shared passion and then the final parting, with no regret or recrimination—exchange all that for the kind of life I have observed marriage to bring? You must be mad!'

'You exaggerate, Charles!'

'Forgive me, but I do not! You cannot say that my father's second marriage was a recommendation! The

scenes, the drama—the poor man never had a moment's
peace! Four of them—my stepmother and her three
dreadful offspring—and they hadn't even a legitimate
claim on him! Forever demanding this, complaining
about that. And then Gervase and his choice. . .' Lord
Aldworth took his hand from the mantelpiece and
moved restlessly about the room. 'Have you any notion
of what it is like at present up at Aldworth? I live in
a. . .a hen-coop, surrounded by squawking, cackling
females. You may put me in Bedlam if I add another to
the collection, to squawk at *me*, to submit *me* to her
freaks and her tempers, to accuse *me* of selfishness and
worse.'

'You've been spoiled, Charles. In my day a man
married first and took his pleasures afterwards. You've
been living like a butterfly for far too long.'

'I believe my work with Castlereagh has not been
without merit, ma'am,' said Lord Aldworth mildly.

'Oh, lord, I'm not denying you've done marvels in
Vienna and elsewhere for your country. But what about
your family? When you were a younger son it was all
very well to carve out a name for yourself, charging
about the Continent, performing heroic deeds. Even
afterwards in Vienna, wheedling trade concessions out
of what is left of my poor France, and seducing the
wives of all the others who are doing the same——'

'The commission has been more than fair with your
poor France, ma'am. As for the rest. . . You overesti-
mate my powers, I assure you.'

'I doubt it,' said the Dowager drily. 'But you must
now put that all behind you and settle down to managing
Aldworth. Good God, you're not trying to tell me that a
few raddled Englishwomen will get the better of you,

when Metternich and his lot have tried and failed, are you? You're a diplomat!'

'Diplomacy plays no part in dealing with the numerous Aldworth widows, ma'am—except yourself, of course. A bludgeon is more their weapon.'

'Well, get rid of them, then,' said the Dowager, losing patience. 'If you were to get yourself a wife they would have to move out of Aldworth anyway. Gervase was far too soft with Almeria and her three harpies. They should have been packed off when he married. And the screech-owl should be given somewhere else to live, too—but not this house,' she added firmly. 'You could settle some of them in the Sussex property, perhaps. Old Millicent Dacre's place—what's it called? Blanchards! That's been empty for years.'

'I went to Blanchards on my way back. It's in a bad way and the caretaker has been negligent—the place was overrun with gypsies—but it could be put right. . .'

There was a silence in the room as Lord Aldworth went to the window and stared out at the rolling Berkshire countryside, at the distant Palladian mansion set like a jewel in its park.

'You know I am right, Charles.' His grandmother's voice was sympathetic but firm. 'The family needs an heir—and an absentee landlord does the land no good.'

'Yes, I know you're right. Of course you are right,' he said finally. 'But not yet, Grand-mère.'

'You can't leave it much longer,' she said unrelentingly. There was another silence. Then she sighed and spoke again. 'What if we were to compromise? If I were to find you a nice, biddable girl—not too sophisticated, one that wouldn't expect much by way of attention, a simple girl who knew her duty, and was prepared to

perform it without fuss, to give you your heirs and let
you go your own way otherwise. . .'

His attention caught, Lord Aldworth came back to
her. 'You would never find such a paragon.'

'I think I might. France was full of them in the old
days—I don't see why England shouldn't have a few.
She has to be well-born, that goes without saying, but
she needn't be rich.'

'All the better if she isn't!' said Lord Aldworth
cynically. 'She would at least have something to gain
from the marriage. But it's a hopeless task. Such a
girl would have to be simple to the point of idiocy,
Grand-mère!'

'Oh, *mon Dieu*, have I misunderstood? You want her
to have brains?'

'Good lord, no! A wife is better off without them.
Indeed, a clever wife is the last thing I should want!'
Lord Aldworth grinned as he entered into the spirit of
the thing. 'Well, Grand-mère, if you can find me a well-
bred, biddable, modest, sweet-natured girl. . .'

'Who knows how to behave. . .'

'But isn't going to argue, or think she knows
better. . .'

'Who is looking for a rich husband. . .'

'And is exquisitely lovely into the bargain. . .'

'I didn't promise that!'

'Well, why not? If we are going to invent an impossible dream, why not have her lovely too?' Lord
Aldworth laughed. 'I'll make a bargain with you,
Grand-mère. If you find such an ideal—I say *if*—I'll
marry her!'

* * *

Lord Aldworth might not have been serious, but his grandmother was. After he had left her to go back to his 'hen-coop', she sat deep in thought for some time. If this was the only way she could persuade her reluctant grandson to marry then she would find a suitable girl, one way or another. It was a pity, though. She had always hoped that he, the best-loved of her grandchildren, would find a woman he was capable of respecting and with whom he would be willing to share his life properly. He would have had much to give and much to gain from such a partnership. Not for the first time she cursed Charles's father's unfortunate second marriage. And as for Gervase and his harridan—the less said about them the better. The only clever thing poor Gervase ever did was to quit the world and leave the way clear for Charles to succeed. . .

Her thoughts had come in a circle back to her present problem. Where was she to find a wife for Charles? It would be dangerous to wait for next season's crop of débutantes, for Charles was not expecting to stay in England for long. He had come home after Gervase's unexpected death to sort out family affairs, but he would have to return to his post in Vienna to deal with unfinished business there. Once in Vienna he might well succumb to the attractions of a dainty *contessa* or an elegant *marquise*, and postpone fulfilling his family obligations in England. Worse still, he might be called on to act in a business which she knew to be dangerous, for all his protests. He must marry soon!

The Dowager spent much of her time during the next few days writing to a number of friends and acquaintances. She also sent instructions for her apartments in the family mansion in Berkeley Square to be aired and

opened. It was tiresome that she would have to spend
time out of season in London, but she was determined
to spare no effort to see that her grandson acquired a
wife. . .

Meanwhile, some eighty miles to the south, the happy
anticipation of Serafina's visit to London was disturbed
by some disquieting news from Oxford. Gabriel's tutor
was uneasy about him, and Mr Feverel hastened up
there to spend some days with his son. When he
returned he was clearly worried, and, since it was not a
matter that he could possibly hide from his wife, both
she and Serafina soon knew it all. Gabriel had fallen in
with a bad set—idlers and gamblers, all of them. The
boy had gone up to Oxford at sixteen, of course, and
had probably been too young and too unsophisticated to
withstand the wiles of those older than himself. Whatever the cause, he had been incurring debts, the sum
total of which was still unknown. It was an anxious time
for them all, for Mr Feverel's resources were strictly
limited. Though his family was an ancient one, the
estate was now small and, since Lucius Feverel had
liberal ideas, a major part of its income was taken up in
repairs and maintenance.

   Serafina hated the thought of leaving her family in
this state, but her mother gently pointed out to her that
Lady Chilham's ambition to secure an advantageous
marriage for her might now be more important than she
had realised. So Serafina satisfied her conscience by
cancelling two of her new dresses and finally set out for
London, determined to succeed. She was kindly
received by Lady Chilham and soon settled into the
house in Curzon Street.

Here she quickly found that Society's rules were
every bit as rigorous as the rules of Latin grammar or
the principles of mathematics, and that learning them
was every bit as demanding. Lady Chilham was as
thorough as Mr Feverel, and much less tolerant. She
took Serafina through the tortuous procedures for
arrivals, introductions, departures and return visits. She
instructed her in what one might say and what it would
be social disaster to say, what one might wear and might
not wear, what was done and what was not done. As
Lady Chilham had feared, Serafina was quick to learn
what was required, but it was difficult to convince her
that the rigmarole was desirable. She was forced to
remind the girl constantly of the goal she and Mrs
Feverel, and Serafina herself, all had in view.

Serafina grew to dislike the very mention of 'an
advantageous marriage'. No girl could grow up in a
family with three younger brothers without knowing
that there were physical differences between men and
women, but nothing in her upbringing had led her to
believe that there should be differences in their mental
attitudes. It seemed laughable to her that men, most of
whom she regarded as reasonable human beings, should
demand such artificial behaviour from the women they
hoped to marry; it was absurd that any man would be
influenced in his choice of a partner for life by the
manner in which she curtsied, or that he would depend
on the opinion of his mother, or his aunt, or the
patronesses of Almack's, or any of the other arbiters of
good behaviour. Then she remembered the young men
in Sussex and her failure to attract an offer from all but
one of them, the necessity for her to make a good

match, and she would sigh and set her mind to satisfying
her godmother.

About a month after Serafina's arrival she came in from
a stolen visit to the British Museum to hear that Lady
Chilham wished to see her immediately. Serafina's heart
sank. How had her godmother found out? But when she
entered the little salon on the first floor she found
nothing to indicate that Lady Chilham was annoyed. On
the contrary, though she was sitting calmly enough in
her customary place by the fire, there was an air of
suppressed excitement about her. She had a letter in her
hand.

'Serafina! The most extraordinary opportunity for
you has arisen. I only hope we may profit from it. This is
from an old friend of mine, Lady Carstairs. Listen to
what she writes. "Do tell me if there is any further news
of Lady Aldworth's quest to find a bride for her
grandson. I am sure it is being treated with all possible
discretion, of course, but such an affair must arouse a
great deal of interest. I should have thought Charles
Dacre was handsome enough to find a girl for himself,
but no, it seems the Dowager has been charged with the
task. Perhaps he is too busy, in every sense of the word,
in Vienna! And the need for an heir is evident. What a
prize! The Aldworth fortune is vast, even allowing for
the Aldworth widows. If only my own granddaughter
were old enough! Don't forget to let me know the
instant you hear a thing."'

Lady Chilham folded the letter carefully and put it
down. 'She rattles on further, but nothing of any interest
to you. You realise what this might mean, Serafina?
Have you heard of the Aldworths? They are fabulously

wealthy, and Aldworth himself must be one of the most
eligible bachelors in England. It would be to aim almost
too high. . .'

Serafina cleared her throat nervously. 'I believe they
own a property in Sussex, ma'am. Blanchards is quite
near where I live.'

'Then you know the family?'

'No, not at all,' said Serafina swiftly, shutting out of
her mind a sudden vision of furious grey eyes under a
dusty crown of vine leaves. 'Blanchards has not been
lived in for as long as I can remember.'

'That is satisfactory. We shall have our work cut out
as it is, without the intrusion of your family
background.'

Serafina stiffened. 'I beg your pardon, ma'am?'

'Well done! That touch of hauteur was excellently
judged. I think you are learning after all, Serafina!'

But Serafina was not to be mollified. 'You referred to
my family, I believe, Lady Chilham. Surely it is at least
as old and distinguished as anything Lord Aldworth can
boast?' She added scornfully, 'It is not rich, of course.'

'I'm sorry if I have offended you, child. There's
nothing wrong with your breeding—on either side. But
your upbringing. . . That is a different matter. You will
naturally deny that there is anything wrong with it, nor
do I blame you for your loyalty. But we both know that
it is not what Lady Aldworth will look for. That reminds
me—I must make a few discreet enquiries. Exactly what
is Lady Aldworth's role in this affair? Lord Aldworth is
certainly not the man to need any help in engaging a
young woman's affections. Rather the reverse, I should
say!'

The result of Lady Chilham's researches was to give

her a very thoughtful air. She sent once again for Serafina.

'How serious are you about wishing to oblige your family, Serafina?'

Serafina looked surprised, and then her quick intelligence made the connection. 'What is wrong with the Aldworth match, Lady Chilham?'

'Nothing at all, nothing at all. It would be many a young girl's dream. It's just. . .'

'Just. . .?'

'Lady Aldworth has a very clear idea of the sort of young girl she is looking for. Her grandson will marry no other.'

'And?'

'You meet her requirements in only two respects. Perhaps three, if you were to concentrate.'

Serafina should have been very glad to hear that she was not to be put forward as a candidate for Lord Aldworth's hand. She was haunted by a secret fear that, unlikely though it was, he might recognise in her the thief in his greenhouse. But this was too much for her natural pride.

'Which are they?'

'You are beautiful, and well-bred. And with some hard preparation I think you could persuade her that you know how to behave in Society.'

Serafina's eyes were glittering as she asked, 'And in what ways would I not satisfy Lord Aldworth's stringent requirements?'

'The tendency to talk like that is one of them,' said Lady Chilham bluntly. 'Lady Aldworth is looking for someone who will give her grandson an heir, is meek, content to let others do her thinking for her, and is

ready to allow Lord Aldworth to continue in his present
mode of life——'

'Stop, stop! You have said enough. Lord Aldworth
obviously wants a. . .a Miss Twitch, but with impeccable lineage and outstanding beauty. I can see that he
and I should never suit.'

'That is not the question. It would be more to the
point to remember that if you could catch him, Serafina,
your family would have no more financial worries. But I
fear we could never persuade him—or Lady
Aldworth—that you were even a suitable candidate.'

'Could we not indeed?' said Serafina, her eyes glittering again. 'I would wager, ma'am, that if I were to set
my mind to it I could play the role of the pretty doll
Lord Aldworth seems to require as well as anyone.
Indeed, I might even enjoy it.'

Lady Chilham looked appraisingly at her god-daughter. Then she said, 'Do you know, I think you just might
do it? I had forgotten your performance as that little
spinster. . . You were certainly most convincingly
demure. . . But no, it would not serve, Serafina! It
would be to deceive him most shamefully.'

'You say he is rich, ma'am? And extremely eligible?
And yet he has such a small interest in the girl he will
make his bride that he asks his grandmother to select
one for him! I think Lord Aldworth deserves no better.
And, as you said, it would, if I succeeded, put an end to
my family's worries.'

The two ladies smiled at each other. 'It would certainly be a triumph to snare the Aldworth fortune,' said
Lady Chilham thoughtfully.

'And how I would enjoy taking Lord Arrogance down
a peg or two!' said Serafina.

'What do you mean? You surely wouldn't cry off at the last minute or anything silly like that, would you?' asked Lady Chilham sharply.

'That is the last thing I should do. What should I gain from that? No, Lord Aldworth would merely gradually discover that he had married more than he bargained for. At the very worst he will abandon me in his country seat, and I shall be free to study as much as I like. And at best he might even come to terms with having a bluestocking for a wife! And until he did one or the other I could make life most uncomfortable for that conceited peer!'

Lady Aldworth, meanwhile, was having small success in her search. The best families in England seemed to be suffering from a dearth of eligible candidates. Miss Trotton de Courcy was malleable and willing, but she had a face like a horse, and laughed like one, too. Lady Amabel Wye was lovely enough, but her manner was imperious, and a disagreeable frown too often marred her fair brow. The Honourable Prudence Carter was too fat, Lord Bacup's daughter too frail. . .and so it went on—each of the girls she had so far seen had some fault or other. In fact, Lady Aldworth was reluctant to give her seal of approval to anyone. Though she herself had suggested such a match, she found it repellent to think of Charles tied to a girl who fulfilled all his selfish requirements. He would need more than such a soulless union to keep him happy for the rest of his life. So it was with no great optimism that Lady Aldworth agreed to pay a call on Lady Chilham. It appeared that there was a god-daughter. . . She asked herself what would be wrong with this one.

Her first impression, however, was good. The chit
was angelically lovely—one requisite more than
adequately fulfilled. Silver-gilt hair, clear blue eyes
under delicately arched brows, a perfectly formed nose
and a beautifully moulded mouth—a fraction too wide
perhaps, but that was better than being too small. The
girl was slender and moved gracefully—her curtsy was a
delight to watch. She looked healthy in spite of her
ethereal air, and her teeth were good. So was her dress
sense. The round gown in pale blue muslin was neither
too plain nor too elaborate, and the Paisley shawl over
it was handled with skill as she sat down on the chair in
front of the Dowager. Good hands and feet, neatly
disposed. Altogether very promising!

'Lady Chilham tells me that you live in Sussex, Miss
Feverel.'

'Yes, Lady Aldworth.'

'Where, exactly?'

'Hardington Feverel, not far from East Bourne.'

'Really? Do you know Blanchards, our estate down
there?'

'Yes, Lady Aldworth.'

'Well, girl? Tell me more. How close is it to your
home?'

'It is quite near, Lady Aldworth.'

'Really? Did my grandson call on your papa when he
was down at Blanchards recently?'

'No, Lady Aldworth.' The girl seemed to be getting
nervous. She seemed almost too simple, thought Lady
Aldworth. Even Charles would tire of these monosyl-
lables. Perhaps she was to be disappointed yet again in
her search? But this Feverel girl was so lovely—she
would try once more.

'Let me see. . . Feverel. Of course! Lucius Feverel, the scholar.'

'You know him?' Suddenly the girl's face came to life. The wonderful eyes glowed and her mouth was curved in a smile. Lady Chilham coughed and Miss Feverel, with an effort she could not quite hide, calmed down into her former insipid manner. Lady Aldworth was intrigued. She decided that this was a promising line of investigation.

'He is a madman, of course,' she said with deliberate provocation. What would be the reply to that? The girl must either agree, thus showing lack of filial respect for a father she was clearly fond of, or dare to disagree with her visitor. Lady Chilham shifted nervously in her chair, but Miss Feverel remained calm. Her answer when it came was a masterpiece of diplomacy.

'I cannot judge what the world thinks of Papa. I have lived in the country until very recently. You may be right, Lady Aldworth——'

The Dowager smiled in grim satisfaction. So the girl was going to sacrifice her father in her own self-interest, eh? Or was she too simple to see the implication? But the satisfaction faded at the unexceptionable words which followed.

'—but I owe him every respect. He has always been a kind and loving father to me and to my brothers and sister.' Miss Feverel had been looking down at her clasped hands but she now raised her eyes and gave Lady Aldworth a look of hurt reproach. Had the Dowager but known it, that look was one of Serafina's most successful weapons. The Dowager barely stopped herself from begging pardon. She pulled herself together.

'Brothers and sister, eh? You like children?'

'I love my brothers and sister, ma'am.'

The conversation continued in this vein for some time, but though Miss Feverel's manners were subjected to some hard testing she did not falter in her modestly polite responses. Only once was there a hint of something else. Towards the end the Dowager snapped out a question intended to disconcert this paragon.

'Well, miss, you know why I am here and I suppose you have considered whether you would like to be the next Lady Aldworth. Should my grandson decide you'd suit, what would you say?'

The blue eyes widened in surprise at this very indiscreet enquiry. The girl gave a slight smile and said demurely, 'Until he does, Lady Aldworth, it would not be proper for me to say. Anyone must be flattered at Lord Aldworth's condescension, of course.'

This time there was something in the voice—a slight irony? Surely not! All the same it was enough to intrigue the Dowager. The girl had a quality unlike any other she had met. She found herself wondering what Charles would make of the chit, and was inclined to risk introducing them. But first she would have some further conversation with young Mademoiselle Feverel! The Dowager had a suspicion that she might have been engaged in a battle of wits during the past half-hour. And if that were so, then this angelic-looking girl had been one of the most cool, most subtle opponents Lady Aldworth had come across for some time.

CHAPTER THREE

A FEW days later Serafina received an invitation to visit the Dowager Lady Aldworth at her house in Berkeley Square. It was made clear that Lord Aldworth would not be present.

'She means to have another look at you, Serafina,' said Lady Chilham. 'On the one hand it is very flattering—you have passed the first test, so to speak, and I don't think any of the others got as far. On the other hand. . . I wish I could be with you, but the invitation only mentions your name. . . Still, you managed the last interview perfectly. We shall just go through the courtesies involved in making a call, if you please. And we must look through your wardrobe. . .'

As a result of Lady Chilham's efforts Serafina arrived at Berkeley Square looking composed and very elegant. The weather had turned cold and she was wearing a velvet pelisse in a very pretty shade of dark lilac over her white muslin dress. Her face was framed in a bonnet of lilac *velours simulé*, lined with white sarsnet, and she was carrying a small white fur muff, borrowed from her godmother. Marbury, the elderly butler, afterwards confided to Mrs Phillips, the Berkeley Square housekeeper, that he had never seen anything so lovely come up the front steps before.

Lady Aldworth had a suite of rooms on the first floor. Attempts had been made, somewhat unwisely, by the other Aldworth ladies to oust her from them, but she had foiled them all, and whenever she was in London she occupied what were, in fact, the best rooms in the house. Serafina followed Marbury up the broad staircase and into Lady Aldworth's salon.

'Miss Feverel! How charming you look—come here and sit down.' After the courtesies were complete Serafina found herself sitting on the opposite side of the fireplace from the old lady, facing the long windows. 'It is pleasant to see another face, Miss Feverel. I have been confined to my rooms in this inclement weather.' After Serafina had expressed her sympathy and they had exchanged pleasantries the Dowager said, 'Tell me, Miss Feverel, would you be willing to do an old lady a favour? My eyes are not what they were and there is an article in *The Times* which intrigues me. As you will have guessed I was born in France, and though I have no sympathy for the regime which was recently defeated by the Allies I am enough of a Frenchwoman still to wish to know what is happening to her now. Would you read it to me?'

Serafina could hardly refuse. She took the proffered paper and began to read. At first she managed to stay in character. She hesitated over words of more than one syllable, she stumbled over foreign names, looking apologetically each time at Lady Aldworth. The Dowager merely nodded. But slowly Serafina's interest was caught by what she was reading. She soon became more fluent, referring easily to Metternich, Talleyrand and Aix-la-Chapelle. The soft, sweetly hesitant tone she had adopted in London disappeared, and indignation was in her voice as she read of Prussia's extortionate demands. The article came to an end, and she looked up to find Lady Aldworth smiling at her grimly.

She had betrayed herself! Oh, how could she have been so careless? 'I. . . I read a lot with Papa,' was all Serafina could find to say.

But to her surprise the Dowager simply replied, 'Of course, of course. You read well, Miss Feverel—after your initial nervousness. Thank you.'

Serafina thought it was time to take her leave. Though Lady Aldworth had not referred to the change in her personality, she must have noticed it. She would certainly not ask to see her again. So it was with astonishment that Serafina heard her hostess suggest a further meeting. 'Perhaps Lady Chilham would be good enough to take you to Lady Carteret's drum, which is to be held at Marchant House in a week's time. I will see that you receive invitations. I am sure you would enjoy the occasion, and I shall try to arrange for my grandson to be there. He is, of course, his own master, but he normally obliges me when he can. I shall not tell him anything beforehand, but I shall take the opportunity to introduce you both.'

Serafina was still perplexed as she took her leave. She was even more astonished when, as she got to the door, Lady Aldworth said, 'Miss Feverel! The manner is very good—just what Charles thinks he is looking for. Don't overdo it—a touch more vivacity would not come amiss.' She chuckled, then added, 'But you must take more care to sustain it. All the time, Miss Feverel! Goodbye—I shall see you at Marchant House.'

After Serafina had gone Lady Aldworth chuckled again, and then grew serious. The girl was very nearly perfect in her role as an *ingénue*. But it was now obvious that it was a role. The real Miss Feverel was more intelligent and better educated than she admitted. What a clever minx she was! Well, it might end in disaster, but Lady Aldworth was inclined to think that Serafina Feverel just might be the perfect answer to Charles's objections to a proper marriage. Meanwhile she, Lady Aldworth, would sit back and enjoy the comedy.

The drum at Marchant House, which took place in November each year to celebrate Countess Carteret's birthday, was not generally held to be among London's most brilliant occasions. The capital was not as full as it would be in spring and early summer, nor were the Carterets, though a worthy enough couple, leaders of Society. But it was usually well-attended, and to one as unsophisticated as Serafina it was immensely exciting. She tried hard to look composed and not to stare as she went through a succession of handsomely furnished rooms to the ballroom at the back of the house. She herself caused no small sensation. Since she had not yet been presented her toilette was modest, but Serafina had no need of embellishment. Her simple white silk dress provided the perfect foil for her beauty, and she was the focus of many admiring eyes and whispered enquiries for her name. Lady Chilham was soon besieged by eager aspirants for a dance with Miss Feverel.

Lady Aldworth was there, of course, but there was no sign of her grandson. She greeted Serafina kindly, though she took care not to give the curious any indication that this was her favoured candidate.

About halfway through the evening there was a stir as a small party of elegantly dressed ladies and gentlemen entered the ballroom. They had obviously been dining together and were all in high spirits. Serafina recognised Lord Aldworth immediately. On his arm as they came into the room was a vivacious, dark-haired woman, dressed in a daringly cut gown of geranium-coloured gros de Naples silk. Diamonds glittered at her throat and in her hair, and she was carrying a fan which she was using to great effect. Even as Serafina watched, the lady spread the fan and gazed mockingly at Lord Aldworth over the top of it.

'There's Lord Aldworth, Serafina,' said Lady Chilham. 'The tall man with the woman in red. Gracious me, that's Louisa Paget, unless I'm very much mistaken. I'm surprised; I thought the Pagets were in Vienna still. Just look at that dress—Paris in every line of it! But then she always did spend a lot on her clothes. Heavens, how she hangs on Aldworth's arm. I wonder where Sir Robert is?'

'Sir Robert?'

'The lady's husband. He's not one of the party, that's certain.'

After a while the little band of revellers split up and wandered round the ballroom, talking to friends and acquaintances. Lord Aldworth stopped at his grandmother's chair for a while but he soon moved on, still accompanied by Lady Paget. Serafina watched him as he shepherded his lady expertly through the crowds, then laughed down at her, put his hand at her waist, and swept her into the waltz which had just begun.

'Just look at those two—they are practically embracing in public! I have never approved of the waltz, however fashionable it may be in Vienna. It gives rise to the sort of scandalous behaviour you see over there,' said Lady Chilham.

'They look so graceful, ma'am—and the gentleman is

keeping the same strict distance from the lady as everyone else is,' replied Serafina.

Lady Chilham frowned. 'That might be so—but they don't look as if they are,' she said somewhat obscurely.

Serafina sighed. Lord Aldworth was more handsome than she had remembered, and his black and white evening clothes suited him even better than his travelling garb. How could she possibly attract him? She could never aspire to the sophistication and elegance of the woman at present in his arms. She sighed again, but then saw that the Dowager was beckoning to her, and with a word to Lady Chilham Serafina went over to speak to her.

Lady Aldworth was frowning, and her bony fingers were clutching her cane so tightly that the knuckles were white. The old lady was clearly in a rage, and Serafina was willing to wager that it had been caused by her grandson's appearance with Lady Paget. What was she planning to do? Serafina felt a touch of apprehension, but smiled dutifully and, at Lady Aldworth's invitation, sat down beside her. The Dowager said abruptly, 'Miss Feverel, if you are willing, I will introduce my grandson to you. I am sure he would like to make your acquaintance.'

Serafina allowed her eyes to rest for a moment on the two circling the floor. 'Really, Lady Aldworth?' she said doubtfully.

The Dowager lips tightened. 'Perhaps I should have told him you were to be here tonight. However, I wanted to surprise him. He will come over when he sees I have someone with me, I am sure.'

Serafina was by no means sure of this, but she was proved wrong. The waltz ended, Lord Aldworth escorted his partner back to her friends, bowed, and could then be seen threading his way towards his grandmother.

Serafina was suddenly in a panic. 'I don't think. . .'

But she subsided when the Dowager snapped, 'Don't be foolish, girl. Stay here!'

Lord Aldworth was suddenly quite near and Serafina clasped her hands together nervously. However, there was no sign of recognition in his face as he looked first at her and then enquiringly at his grandmother.

'My grandson, Lord Aldworth—Miss Feverel.'

The usual courtesies were exchanged, then Lord Aldworth took a small step back and examined Serafina. 'I congratulate you, Grand-mère,' he said. 'Miss Feverel is charming.'

Serafina supposed that she deserved his patronising tone, for it was well-known to all three of them that she was a candidate for marriage, but, try as she might, she could not suppress a feeling of resentment. A faint flush of anger appeared in her cheeks, but Lord Aldworth seemed to regard this as one of maidenly modesty.

'Delightful!' he said.

'Miss Feverel is staying with her godmother, Charles.'

'Really? Now that is good news,' he said. His tone was still one of patronage and Serafina felt a strong desire to box his ears. Since this would hardly further her cause, however, she hid her feelings by looking down shyly at her hands.

'But don't you find it rather boring in London at the moment, Miss Feverel? There are so few entertainments for such a lovely young lady.' She looked up again to find that he was smiling down at her—a ruefully lopsided smile—and for a moment she felt the pull of his charm.

'I am enjoying it, Lord Aldworth,' she said, stammering a little.

'That's good! That's very good. Er. . .where do you come from? The Home Counties?' Lord Aldworth's tone was kind but it was obvious that he was making conversation, and Serafina doubted that he was really interested in her answer. However, much could be forgiven of a man who continued to smile at one in that devastatingly attractive way.

'She comes from Sussex, Charles,' said the Dowager.

'How very interesting!' His eyes strayed a little, and Serafina saw that he was watching Lady Paget, who was taking the floor with another member of her party—a handsome man in his forties. 'Er. . .would you dance with me, Miss Feverel?'

They joined a set of country dances. Serafina was not sure how, but they ended up in the same set as Lady Paget, and it was obvious that Lord Aldworth's real purpose was to keep a close watch on what was happening at the other end of the set. Though she could do little about it, this annoyed her. But after a while he pulled himself together and spoke.

'Did my grandmother say you came from Sussex, Miss Feverel? You are not a smuggler, I hope!' An avuncular grin was meant to convey that, in case she thought he was serious, this was a joke.

'Oh, goodness me, no, Lord Aldworth!' she exclaimed, looking at him in well-simulated horror. 'Ladies in general are not, you know.'

'No, of course not. Stupid of me. Er. . .so where do you live?' His eye moved to the head of the set.

'Feverel Place at Hardington.'

'I see.' Serafina waited in vain for any comment on

this. If he had been listening with any concentration, he must have asked if she knew Blanchards—Hardington was not all that far from the property. But he said nothing, and she began to feel angry again.

'And what do you do with your time in London?' he asked at last, turning to her with another charmingly avuncular smile. Before she could reply Lady Paget's delicious laugh rang out and his head turned swiftly towards the sound.

Serafina took a deep breath and said diffidently, 'I clean the streets and sweep chimneys.'

'Good, good! I expect your godmother has arranged a good few things of that nature.'

Serafina almost spoilt everything by laughing out loud. What a conceited, rude man this was! He had obviously written her off as a mindless nonentity, and was treating her accordingly. She would enjoy the dancing and forget him, and she managed to do so for a while. Then he seemed to pull himself together and make a genuine effort to talk to her, but though she risked no more nonsensical replies it was not difficult to keep up her role of *ingénue*. He said little that would not have been instantly understood by a five-year-old child. The set of country dances finally came to an end and they returned to the Dowager, who was talking to Lady Chilham.

'Thank you, Miss Feverel. I enjoyed that enormously. We must try it again some time. Now, if you'll excuse me. . . Your servant, Lady Chilham. . . Grand-mère.' He was gone. Not five minutes later they saw him escorting Lady Paget from the room.

* * *

When Serafina came downstairs the following day, she was greeted with the news that the Dowager Lady Aldworth had just arrived and was waiting to see her in the salon. Surprised, she went in to find her godmother and the Dowager in earnest conversation. But Lady Chilham excused herself after a short while, and Serafina was left alone with her visitor.

'I've come to talk to you about my grandson,' began Lady Aldworth briskly. 'Lady Chilham has told me that your father would not object if Aldworth were to make an offer for you, though naturally they would have to meet first. I should like to know how you would view such an offer.'

Serafina would have spoken but Lady Aldworth held up her hand. 'I know that I have asked you this once before, Miss Feverel, and was refused an answer. At the time I was content to let matters take their course. But the situation was not as urgent then as it is now. Unless I act swiftly this new affair of his will distract Aldworth, and once again he will delay fulfilling his family obligations. You see—I am being frank with you. I can hardly be otherwise. You can't have failed to observe his conduct last night with that creature.'

'Do you mean with Lady Paget?'

'So you know her name? It's an old name, a good name. She has no business to be exposing it to gossip, and nor has Charles. Why the devil couldn't he confine his affairs to Vienna or Paris?' She stopped, glared at Serafina, and then made an effort to speak more calmly. 'But that's a matter between my grandson and me. I haven't come here to talk of that. I'm here to ask if you are serious.'

'Serious? I'm not sure what you mean, Lady Aldworth,' said Serafina with a wide-eyed stare.

'For the love of God, don't play-act! There isn't time for it. That innocent gaze doesn't fool me, Miss Feverel—we both know that you are far cleverer than you pretend. I'm not sure I approve of your attempt to deceive me, but that's water under the bridge now. I have come to the conclusion that you are the very girl for my plans.'

Serafina said calmly, 'What plans, ma'am?'

'To get Charles married, of course. I realise now that a genuinely simple girl would never do! Charles would get bored in five minutes and I would lose him before he ever got round to offering for her. I need someone who can appear to be what he wants, yet is clever enough to hold his interest afterwards, and I'm inclined to think that you are the very one. I wish to know if you are serious in your wish to marry Aldworth.'

'I. . . I am serious in my wish to marry well, ma'am. I too have an obligation to my family. But whether it should be to your grandson is another matter.'

'Listen to the chit! Anyone would think eligible bachelors grew on trees, ready for the plucking! You're not in love with any one else, are you? There are no complications of that sort, I hope?' Serafina shook her head, and Lady Aldworth continued, 'Good! Well, now, Aldworth is a man who keeps his promises, and he has promised me that he will marry. I think I can persuade him that you are suitable. He trusts me, I believe.'

Serafina gave a laugh. 'Wait, wait! Unlikely though it may seem to you, you might have to persuade me that your grandson is suitable for me! Marriage to such an unwilling suitor does not seem very attractive!'

'He is worth a little effort, Miss Feverel. He is well-born, handsome, and rich, as I am sure you already know. But he is not just the charming rogue most people see. He is a skilled and intelligent diplomat, and deeply committed to his country's interests. Given the right partner he could be equally committed to his marriage.'

'Then tell me why he delegates this important decision to you, Lady Aldworth,' Serafina asked bluntly, abandoning her pose completely. 'I have my own reasons—family reasons—for wishing to marry for wealth rather than love, and if Lord Aldworth seeks a. . .a doll, then I am prepared to be one. But why does he wish for such a bride? I hardly think a doll would be the right partner for a man as intelligent as you claim Lord Aldworth to be.'

'Exactly! But Lord Aldworth does not wish to marry at all! I have won his agreement on condition I can find a bride who is silly enough not to interfere with his present way of life.'

'Silly?' asked Serafina in astonishment.

'My word for it, not his. His is "biddable",' explained Lady Aldworth.

Serafina gave an exclamation of disapproval.

Lady Aldworth hesitated, then went on, 'There are good reasons for his attitude, which I will not go into at the moment. But. . . But, Miss Feverel——' she spoke with emphasis '—I think it would in fact spoil his life to marry such a girl. He is already somewhat selfish, and slightly arrogant——'

'Somewhat! Slightly! You are over-partial, Lady Aldworth.'

The Dowager, far from resenting this, smiled. 'If you would agree to get to know him better, I think you would find it possible to tolerate him. His preoccupation with that creature last night was unfortunate, but I shall deal with that. Once Lady Paget is out of the way I think you would find him attentive enough. Will you try it? I have to know.'

Serafina hesitated.

'I shall see that there are handsome settlements, Miss Feverel.' Then, when Serafina still didn't speak, she sighed and said, 'Will you at least agree to see something more of him?'

This Serafina agreed to do.

Lord Aldworth's interview with his grandmother that same day was much less friendly than their earlier discussion. She received him coldly, and began without any idle preliminaries.

'I have found the girl I consider to be ideal for you, Charles. You met her last night—if you were aware of her existence.'

'What do you mean, Grand-mère? I even danced with Miss Feverel!'

'Oh, so you remember her name, do you?' she said sardonically.

'She's a very pretty girl——'

'She is exquisitely lovely, well-born, sweet-natured, and she has all the other qualities you need, Charles. I expect you now to keep your word, and see if the girl will marry you. I only hope you haven't put her off by your obvious preoccupation with someone else.'

'Surely the bargain was that I should be free to go my own way?'

'But even you, Charles——' Lady Aldworth's voice was scathing '—even you would surely not intend to flaunt your amours in front of the girl's very nose?'

Lord Aldworth stiffened and said, somewhat defensively, 'I was not aware that you were about to produce a prospective bride for me so soon. Lady Paget happened to be in London, and is an old friend of mine——'

'And Sir Robert? He is still in Vienna, I hear. Is he a friend of yours?'

'Why, yes.'

'And you think it the act of a friend to expose Sir Robert—a senior diplomat and distinguished servant of your own country—to expose such a man to ridicule, and his wife to gossip and scandal? I am surprised and grieved, Charles. Your affairs in Vienna are, I suppose, your own concern——'

'Indeed they are, ma'am,' said Lord Aldworth angrily.

But Lady Aldworth continued as if he had not spoken, 'I have regarded your career as something of a Don Juan with tolerance, Charles. I have even been amused at the reports of your escapades which kind friends send me from time to time. But this affair with Lady Paget is very different. Your behaviour in this matter is not honourable, and I find it singularly unamusing. In fact I find it distasteful, and I begin to wonder what sort of man you have become.'

Lord Aldworth flushed. 'You are doing me an injustice, Grand-mère. In spite of what you saw, Lady Paget is not my mistress.'

'And you are not attracted to her?' There was a pause. When he remained silent, she went on, 'Leave her to her other friends, Charles, before it is too late.

Concentrate instead on your promise to me. Miss Feverel would make you a perfect wife. Spend time with her instead of bringing discredit on the family name with such a dubious liaison.'

There was a long silence. Lady Aldworth was content to have it so. Charles was usually honest with himself. He would admit that her analysis of the situation with Louisa Paget was a fair one.

'Where shall I find Miss Feverel?' he said eventually.

CHAPTER FOUR

AFTER that Lord Aldworth was a frequent visitor at Curzon Street. He remained patronisingly avuncular, and Serafina often had to grit her teeth to stop herself from dropping her pose and saying something outrageous. But as time went on she began to enjoy his company. It was not only that she found it amusing to pit her wits against his. When he put his mind to it he could be a very charming companion, willing to do what he could to entertain her. It was considerably easier to gain admission to various exhibitions and museums under the aegis of a peer of the realm than it would have been on her own, and she soon learned to use her ingenuity to ensure that their various outings were to more interesting places than he thought suitable for her amusement.

She shuddered to think what her father would have said if he had been there to hear the inanities she uttered and the naïve questions she asked. But in the end she could pride herself on the fact that, though Lord Aldworth was frequently amused by what she said, he never for one moment suspected that she was not all that she seemed. In this she was helped by the fact that he did not, basically, see her at all as an individual. He might, as she had heard, have abandoned his pursuit of Lady Paget, but he had certainly not transferred his interest to the girl he was considering as a bride.

Lady Paget herself was less indifferent—or more

personally interested—and indeed on one occasion Serafina felt she might have gone too far. They had met Lady Paget and her escort by accident at Somerset House. Lady Chilham, who was also one of Serafina's allies, had asked Lord Aldworth to take them to view a private exhibition there.

'How odd to meet you here, Lord Aldworth,' said Lady Paget. 'I had quite thought you had gone into the country.' Her green eyes rested on Serafina, and Lord Aldworth was forced to introduce them all.

'What a pretty girl! Your niece? Are you here for an educational visit, child?'

'No, Lady Paget. I am staying with my godmother.'

'Ah, yes! Uncles, aunts, godmothers—they are all pressed into service to educate the unwilling young! Poor Aldworth! How we suffer!'

'I should imagine,' said Serafina, with a look of innocently glowing admiration, 'that your fortunate companion must feel proud to be seen with such an elegant guide. I only wish my own aunts were half so lovely—or is he your godson?'

Since it was unfortunately true that Lady Paget's friend was considerably younger than she was, this caused some coldness on the part of the lady, and she withdrew shortly afterwards.

'That was not well done, Serafina,' said Lady Chilham severely.

'Why, ma'am?' Serafina faltered. 'Was I. . .was I too forward? But Lady Paget is lovely! Should I not have said so? She is offended with me?'

Lady Chilham pursed her lips disapprovingly, and walked away to examine one of the pictures. Serafina looked at Lord Aldworth, who was suppressing a grin,

but when he saw Serafina's look of hurt reproach he
tried to explain.

'Lady Paget is with someone she regards as a friend,
Miss Feverel, an equal. Not as someone who needs
looking after. I think she was slightly put out at your
remark, but do not worry about it. I'm sure she realises
that it was innocently meant.'

Serafina was relieved that Lord Aldworth was not
there to hear her godmother's subsequent remarks.

With this and other diversions the time passed.
November was drawing to its end, and Serafina would
soon leave London to spend Christmas at home. Lord
Aldworth was a frequent escort, and London was
beginning to speculate on their friendship. But he had
so far not committed himself.

This somewhat unsatisfactory state of affairs was
brought to a close by a message from the Foreign Office.
Lord Aldworth's presence was urgently needed in
Vienna, and he was to set off immediately. His grandmother was annoyed. Lady Aldworth had hoped that
her grandson would visit Serafina in Sussex after
Christmas and meet her family—in particular, Mr
Feverel. But there was little Lord Aldworth could do
about this call to duty. Some highly delicate negotiations
were in hand, and he was essential to their successful
conclusion. He promised his grandmother that he would
seek out Miss Feverel as soon as he returned, and
pursue the acquaintance with a view to marriage.

'If she is still available it will be more than you
deserve, wretched man!'

'I shall return as soon as I can, Grand-mère. Miss
Feverel tells me she will be in Sussex till March. She

won't meet anyone there. I should be back by then—or shortly after.' He left with a grudging blessing from her.

The Dowager, anxious to make sure that her plans were not spoiled, assured Serafina before she left that Lord Aldworth had every intention of making an offer when he returned at the end of March. Serafina did not know whether she was pleased or sorry. She was eagerly looking forward to being with her family, and even more to acting naturally again. This eagerness gave her some pause for thought. Did she really wish to spend the rest of her life with a man who was both intelligent and perceptive, but who was neither as far as she was concerned? He was superficially so attentive, yet in reality so indifferent to her that he had never observed her closely enough to see how she was deceiving him. She decided that she must give the matter of their relationship some serious thought in the next few weeks. She was prepared to marry for her family's sake, but not if it meant she would be actually unhappy.

However, all thought of rejecting Lord Aldworth was dismissed when she arrived home. Gabriel's affairs were more desperate than anyone had realised, and Mr Feverel had been forced to dispense vast sums to buy him out of trouble. The family's capital, never large, had been seriously eroded and, though the thought was highly distasteful to Mr Feverel, Serafina's marriage might be their only salvation. . .

January and the first half of February passed too quickly. Serafina wandered the fields with the rest of the family, skated and sledged, spent a good deal of time over Christmas rehabilitating Gabriel in his father's regard, and talking at length with her mother. She never once expressed any of her doubts about Lord Aldworth, though she did say that he expected his wife to be a model of decorum. This gave rise to some mirth until Serafina showed them just how much she had learned, and even instructed Angelica in some of the arts. But most of the time she behaved as she had before she had gone to London, ignoring the rules she had painstakingly acquired, and determined to enjoy to the full these last weeks of freedom.

There came a day of brilliant sunshine, though the wind was cold. The children were well wrapped up in woolly caps and scarves for their afternoon walk, and Serafina kept up a brisk pace. She was in charge, for her father was once again with Gabriel in Oxford. As they came back up the drive to Feverel Place Rafe suddenly said, 'Race you up the oak tree, Sally!' This was a time-honoured challenge that no Feverel could resist. Up to now Rafe had always been too young to race Serafina, and she knew how important it was to his pride that she should not reject him.

'Right, my boy! Mick, Angy, you be the judges. Come on!'

Encouraged by the shouts and cheers of the judges, Rafe and Serafina, one each side, started scrambling up the old tree which stood at the beginning of the drive. Serafina was badly out of practice and Rafe forged ahead, dodging nimbly between the branches. The light was no longer so bright, and Serafina, in her excitement, misjudged her distance and found herself falling. She quickly grabbed a branch, swung on it, glanced down and had the impression of a figure below her. She yelled, 'Watch out there, Mick!' and let herself drop to the ground. There was little danger—all the children were well used to this technique. So Serafina was surprised and angry when, instead of leaving the way clear, Michael stayed where he was. As a result he lost his balance as she swung herself with some force against him, and they both tumbled to the ground. Serafina was furious as she scrambled inelegantly to her feet.

'What on earth are you thinking of, Mick? Why didn't you m——?' Her voice died away as she became aware of the well-dressed but slightly dishevelled figure on the ground. Michael was some feet away, standing dumbfounded next to a wide-eyed Angelica. From above came Rafe's voice.

'Sally! Sally! Are you hurt?'

'Don't worry, Rafe,' Serafina answered automatically. 'I'm quite safe.'

Lord Aldworth got up, dusted himself down, then looked at them all. Serafina was staring at him in horror, her mind racing. Whatever was Lord Aldworth doing here in Sussex, long before he was even due to be in England? And how was she to explain her behaviour? This must surely be the end of any ambition to marry the man. Why didn't he speak? 'Are you. . .are you all right?' she croaked.

'Of course I am,' he replied in an irritated voice.

'I'm. . .sorry.'

'You're the girl from Blanchards' garden, aren't you? Tell me, do you make a habit of knocking people down, or is it a particular vendetta against me?' When Serafina continued to stare at him, he said, 'Never mind. What are you children doing here? Is this the entrance to Feverel Place, or have I lost my way? I wish to see Mr Feverel.'

'We are the Feverels, sir,' said Rafe, who had just come down from his perch. 'And I won, Sally!'

'The Feverels!' Lord Aldworth looked more closely at Serafina. 'Take that cap off,' he said suddenly.

'Why?' said Serafina defensively, though she knew very well why he wished to see her hair. Lord Aldworth was not in a mood to stand any nonsense. He stretched out and removed the woolly cap himself. The hair tumbled down in a riot of silver-gilt curls.

'Good God! Am I dreaming? Miss Feverel!' He looked incredulously at the figure before him—its tangle of hair, its jacket covered in green stains, its torn skirt, and Michael's old boots on its feet. 'But no, you can't be, surely! Didn't I hear the boy call you Sally?'

'That's what we call her——' began Angelica.

Serafina came to life and trod on her sister's foot. She had resolved on a desperate course of action. 'Miss Feverel is my sister, sir. My elder sister, Serafina. People who do not know us well often confuse us—we are very alike. Have you come to see her? I'm afraid she has gone to Oxford with my father.' Behind her back she was making discreet signs to the others. Then she went on, 'Can I help you? I am Sally Feverel, and these are my brothers and sister. May I have your name?'

'I'm Aldworth. I own Blanchards. I met your sister in London before Christmas.'

There was a long indrawn breath from the other three children, and they drew closer to Serafina. She took a deep breath and said, 'I am sorry you have had such an unfortunate first acquaintance with the rest of us. Will you. . .do you have to tell Serafina about it? She'll be distressed at my behaviour—but then she so often is. I'm afraid I'm a sore trial to her and to my parents.'

There was a stifled laugh from Rafe. Serafina turned on him. 'Go on, laugh!' she said fiercely. 'But it's not at all funny—we'll all be dished if today's events get out. Take him back to the house, Mick, and tell him not to say anything. Don't give him any chance—you know how he talks.' Rafe was efficiently removed out of harm's way by Michael, and Serafina was left with Angelica and Lord Aldworth. 'I hope you don't mind. Rafe gets in the way. . .'

'And you are hoping to cozen me into keeping quiet. Yes, I understand perfectly.' His sudden grin flashed out. 'I'm no tale-bearer, Miss Sally.'

'Thank you! You're a trump!' She grinned back at him. 'I know it's more than I deserve. I'll return the favour some time, I promise.'

'By all means, if it is ever necessary,' said Lord Aldworth, looking amused. 'Now, did you say your father is not at home?'

'He is in Oxford, Lord Aldworth.'

'When will he be back?'

Left to herself Serafina would have said that her father was to be a month in Oxford—she wanted no other meetings between her family and Lord Aldworth in the immediate future. But Angelica, who, as Serafina later told her, was occasionally unbecomingly forward, added her voice. 'He's due back tomorrow!'

'Good! I shall call in two days' time, then.' He turned to go, but, seeing Serafina's worried expression, he attempted to reassure her. 'I shan't tell on you. Your secret is safe with me! Goodnight!' He walked off towards the road.

'I hope your secret is safe *from* him, too!' muttered

Angelica when he was out of earshot. 'Sally, whatever possessed you to tell such a whopper?'

'What else could I do? Throw myself on his mercy? Ask for his understanding? You don't know him, Angy. Lord Aldworth would have no sympathy. He's selfish, arrogant and quite ruthless. He would have cast me off without a second thought, and what would we do then for money?'

'He seemed quite nice to me,' said Angelica.

That night three of the Feverels held a council of war — Rafe was considered to be too young, and was left asleep. In order to explain her actions, Serafina had to tell the other two a suitably edited version of Lord Aldworth's plans for marriage to her. Mistresses and the like were, of course, not mentioned. Instead, she drew a picture of a career diplomat, performing great deeds in Vienna, needing an heir, but unwilling to be tied to his wife and family.

'So you see,' she concluded, 'he has to find a. . .a biddable, meek little wife to stay at home and look after the children. And that is what I must appear to be.'

It was generally agreed that, in the circumstances, Serafina had acted with great presence of mind that afternoon. But, though she had solved the immediate problem, they were now left with a much bigger one — how to sustain the fiction.

'I don't think Lord A will stay long down here,' Serafina said thoughtfully. 'I think this was in the nature of another call *en passant* on his journey from Newhaven to London. He probably wished to pay a brief visit only to make Papa's acquaintance — nothing — nothing of a more serious nature.'

'You mean he isn't going to offer for you yet?' asked Angelica. Since the afternoon she had become very eager to see Serafina married to Lord Aldworth and had made her approval of him plain.

'I shouldn't think so.' Serafina put on Lady Chilham's voice. 'Goodness me, Angelica, you are precipitate! An important personage such as Lord Aldworth does not make an offer of marriage without a great deal of thought and preparation. He must consult his grand-mother, his lawyers, his chaplain, his agents——' Her voice suddenly changed and she said somewhat bitterly, 'Anyone but the one other person most concerned—his bride!'

'You're not unhappy about it, are you, Sally?' asked Michael. 'I'm sure Papa could find another way. . .'

'You must not even think like that, Mick! No, of course I shall be happy! Lord A has at least as much address as Hartley Pennyworth.'

The Feverels all collapsed into giggles at this. Serafina's 'beau' was a family joke.

'No, I'm serious, Sal,' Michael persisted.

'I shall be very happy to marry Lord Aldworth, if he asks me. He is much the best chance I shall have of repairing the family fortunes, and also of satisfying my own ambitions. Is that serious enough? But, unless we are very clever, I will not have the opportunity. And that is very serious indeed! What about Mama?'

There was a silence. Mama was most unlikely to agree to any form of deception. Then Angelica said slowly, 'Mama might be persuaded at least not to inform on us.'

Serafina was sceptical. 'I can't imagine how!'

'If we could convince her that it would break your heart not to marry Lord A. You could say that you had fallen hopelessly in love with him, and you would die if you had to part from him.'

'You've been reading too much poetry,' said Michael in disgust.

'No, Angy's right!' said Serafina. 'Mama has a very tender heart herself. She would understand that.'

'But you're not so stupid as to have fallen hopelessly in love, Sally!'

'Good lord, no. It has always seemed the greatest folly to me, and I've never had the slightest inclination to do so.'

'But Papa and Mama love each other,' cried Angelica.

'Of course they do, now. But I remember Mama telling me once that their marriage was arranged—she hardly knew Papa before she married him. And I think that might be the best way love is to be found. Marriage to an intelligent man, with whom one can share one or two interests. . .'

'From the sound of it, Lord A isn't going to share many interests with you, Sally,' said Michael bluntly.

'Well, no. But I think he will be abroad a great deal of the time, and I should be free to read and study. The library at Aldworth is famous. I shall visit you here quite often. . . No, don't worry, Michael, I am very happy to be left to my own pursuits.'

'Wouldn't it be splendid if you did fall in love with him?' said Angelica dreamily.

'On the contrary—it would be disastrous! And most unlikely. But I think I could pretend to have done so.'

'Pretend? To Mama?'

Serafina pulled a face. 'I wouldn't enjoy that part of it. But what else can we do?'

'Perhaps Lord A won't meet her?' suggested Michael.

'Papa is bound to introduce them,' Angelica said. 'You know how proud he is of her. No, we must persuade Mama that it would be unkind to spoil Serafina's chances. I'll help!'

Michael was still not happy. 'As long as you leave me out of it,' he said finally.

The conference decided that Papa, if approached in the right manner, would probably not interfere.

The conspirators suffered a set-back when Mrs Feverel categorically refused to have anything to do with the deception.

'But Mama,' cried Angelica dramatically, 'Sally is deep in love with Lord Aldworth. You cannot condemn her to a life of misery!'

'Don't be so silly, Angelica. Serafina is far too sensible a girl to allow her emotions to get the better of her. If Lord Aldworth is so unreasonable then she is better off without him. Now fetch your mathematics primer and go to the schoolroom. I think a little rational study would not come amiss. Where is Serafina?'

'In her room. She really is unhappy, Mama.'

'Bring her here.'

When Serafina entered her mother's room her face bore a look of determined cheerfulness. Mrs Feverel eyed her sharply. 'What is wrong, Serafina?'

'Nothing, Mama. I. . . I think I must have a cold.'

It was true that Serafina's eyes and nose were pink—she had worked hard to make them so.

'Do you truly wish to marry Lord Aldworth?'

This time Serafina's answer was heartfelt. 'Oh, yes, Mama!'

'Then why did you play such a foolish trick on him? And what are we to do about it?'

'I don't know, Mama! I was in a panic, I suppose, at the thought of losing his regard. And at the moment I should certainly lose it if he were to think me a hoyden. In London I have worked very hard to deserve his admiration, and it seems so sad that it will all be wasted.' She hung her head. 'I wish Rafe had not challenged me, but I couldn't refuse, could I?'

Mrs Feverel said drily, 'No, I don't suppose you could. Nor do I suppose you wanted to!' She looked at her daughter's bent head. 'Perhaps I could speak to Lord Aldworth for you?'

'Oh, no!' cried Serafina. 'I mean, Lord Aldworth has not the least notion that I am in love with him! And at the moment I am sure his instant reaction would be to withdraw. You must not, Mama!' There was a silence. Then Serafina said, 'It is such a pity—he is only at Blanchards for such a very short visit. Oh, *why* did he have to come here yesterday?'

'A short visit?'

'Three or four days, I believe.'

'And if nothing occurred to reveal the truth to him this time, when would you tell him? Soon?'

'If only I had time to give him confidence in me! Later, I am sure, I would be able to confess everything to him, but we don't yet know one another well enough. Oh, Mama, I could not deceive him forever. I only need a little time!'

'Hmm.' Mrs Feverel frowned. 'I will not join in a deliberate deception, Serafina. I wish to make myself absolutely clear on that point. But if your Papa agrees, and on condition that you tell Lord Aldworth the truth before he commits himself to you, I will help you. I find I shall not be able to receive visitors for a few days. Much as I should like to meet Lord Aldworth, I'm afraid my health is about to deteriorate.'

Serafina's smile was brilliant as she leapt up and embraced her mother. 'Oh, thank you! Thank you, Mama!'

That night it snowed quite heavily. When the Feverel conspirators got up they found nearly a foot of snow on the ground.

'Perhaps Pa will be delayed?' said Michael hopefully.

Serafina shook her head. 'He might, but I don't think we should count on it.'

'Well, perhaps Lord A won't come visiting in the snow?'

'You may be doing your best to console me, Mick, but it isn't good enough! Think! Lord A travels at all seasons all over Europe. He isn't going to be put off by a little snow over a distance of two or three miles! Oh, I know it's further round by the road, but it still isn't far enough to stop him coming. No, we have to prepare for the fact that Lord A and Papa are going to meet tomorrow or the day after.'

'I still think Lord Aldworth has a nice face,' said Angelica. 'He looked as if he had quite a sense of humour. And look at the way he agreed not to tell Serafina about you.'

'About me?' asked Michael, startled.

'No, stupid! About Sally.'

'Of course. Sorry. I was just confused for a minute. There are really four of us here, though I can only see three—Michael Feverel, Angelica Feverel, Sally Feverel and Serafina Feverel.'

'You're wrong. Serafina Feverel is in Oxford,' said Serafina absent-mindedly. She was working on another idea. 'He did, didn't he?'

'Did what?'

'Agree not to tell. I wonder if I could use that again? If I could get him not to mention Sally when he is talking to Papa?'

'You couldn't!'

'I could try. I don't think Papa would betray me, but it would be better if the occasion didn't arise. He might find it difficult. It would certainly help if Sally wasn't mentioned. . .'

'I'm tired of this,' said Michael suddenly. 'I want to go sledging. We're wasting the snow, and once the sun comes out it won't last long.'

'Of course!' Serafina's eyes lit up. 'We shall go sledging! Fetch Rafe and we'll all go up Pett's Hill. Then you three can sledge down this side and I'll go down the other side to Blanchards. Sally will pay a call on Lord Aldworth this morning.'

'You can't!' said Angelica. 'That's one of the things you told me were never done. A young lady never calls alone on a gentleman.'

'Serafina wouldn't dare, certainly. She's a lady. But Sally. . . Sally isn't—she's a hoyden. Let's get Rafe and the sledge. I'll see Mama.'

Conversation was not easy as they trudged through the snow up the hill which divided the Feverel lands from those of Blanchards, and it was made more difficult by the presence of Rafe. So Serafina's co-conspirators

forgot their problems and enjoyed the rare sight of a
Sussex landscape covered in snow. At the top they
parted company, Michael and Rafe setting off first down
the hill, and Angelica following soon after. Serafina saw
them off, then walked over to the other side, and viewed
the path down the south-eastern slope. She had to screw
up her eyes as she did so, for the sun had come out and
its rays dazzled her. This particular run was unfamiliar,
but it looked fairly straightforward—a shallow incline at
first, followed by a steeper slope leading into the field
behind Blanchards' walled garden. She got on her
sledge and with a whoop she pushed off.

Lord Aldworth sat at breakfast in Blanchards' small
parlour—the only room on the ground floor that was
habitable. He had risen early, for he wanted to see more
of the men who would be working on the house. He was
in Sussex for a number of reasons. The routine work in
Vienna had been dealt with more expeditiously than he
had expected. The other matter had also gone well,
except for some unpleasant suspicions about the people
involved. At the very least there had been some careless
talk, and perhaps there had been worse. How had his
grandmother heard about what she had called 'the
South American business'? But for those doubts, he
could reasonably have stayed abroad for another
month, enjoying the company of his friends. Indeed, he
had been strongly tempted to do so. But his doubts,
combined with his promise to his grandmother to marry
soon, had brought him back early. He was not a man to
shirk his duty, and he had come to the reluctant conclusion that his duty lay for the moment at Aldworth.
Serafina Feverel was exactly what he had stipulated—

more than he might have hoped for, in fact. Her beauty was undeniable and, though at first he had been bored at the thought of spending time with such a featherhead, she had in fact quite often amused him with her naïve comments. How long this would last once they were married was another matter, but he could surely endure it until he had acquired an heir!

His grandmother's picture of his association with Lady Paget had not been attractive, either. She was right; he had been in some danger there. When he'd heard that Louisa Paget was shortly due back in Vienna it had strengthened his decision to leave early. With time to spare before he was due back in London, he had decided on impulse to break his journey in Sussex for a day or two. If he was planning to marry, then the sooner Blanchards was ready for occupation by one or other — or all — of the ladies at present living in Aldworth House the better. Work on the house in Sussex had been delayed by his preoccupation with affairs in London before Christmas, followed by the trip abroad, and he wanted to set things in motion again. With luck it would now be ready by Easter.

There had been another motive, of course. He had wanted to have an informal look at the home of the girl who was probably going to be his bride. It was a pity she and her father were away, but he had been wrong to call without first sending his manservant with a note. He hoped Mr Feverel would not take it amiss. . . Then he smiled cynically. Surely no father would take it amiss that a rich suitor was impatient to see his daughter! But how did Serafina, who was the epitome of correct behaviour, come to have such a sister? Sally, she was called. A pity the girl was such a hoyden; there was something appealing about her. He smiled as he recalled her woolly cap, her old jacket and bedraggled skirt, her unladylike yell as she had landed on him, and later the frank appeal for his help. So like Serafina in feature, and so unlike her in everything else!

A drip of water splashed down, just missing the breakfast-table. Devil take it! The unexpected fall of snow had found every hole in the roof of the house, every crack in the masonry. Of course Blanchards lay in a hollow; that was part of the trouble. He wondered whether the field behind could be drained and a conduit put in to lead the water from the hill away from the house. He ought to inspect it—he had never looked beyond the garden. But surely this was hardly the weather for any inspection of the ground. He looked out of the window. The morning had been grey, but now the sun had appeared and the sight of the countryside, dazzling in its mantle of snow, called to him. Putting on his heaviest boots, he went through the garden and out into the field. At least from this slightly higher ground he could see the state of the roof from outside. He turned round and contemplated the house. . .

A sudden and strangely familiar yell caused him to turn round. It was a shock to see a colourful figure on a sledge hurtling towards him. . .

CHAPTER FIVE

LORD ALDWORTH leapt easily to one side. But it was unfortunate that the sledge also veered to the same side, and as it overturned and slid to a stop it took his legs from under him. Sally Feverel—for it was she, of course—came to rest in a flurry of snow a few feet away. They looked at one another in silence. Then the girl suddenly burst into a peal of laughter, and after a moment Lord Aldworth joined in.

'I have never in all my life met anyone so prone to mishaps!'

'It's you who are prone, sir. . .' And she went off into another peal.

Lord Aldworth regarded her with fascination. The bright red cap was awry, and wisps of her hair, caught in the rays of the sun, looked like strands of spun gold. Sparkling eyes, the colour of the sky, laughed at him out of a delicately shaped face with cheeks which were rosy with fresh air and exercise. He had never seen anything so. . .so alive! A sudden and strong pull of attraction, not quite like anything he had ever felt before, took him by surprise.

'It's very sad!' she continued. 'I was going to beg a favour of you, too!' Laughter bubbled out of her again, and he was hard put to it not to say that he would grant her anything she asked. Instead, he got up and offered her a hand.

'Let me ask first,' he said. He could feel himself smiling at her like an idiot! 'Are you all right?'

She allowed herself to be pulled up, and they brushed the snow off their clothes. Then she became serious. 'I could have injured you—I'm sorry, truly sorry. I thought I could avoid you by turning the sledge over.'

'You might have injured yourself a lot more. Are you mad?'

'You could say so, I suppose. But you don't grow up with four brothers and sisters without getting used to a few spills and bruises.'

Surprised, he asked, 'I thought there were six Feverels?'

'Oh! Oh, yes,' she said. 'I wasn't counting Gabriel. He has been away for such a long time.'

'What about Miss Feverel? I can't imagine her suffering spills and bruises?'

'No, no. Oh, good lord, no! Serafina was the one who comforted us when we were hurt. You wouldn't believe how good my sister is, Lord Aldworth. It's very hard for me to live up to her.'

'I am sure Miss Feverel is as good as she is lovely. But I shouldn't think you need worry about a comparison. Do you?' The girl before him blushed and looked confused. Delightfully, deliciously confused.

She stammered, 'W-we are so different, Serafina and I. She tries to satisfy every canon of propriety. People would never see her climbing trees, or arguing about philosophy, or any of the other things which are not considered suitable. Whereas I am forever offending. That's why I wanted to ask a favour. . .'

Lord Aldworth became cautious. 'What is it?'

'Well—er—do you think you could avoid mentioning

my name to my father when you see him? I love him
dearly, but he is so proud of Serafina, and I am such a
contrast to her. He will only get angry, and I would
rather not have that—especially when you are there.
Could you do that?'

'An acquaintance with you, Sally, may not be dull,
but it certainly leads to complications! If I do as you ask,
conversation with the two people I chiefly wish to see is
going to be very difficult. First you ask me not to
mention you to your sister Serafina, and now you wish
me to avoid your name with your father. . .' He studied
the face turned up so pleadingly to his, and found it
impossible to disappoint her. 'I suppose I could try. I
certainly won't volunteer anything about our. . .
encounters. Will that do?'

'But you are nice!' she said, looking astonished.

He was curious, and slightly offended. 'Has your
sister told you I am not? I don't think I have been
unkind or rude to her, surely?'

'Oh, no! She. . .she thinks you're perfect! Only I
thought you sounded. . .sounded. . .'

'Go on.'

'Well, stuffy, and not very interesting.'

'I beg your pardon?'

'You take her to such dull places—to shops and
parties, and to see the animals at the Tower, and to
Astley's and all the other childish things.'

Lord Aldworth tried, and failed, to suppress a feeling
of annoyance out of all proportion to the criticism. He
had done his best to amuse Serafina Feverel, at some
cost to his own inclinations. Did this chit think he had
gone to those places to amuse himself? That his level of
intelligence was so low? How dare she? He found

himself growing so angry that he decided it would be better to send her home before he said something he would later regret. 'It's getting colder,' he said, turning towards the house. 'I think we should start thinking of getting you home. I cannot imagine you will wish to climb that hill again, so we'll go this way.'

As they went through the garden he said as calmly as he could, 'I am sorry if your sister has found my company boring. . .'

'Oh, goodness, my stupid tongue—I've made you angry, and that was the *last* thing I wanted! Serafina has not said any such thing! Please do not be offended, Lord Aldworth. My sister would never forgive me if I gave you the wrong impression. She has found great enjoyment in your company, truly. I was speaking for myself. It all seemed such a waste. . .'

Really, the girl was impossible! There was a bite in his voice as he asked, 'And what would Madam Impertinence do with her valuable time?'

'Don't be angry with me, please! If you only knew how I long to visit London! To hear a debate in the Palace of Westminster—particularly one on Foreign Policy—with someone like you who could explain the people involved——'

'Alas, ladies are not allowed in the debating chamber.'

'How unfair! As if we are not allowed to take a sensible interest in what is happening to our own country!' Her voice trembled with real anger and he attempted to distract her.

'What else would you do in London?'

'There are all sorts of buildings I should like to visit—Westminster Abbey, the Royal Exchange, the

Guildhall. . . I would go to the theatre to see Shakespeare, not farces, and spend as much time as I could spare in the British Museum——'

'If you are suggesting that I should do all this with Serafina, you are being absurd! Your sister would die of boredom before we had done the half of it.'

She looked at him strangely, and her voice was sad as she said, 'Yes, she would. And gentlemen do not appreciate it when young ladies take an interest in such things. It is better to be Serafina.' She was quiet then until they reached the high road, and he found himself softening towards her again. He wondered if she was tired.

'Would you like me to get out the gig and deliver you to your home?'

She shook her head. 'Thank you, but no. I like walking.'

'Then allow me to escort you.'

'I am obliged for the offer but no, thank you,' she said with great determination.

'I must!'

'On no account! I—er——' She gave him a comic look. 'I am very familiar with the road to Blanchards, you know. I have visited it quite regularly, especially in the autumn. All those grapes. . . And if anyone from the family saw me with you I should be in trouble again. No, I will not hear of it! Goodbye, Lord Aldworth, and thank you again for promising not to mention me.' She took a step, then paused and said, 'Tell me, do you enjoy your conversations with her? Serafina, I mean.'

Lord Aldworth could not immediately recall ever having had what he would call a conversation with Serafina, but he put as much conviction as he could into his reply. 'Of course! What a strange question! Why do you ask?'

'Oh, no reason. It's just that I cannot imagine what you talk about. Goodbye again.'

'Goodbye. . . Sally. Shall I see you tomorrow?'

'I don't think so. I shall keep out of the way.' Her grin flashed out. 'I'm regarded as a liability rather than an asset in elegant company, Lord Aldworth.' She set off at a brisk pace up the road.

After she had gone Lord Aldworth felt dissatisfied. He should have gone with her, at least to her gates, but she had been quite decided in her refusal. *Very* unlike her sister. . . What an annoying baggage Sally Feverel was! He should be grateful that his grandmother had found the right member of the Feverel family—Miss Independence and he would soon be at odds with one another. He started back towards the house, but then stopped in thought. That extraordinary feeling of attraction he had felt towards her—he had almost kissed her there in the snow! That was very strange. The girl was nothing like any of his previous amours. . . What was he thinking of? Sally Feverel was the younger sister of the girl he was planning to marry. . .some time. He walked briskly up the steps to the door, determined to put them both out of his mind for the moment. But the animated little face, so like and yet so unlike that of her sister, floated before his eyes. She was an interesting little thing. . . What a strange question she had asked at the end! He stopped yet again. What the devil *did* he and Serafina Feverel talk about?

Serafina felt dispirited as she walked back to Feverel Place. She had enjoyed sparring with Lord Aldworth and, even more, she had enjoyed expressing her real feelings about their activities in London. But the situation was fraught with danger, and if he once found out before she had had time to lay some sounder foundations for their friendship. . . Strangely, it seemed more important than ever before that she should marry this man. However, when she reached the house and saw that her father had arrived home, she put all thought of Lord Aldworth out of her mind.

In answer to the family's eager questions Mr Feverel told them that Gabriel was clearly back on the right track again and working hard.

'I shouldn't be surprised if they offered him a chance to do a further degree. His professor is very taken with his work. There's the problem of the estate, though. I really need his help here. Still, it would be an honour.' He turned to Serafina. 'What's this I hear about a visit from your suitor?'

Serafina gave Angelica a look of burning reproach. 'Not me,' mouthed her sister. 'Rafe.'

'I think he's coming to see you tomorrow, Papa. But I don't think he's quite ready to offer for me yet. He is really just paying a social call, as a neighbour, on his way to London. We were. . .we were quite taken by surprise when he came.'

'I should think so, indeed! In my young days gentlemen didn't pay visits to perfect strangers without checking first that they would be welcome! Still, you were pleased to see him, eh, puss?'

'Oh, yes, Papa,' said poor Serafina. 'Er. . .may I have a word with you in private, Papa?'

Once in the library she was unable to stop herself from telling her father the whole. To her relief he took

it very well. Indeed he laughed so heartily at one point
that she grew quite resentful. 'But Papa!' she protested.
'It really isn't funny at all. Lord Aldworth would be
extremely angry if he knew.'

'I should imagine he would,' said her father. 'And
with some reason. So what will you do about it? Or are
you expecting me to sort it out for you?'

'I don't think anyone could,' said Serafina gloomily.
'Not before Lord Aldworth and I know one another
sufficiently well for me to tell him myself.
Meanwhile. . .'

'Meanwhile you want me to carry on the fiction, is
that it?'

'You're too clever, Papa. Yes, that is what I would
prefer.'

'Is he such a coxcomb, Sally? I wouldn't like you to
marry someone you disliked.'

'I. . . I told Mama that I loved him. That wasn't quite
true. But when I was talking to him this morning, when
I could speak to him like a sensible human being, I liked
him very much.' She paused and thought about it. 'Very
much. I think I could be quite happy with him, Papa. If
only I can tell him about my deception in my own time.'

'You've asked him not to mention the name Sally to
me, you say? That was cunning. Not honest, but
cunning. And the poor man isn't to mention Sally to
Serafina!' Mr Feverel almost went into another parox-
ysm of laughter, but sobered when he saw Serafina's
face. 'I should say, rather, "poor Sally"! Very well, I
shan't go out of my way to betray you. But I won't tell
any lies, mind. Do you wish me to have a word with
your mother? She will not be so easy to persuade,
though I know she wants you to marry the fellow.'

Serafina then informed her father of her arrangement
with her mother. He frowned at first, for he disapproved
of making capital out of Mrs Feverel's illness. But he
was finally won over.

'Our name won't be worth much if this ever gets out,
Sally. I hope you realise that. But there, I never cared
for what people in general thought of me. A poor lot,
people in general. Now, tell me what you've been
reading while I've been away. I have some new German
books from Oxford for you—there's a particularly fine
copy of *Werther*. Now there was a madman—dying for
love, the fool! It's well-written, however.'

When Lord Aldworth called the following day the stage
was well set. The snow had gone, and Angelica and
Michael had taken Rafe for a walk—a long walk. Mrs
Feverel was in her room, with a collection of books and
periodicals to amuse her, and a bell was to hand for her
to call one of the maids if she needed anything. Serafina,
dressed in one of her London muslins which had been
freshly laundered the day before, was sitting in the
library with her father. Her hair was smoothly caught
back in a pink ribbon, in marked contrast to the recent
riot of curls under the woolly cap. Maggie, her mother's
maid, had applied a little Gowland's lotion to Serafina's
cheeks to remove the hint of colour brought about by
her adventure in the snow. Pink ribbons trimmed her
dress and tiny white slippers were on her feet. A piece
of her mother's embroidery was in her hands.

'Don't set any stitches I can't afterwards remove, for
heaven's sake, Serafina. It's a particularly pretty design,
one of my favourites, and you know what you are,' her
mother had said as she'd given it to her.

Serafina broke the silence that had fallen on them after they had left her mother. 'Remember not to call me Sally, Papa,' she said nervously. 'Also that I have never willingly opened a book in my life, nor am I at all clever or knowledgeable. Modish young ladies aren't.'

'You have reminded me so often that I should have to be a dolt myself to forget,' said Mr Feverel somewhat testily. 'Though why the devil the man would prefer such a simpleton I cannot understand. But there's not the slightest need for you to look so anxious; I'll accept what you say. Pick up your embroidery, *Serafina*; I see someone coming up the drive. But you in turn must remember this—I will tell no lies, not even for you.'

There was no time for more. Lord Aldworth was being announced.

Serafina took a deep breath and set herself to act as she had never acted before. This man was no fool. It had been comparatively easy yesterday and the day before to persuade him that Serafina and Sally were two different people, for he had never been really interested in Serafina as a person, and in any case he had not seen her since before Christmas. But he had seen Sally twice at close quarters very recently, and the resemblance between the two sisters must seem almost incredible. Only twins could be so alike, and Lord Aldworth knew that Serafina was not a twin. She must convince him of their separate identity by character-acting alone. Sally's carelessness in dress and appearance, her frank, uninhibited manner of speaking, her interest in the world of books and politics were already a contrast to Serafina's exquisite neatness and propriety, her sedate modesty, her lack of interest in anything intellectual—but she must now underline this contrast with her voice and manner. Her nervousness was not assumed as her father went to meet his guest.

'Aldworth, how kind of you to call! At last, after all these years, we meet our neighbour from over the hill!'

'Mr Feverel, your servant, sir. I am sorry that my brother's preoccupations in Berkshire left him little time to visit Sussex. And if I am honest I have to confess that I would have postponed our meeting until I had more time down here—except that I had another reason. . . Miss Feverel, I hope I see you well?'

Lord Aldworth came over and took Serafina's hand to his lips. She blushed, looked down and murmured something suitable. As he looked at her an expression of disbelief crossed the handsome features. 'Amazing!' he said.

This was the moment. She must bear it in mind that Sally would not have talked of meeting Lord Aldworth. As he continued to stare she looked up with an air of slightly embarrassed bewilderment. 'Sir?' said Serafina. 'What do you mean? Is there. . .is there something wrong?'

'You are so like——' He stopped. Serafina continued to look puzzled, while he obviously wrestled with a problem. How could he even mention Sally, when he had promised not to? Even though she was nervous of the outcome, part of her was enjoying his dilemma. But she had to admire his sang-froid as he went on, 'So like a picture I saw recently in Vienna. Botticelli, I think it was.'

'Bottic——?' Serafina's anxiety at an unfamiliar name was patent.

Mr Feverel intervened. He came over to his visitor with a glass of wine and said genially, 'Ah, Vienna. I hear you have recently come from there, Aldworth. You've been working for Stewart and Castlereagh, I believe. How are we doing?'

Lord Aldworth was finding it difficult to take his eyes from Serafina, but he turned to his host at this. 'As well as we could reasonably hope, sir, though it's a slow business. As I understand it, the chief difficulty lies with Prussia. We and the other Great Powers are doing everything we can to persuade her to moderate her claims for reparations from France, but she is very reluctant to forgo anything. It is uphill work.'

'Difficult lot, the Prussians. You only have to read their so-called literature. But I'd have thought Wellington wouldn't stand for any nonsense?'

'He does his best, though he sees everything from a military point of view, of course.'

'It was a good move to withdraw some of the occupation troops from France, wouldn't you say?'

'Indeed. The people are growing resentful of these foreigners living off their country. It's natural enough, I suppose. But a resentful population and a weakened regime in France won't help anyone. Unless we do something about supporting Louis we shall——' He stopped suddenly. 'But where are my manners? I am sure I must be boring Miss Feverel!'

'Oh, no!' Serafina said in her shy, slightly high-pitched voice. 'I like to hear gentlemen talking.' She added with simple pride, 'And I know of the Duke of Wellington.'

Mr Feverel frowned. 'I should hope so, indeed.'

'All the same, I shouldn't like your daughter to think that I came to visit her only to ignore her, or, worse, to bore her!' Lord Aldworth came over and sat down beside Serafina. 'That is a pretty piece of embroidery, Miss Feverel,' he said. 'And executed with skill.' Serafina's blush was wholly natural. If he only knew!

Under the pretence of examining the work Lord Aldworth was having a close look at the face bent over it. 'Remarkable! Quite remarkable,' he said, frowning. 'Tell me, are all your family as handsome, Feverel?'

Under her demure front Serafina was indignant. This was cheating! He might not have mentioned Sally's name, but he was deliberately inviting her father to talk of the rest of the family. She waited apprehensively for the reply.

'I believe they are,' replied Mr Feverel indifferently. 'I have never paid much attention to their looks. Serafina resembles her sister, I believe.'

This was perfectly true—Serafina and Angelica were quite alike—though it was not what Lord Aldworth understood from the remark. 'Astoundingly so!' he said, taking his eyeglass and examining once again the young lady sitting next to him. Serafina was grateful for her father's evasion but thought it was time to change the subject.

'Would you like me to see if Mama requires anything, Papa?' she said nervously.

'If you wish to, my dear. But come back soon. I am sure that Lord Aldworth and I have a great deal to say to one another, but he might object if you were absent for too long. And don't you want to hear what your father says about you?'

'Oh, Papa!' said Serafina, looking reproachful. 'You are a tease. I am sure Lord Aldworth is too kind to listen to your stories! I expect you will talk about politics or books or sport, not about a silly girl like me.'

'Well, off you go!' Serafina made her escape. As she went she heard her father say, 'My wife is an invalid, Aldworth. I should have liked to have you meet her, but that is unfortunately not possible today. Perhaps the next time you call? Are you planning to stay in Sussex long?'

'I'm afraid not. I leave for London very soon. . .' The conversation continued as she went up the stairs.

Her mother was naturally very interested in their visitor. 'Hetty says he is very handsome. Do you think so?'

'Of course. And Papa seems to like him. I wish you could meet him, Mama, but I'm glad you agreed not to see him this time. I heard him say he is going to London within the next day or two.'

'So soon! So your problem will be solved—temporarily?'

'Yes. . .'

'What is wrong, Serafina? You are surely relieved that Lord Aldworth will soon be gone, aren't you? Or will you miss him?' Mrs Feverel's voice was sympathetic, but amused. 'Oh, dear, it is hard enough to be in love! But only you, Serafina, could have made it so complicated too!'

'In lo——? Yes, you're right, Mama. It is hard—very hard. But I am glad he is going. I shall be glad not to have to pretend to him any more.' She paused. Why wasn't she more convinced of this? Her mother raised an eyebrow, seeing her daughter's uncertainty and waiting for her to say more. Serafina went on slowly, 'But you're right, I shall miss him. He is different, somehow, down here in Sussex. I like him better. . . I mean, even better. And. . .and what if he is angry with me for the deception and refuses to see me any more?'

'I should imagine that he will indeed be angry. Very angry! But if you truly love each other you can solve that problem.' Serafina looked doubtful. 'You must confess the truth to him, my dear.'

'I will, I promise.'

As Serafina went back downstairs she was hard put to it to know what she felt. Talking to her mother had made her face the problem more clearly herself. What she had said was no less than the truth. On the one hand she wanted Lord Aldworth out of Sussex as soon as possible—the risk of discovery was too great. She had been lucky that Blanchards was comparatively isolated, and that he apparently did not as yet wish to make the effort to meet the other families of the neighbourhood. His arrival at Blanchards had been unplanned and she doubted that it was generally known. But it only needed one question to an innocent neighbour for the whole subterfuge to be exposed. The sooner he was in London the better!

On the other hand. . . As Sally in Sussex she had a chance to talk to him as she really was, and she was finding the experience more stimulating than she could have imagined. He was a different person when he dispensed with the air of indulgent indifference he adopted towards Serafina, and behaved naturally.

As she came into the room Lord Aldworth was saying, 'The trouble is, sir, that the present powers that be in Europe are all so damned autocratic! They have no moderation—I would say not even much sense! Ferdinand of Spain is the worst—he's going to give us real trouble soon. He's an unpleasant character, and not at all popular with his people. We can't interfere, of course, but we're very keen to keep our trade links with the Spanish American colonies. There's something brewing out there. . . That's the reason I had to go back to Vienna in such a hurry, to be honest. We wanted to get something signed and sealed before. . . Ah, Miss Feverel. How is your mother?'

'Feeling a little better. She sends her apologies to you, Lord Aldworth, and hopes to be able to see you before you go back to London.' This was sheer bluff on Serafina's part, for she knew very well that Lord Aldworth would have to make his excuses.

'Alas, that is impossible. I was telling your father that I am going to London quite soon. I've done all I can to set things going at Blanchards for the moment. But I hope. . . I intend to come back a little later in the year, and perhaps then. . .? Shall I see you in London before then, Miss Feverel?'

She lowered her gaze. 'I hope so, Lord Aldworth. If Papa permits.' She said in her soft, slightly higher Serafina voice, 'I enjoy life in London. And Lady Chilham says there are even more parties once the season starts.'

'Tell me. . .tell me what you most like doing. In London.'

So Sally's comments had met their mark! Serafina kept her amusement at this request well-hidden as she replied vaguely, 'Everything. Shopping, I suppose. And I like it when you take me to places you enjoy visiting. The animals at. . .the Tower, was it?. . . were nice. . .' She smiled in sweet reminiscence.

Lord Aldworth sat back, looking satisfied. 'I thought as much,' he said. 'We shall see some more of London when you return to the capital, if Lady Chilham permits. Would you like to visit the British Museum again? Or somewhere else—the Palace of Westminster, perhaps? Or the Royal Exchange?'

The avuncular tone again—he deserved to be deceived! Serafina's response was a masterpiece of reluctant compliance as she said, 'If those are places you would like to visit, Lord Aldworth,' adding despondently, 'I am sure they would all be very interesting. What is the Royal Exchange?'

Mr Feverel, who was clearly not comfortable at this deliberate misrepresentation of his daughter's character, frowned again. He suddenly said, 'Serafina, would you get me the *Cogitationes*? There's something in it which I wish to show Lord Aldworth before he leaves. Something about Spain. It is apposite to our present situation, I believe.'

Remembering to walk with the graceful but slightly mincing gait that she had been taught in London, which was so different from Sally's free stride, Serafina obediently fetched the copy of Bacon from the shelves, and gave it to her father with a charming little curtsy.

'Do you know where all your father's books are, Miss Feverel—even one in Latin?' asked Lord Aldworth, with a look of surprise.

She had not thought to ask where to find the book first! What a fool she was! Serafina looked suspiciously at her father—had he done it deliberately? He knew she had been referring to the work that very morning. . . Lord Aldworth was waiting. . .she must think of something quickly—her movement had been too confident to deny that she had known where it was.

'Oh, yes, indeed!' she said proudly. 'I dust them very

frequently, Lord Aldworth. Papa doesn't trust the servants to do it. I know all their covers.' She looked at the copy of Francis Bacon's book. 'Especially the pretty ones.'

Mr Feverel leafed through the book and said, 'Ah, yes! Here it is. Read that, Aldworth.'

While Lord Aldworth's attention was on the book Serafina stole a look at her father. He was regarding her with disapproval mixed with admiration—so he *had* tried to trap her! But why?

After Lord Aldworth had left Serafina tackled her father about it with some indignation.

'Sally, I just couldn't sit there watching you make a fool of him. I liked him. He talked like a sensible man about the international situation, and he obviously feels deeply about his work. And you were so. . .so. . . cocky. When I agreed to help you I thought you were distressed, but this afternoon you were actually enjoying yourself. So I gave you something to think about.' He smiled at her in triumph. 'And you failed! You walked straight to that book, as I knew you would.'

'You'll admit that I soon recovered my position, Pa!'

'Magnificently! "Pretty covers" indeed!' He chuckled. Then he said more seriously, 'However, I warn you that I won't have much more of this nonsense. When Lord Aldworth pays his next visit I hope he will have been told, by you or someone else. And Sally——'

'Yes, Papa?'

'I approve very much of Lord Aldworth. I like the idea of having him as a son-in-law, and not just because he is rich, either.'

For the rest of the day Serafina was restless. Her encounters with Lord Aldworth had stirred feelings she

had not before experienced. In London she had felt a
tug of attraction at their first meeting, but that had soon
been overlaid with irritation at his lack of interest in her,
at the low level of intelligence he expected of her. Here
in Sussex she had met him as a different person, and the
tug of attraction was even stronger. Her father was
right—she had enjoyed the meeting in the library,
dangerous though it had been. She had felt alive! Here
was a man who was worth challenging—she felt it, and
her father also felt it. Her charade had been born of
desperation, but now she would not have missed it for
the world. For the first time she saw what Lady
Aldworth had meant when she had said that Charles
was worth an effort. But that was not the Charles
Serafina would know—Sally was the girl who had caught
a glimpse of the real Charles Dacre.

So it was not really surprising that Sally should decide
to risk meeting Lord Aldworth once more before he left
Sussex. Who knew what would happen before she saw
him next?

CHAPTER SIX

THE snow had completely disappeared, and the mud and slush which it had left on the roads had also gone. The sun was bright in the sky when Serafina walked over to Blanchards the next day. She would have ridden, but she dared not let Lord Aldworth see her in her riding-habit and the very elegant riding-hat that Papa had been good enough to give her the Christmas before. In them she looked too much like Serafina. So she marched over the hill in her woolly cap and the same old jacket and skirt—which were even more the worse for wear since her accident with the sledge. At the gate into Blanchards she paused for thought. She could hardly go boldly up to the front door and ask for Lord Aldworth!

With a shrug she climbed up her usual bit of wall and sat on top of it for a minute or two, grimacing as she saw the bare expanse where the greenhouse and vine had once stood.

'Regretting your past escapades, Sally?'

Startled, Serafina turned her head. Lord Aldworth was standing at the far entrance, her sledge at his feet.

'Have you come for this? I found it in the field and was about to come looking for you to return it.' He came through the garden towards her, staring hard. With a touch of suspicion in his voice he said, 'You are astonishingly like your sister!'

Serafina laughed in apparent delight. '*Merci du compliment, monsieur*! I know our features are almost identical, but it's the first time that anyone has thought me as elegant as my elegant sister! My mother says that I even lack elegance of mind. But it's so stuffy to be proper. And, though Serafina is so much more presentable, I do think I am just a touch quicker of understanding, don't you? May I come in?' He nodded and made to go to the gate, but with a laughing protest Serafina climbed nimbly down the tree on the garden side of the wall and jumped to the ground. Here she stood facing him, a frank, open smile on her face. 'Can you imagine Serafina doing that? She would sooner die!' With great daring she said, in a travesty of Serafina's somewhat childish voice, 'Oh, Sally, please don't be such a hoyden! What will people think?'

Lord Aldworth, much to Serafina's relief, laughed. 'You're a minx, Sally Feverel! Your sister is right—you should learn to behave.'

'Well, I shall, but not yet. Besides, you already know me as I am—it would be a waste for me to try to behave properly with you! Your visit yesterday went well, I hear.'

'Where were you?' he asked casually.

'I told you—the family usually tries to keep me out of the way when elegant company is expected. Serafina and Pa were considered to be company enough—the rest of the family had to go for a walk! But from what he said afterwards Pa liked you a lot. He thought you intelligent.'

'You sound doubtful. Does my choice of excursions in London still cause you to think me "stuffy"? Lacking in intelligence? You are wrong if you do. Your sister enjoyed those excursions.'

'Did she say so? I expect she was trying to please you.'

'On the contrary. The suggestion that we should visit some of the places you mentioned—the Royal Exchange and so on—appalled her. It was at that point that she tried to please me—she did her best to disguise her feelings, but her reluctance was obvious.'

'In that case, I suppose you were right. But wouldn't it be more intelligent to. . .? Have you never thought of educating her?'

'What on earth for? She is perfect as she is.'

'Oh. I see. Er. . .for what?'

'I don't think that need concern you,' said Lord Aldworth coldly.

'But it does! Serafina is important to me, and I wish to be sure that she will be happy with you.'

'You are being precipitate, Sally——What are you laughing about now, for God's sake?'

'Precipi. . .precipit. . .' Serafina could not get the word out for laughter.

He said haughtily, 'I suppose you will explain, when you have recovered yourself?'

These words, uttered in such a tone, sent her off into another gale of laughter. How could she explain? To say that she had used the word in order to make fun of him to the children? 'Goodness me, Angelica,' she had said, 'you are precipitate! An important personage such as Lord Aldworth. . .' And she had used just such a haughty manner, too. But to tell him this would hardly help to soothe him. She made an effort and said, 'I beg pardon. Only—you sounded so. . .so stuffy!'

'Stuffy!' She had been right. He was angrier than before.

'I am sorry, truly I am, but you should not provoke me. What shall we talk about? Your visit yesterday? Pa said you had discussed the international situation. He must have enjoyed talking to someone who is right in the centre of affairs. Is there really a prospect of further trouble? War, even?'

'No, I don't think so. That would be in no one's interest.'

'I suppose it's important to keep a balance between all those who might wish to pursue their own profit at the expense of the others? Do we? Pursue our own profit, I mean?'

'Of course not! Except perhaps in trade. That's where our interests lie—markets and goods for our merchants. There's a situation brewing in South America——' He broke off.

'Papa told me something of it. The Spanish colonies out there wish for independence. Do you think they should be supported?'

'At the moment,' he said carefully, 'our official position is to support the sovereignty of Spain—though I am not sure how long that will last. Sally, I would much rather not say anything more—we have to tread very warily, and with as much cunning as in any wartime campaign. There are any number of wolves and traps, and I'm doing all I can to see that we avoid them at the moment.'

'You'll have to learn from the lion and the fox, won't you?'

He looked at her in surprise. 'You read Machiavelli?'

'Have I shocked you? A girl, and so well-read?' she mocked. 'Allow me to tell you that I wouldn't let you treat me the way you think Serafina should be treated. I read anything and everything, the more the better. Indeed, "I have studied books rather than men", and I sometimes think I have been right.'

'What a waste of so much beauty!'

'Don't you dare patronise me! Serafina is the beautiful one. Keep your empty compliments for her.'

'You are her equal in beauty, Sally. Or you would be if——'

'If I cared more for such things, Lord Aldworth. But I am not content to be a. . .a plaything. When I marry it will be with the intention of having a true partner for a husband, one who will share his life with me, share his worries and his triumphs, share his interests and work, not. . .not someone who would put me in his home and then forget about me except when he wants heirs!' She came to a sudden halt as she realised that she had allowed her feelings to get the better of her. If Lord Aldworth did marry Serafina, that was exactly what he intended to do with her. This thought was so depressing that she had to turn away from him to hide sudden tears.

'He would be a fortunate man, your husband,' said Lord Aldworth slowly, and turned her gently towards him. 'Look at me, Sally. Why are you crying?'

'I doubt my ability ever to find such a man.' It seemed quite natural that he should take her in his arms to comfort her.

'That is nonsense!' he said softly. 'You could do anything! When the time comes for you to marry——'

'I shall no doubt be forced to compromise.'

Lord Aldworth seemed not to have heard. His arms tightened round her and his eyes were on her lips. He bent his head. His own lips were very close. . . Serafina stared up as if mesmerised. A sudden excitement was

racing along her veins. Something momentous was
happening. . . Then Lord Aldworth gave a groan,
released her, and moved away. 'I must be mad,' he
muttered. 'Quite mad!' Without looking at her, he went
on, 'Will you take the sledge back with you now? There
would be room for it in the gig. I'll get one of the men to
take you home.'

Serafina was dazed. Nothing had really happened and
yet she had caught a glimpse of something she had never
before even dreamed of. It had nothing to do with
reason or logic but, whatever it was, it threatened her
sane, rational view of life as nothing else ever had. She
shivered and said in a subdued tone, 'Yes. Thank you.'

'Sally!'

'Yes, Lord Aldworth?' she said, looking at him.

'I. . . I'm sorry if I frightened you.'

'You didn't frighten me. I. . . I wanted you to kiss
me.'

'Oh, God, Sally, I can't! I mustn't!'

'No, of course you must not. I know that.'

She raised her head and looked at him gravely. He
went to say something, hesitated, then shook his head.
When he finally spoke he sounded angry.

'Come, I'll take you to the stables. There'll be
someone there.'

The stables were on the other side of the house. They
went through the walled garden and out into the
overgrown shrubbery—at this season a tangle of
branches and dead leaves, interspersed with laurels.
Lord Aldworth kicked a dead branch off the path with
unnecessary violence. 'This will all have to be pruned
and cleared. There's a mountain of work to be done
before——' He cut himself short and they walked on in

silence. They came to a place where the path was so overgrown that it had narrowed to a single track. 'I'll go first—there might be some more rubbish in the way,' he said. But a few yards on the path was completely blocked, and he was forced to stop. Serafina, who had been watching where she put her feet on the muddy track, walked straight into him. She slipped and would have fallen, but he caught her.

It was like putting a match to tinder. There was no pause for thought, no hesitation, no holding back. She was seized in his arms and he kissed the breath out of her body. For a moment she had no thought of resistance, indeed no thought at all. She was swept along on a tidal wave of emotion such as she had never before experienced. He was holding her so tightly that she could not move, and yet she wanted to be even closer. He was trembling as he parted her lips with his own. . .

Serafina *was* frightened now—frightened by the sudden force of an experienced man's passion, and even more frightened at the depth of response it had aroused in her. She was torn between an intense desire to let this man do anything he wished with her and an equally strong fear of this total loss of control. She gave a little cry and sought to free herself—and the instant she did he let her go.

'Sally, I. . . Oh, God, what can I say? You're just a child. . . I. . . I don't know what came over me.' He turned away from her, cursing under his breath. Then he turned back and said desperately, 'Such a thing has never happened before, I swear. I behaved like a schoolboy, grabbing what he wants with no thought or care. Have I hurt you?'

The polished, urbane man of the world had vanished.

He looked much younger, almost vulnerable, as he stood before her, making an obvious effort to regain his composure, an expression of contrition and concern on his face. Her heart gave a sudden pang and she forgot her own fears in a desire to reassure him. Forcing herself to speak normally, she said, 'Hardly a schoolboy. Not like any schoolboy I've known, at any rate. No, you didn't hurt me. And. . .and I understand what you mean—I felt it, too.' A shiver went down her spine. 'Nothing like that has ever happened to me before, either.'

'But you are still so young! I'm the one who should have known better. And I didn't. Was that your first kiss, Sally?'

Serafina was still so dazed that she answered him with complete honesty. 'The first which. . .made me feel like that. I'm. . . I'm not sure I like it. It wasn't at all sensible. And it doesn't fit in with my ideas of. . . With what I wish to do with my life.'

An unwilling laugh escaped him. 'I'm afraid life doesn't always let us dictate our own terms, little Sally. Surely your reading has told you that? Feelings have a way of coming into conflict with what one knows to be safe, or sensible. And,' he said, with a sudden note of bitterness, 'one's duty. My God, I know about duty only too well. But that's another question. Tell me what I can do to make amends to you.'

Serafina had been reminded by this speech of Lord Aldworth's own determination to live his own life, but she made herself remain calm. 'You don't have to make amends to me, Lord Aldworth. After all, it was——' she swallowed '—only one kiss.' She stared, fascinated, as his eyes dropped to her mouth, and her own treacherous emotions started to respond once again. She took a hurried step back, and said with decision, 'But I think it has given me some right to be plain with you. Plainer than I would otherwise be. I have heard things about you—about your behaviour in Vienna and other places. You needn't think Serafina has been telling tales, either—she thinks you perfect. But I write—and receive—letters, you know. Your association with Serafina in London has naturally roused a certain amount of interest, and there are always some who like to gossip, and others who pass the gossip on. Young ladies are not supposed to know about affairs and. . . and mistresses, and certainly Serafina would never dream of mentioning them to you, even if she knew about them. But, as you know, I am no lady, and I do ask you about them.'

He had been listening intently, but now his face closed up and he said coldly, 'Forgive me. What happened just now gives you no right whatsoever to ask anything of the kind! It was another thing entirely!'

'Was it? I fail to see the difference.'

'That kiss was the impulse of a moment,' said Lord Aldworth grimly. 'I am sorry it happened, and I shall certainly take care that it does not happen again. But my affairs are exactly that, Sally Feverel. *My* affairs. They have nothing to do with you or anyone else!'

'They surely have something to do with your wife!'

'I do not yet have a wife. In any case, neither that kiss nor my affairs have any relevance to my marriage.' Serafina gave an exclamation of disgust and turned away. There was a difficult silence. Then he sighed and said, 'I suppose I haven't been making allowance for your youthful idealism. I can't blame you for asking the question. Look at me, Sally.'

She turned round with obvious reluctance.

'I can't justify kissing you, and I dislike myself for having done so. But believe me, I meant no disrespect. It was an. . .an overwhelming impulse, and even now I cannot account for it. Can you forgive me, and forget it happened?'

Serafina's delicately balanced composure suddenly snapped. 'I'll forget it! I'll forget it willingly! I don't wish to remember it. But how many other unaccountably "overwhelming impulses" is poor Serafina to put up with if you do marry her? How many affairs is she to hear about from the gossips? Tell me that! No relevance to your marriage, indeed! But don't bother to say anything more. I don't wish to hear it. I must go!'

She tore past him and ran to the stables. When he caught up with her she was standing by the groom. She looked at him stony-faced and waited while he gave orders that Miss Sally Feverel was to be conveyed home. There was a slight delay while the sledge was fetched from the garden where they had left it, but conversation between Lord Aldworth and his visitor was minimal.

Lord Aldworth went back into the house feeling more unlike himself than he had for a long time. For years he had known what he wanted and had used his considerable charm and abilities to get his way. The nature of his work abroad would have made a long-term commitment to one person inadvisable and, in any case, his father's second marriage had given him a horror of that institution. While his brother Gervase had been alive Charles had always sworn that he should not be caught

in the same trap as his unhappy sire. Fortunately, he
had never met anyone with whom he wished to spend
more than a delightful interlude, and all his affairs had
been with mature, experienced women of the world—
women who knew the rules and kept to them. It had
seemed to him that this was an ideal life—work he
loved, and pleasure where and when he chose to find it.

But Gervase's death had changed all that. Marriage
and an heir for Aldworth were imperative and, though
Charles was reluctant to face the prospect, he acknowl-
edged the justice of his grandmother's views. Life was
always uncertain, and the sooner the Aldworth succession was ensured the better. Serafina Feverel had
seemed to represent a suitable compromise. A lovely,
well brought up bride of impeccable lineage, a couple of
healthy children born as soon as possible afterwards,
and then a life of domestic preoccupation for his wife,
and freedom for him to find congenial company elsewhere—even, perhaps, to take up the work he loved
again. Not ideal, but the best one could do.

Now Sally Feverel had dared to cast doubt on it all. A
slip of a girl, impudent, indecorous, ungraceful—no,
not ungraceful. Though they were not what was
expected of a young lady, her movements had a wild,
free grace of their own. But she was frank to the point
of rudeness, she was over-educated, opinionated, lacking in any sense of dress or occasion. . . She had dared
to question what had seemed to him to be a very
sensible arrangement, and, what was worse, she had
made him begin to question it himself!

When he had first seen Serafina in her father's library
he had found the resemblance to Sally almost too much
to credit. Could two girls who were not twins possibly

be so alike? But he had soon dismissed his doubts. The very different way he felt about each of them had convinced him. Serafina was placid, gentle and undemanding. Her understanding might be a trifle limited, but she would never argue with him. Life with her would be easy, if somewhat boring. Dull. In fact, he had recently found himself wishing that Serafina were not quite such a mouse, that she were a little more like her sister. . . But no! A wife like Sally Feverel would drive him insane in a week!

On the other hand. . . Sally would never be dull. She might be infuriating, but he had never yet been bored in her company. She was almost as lovely as her sister, and equally well-born. Dammit, she was fun! And that kiss. . . His blood quickened at the thought of it. Young and inexperienced though she might be, she would be his equal in passion, he was sure. He smiled as he thought of her laughter, the animation in that delicately moulded face in the snow, her fiercely loyal defence of Serafina's interests. What a girl she was! What. . .what if he were to change his mind and marry the younger Feverel sister. . .? He was tempted; he was strongly tempted. . .

What was he thinking of? It would be the very trap he had so sedulously avoided! Sally Feverel would never meekly acquiesce to his will; she would expect—no, *demand* to be consulted on anything and everything. She would not agree to stay at home while he was abroad; she would want to be with him—if only to see the world. And what a disaster for his career she would be, with her unconventional behaviour and lack of Society manners! He shuddered as he visualised the effect of Sally's impetuous ways on the rigid protocol of the diplomatic circles of Europe. He was willing to wager that she would never be content to come second in his affections, but would want him to dance attendance on her all the time. And though at the moment he felt that he might want nothing other than this, what would be left when this present infatuation, this *madness*, had worn off, as it surely would eventually? He would be tied to a wife with a mind of her own, a wife who would demand to know what he was doing and why, and who would fill the house with her accusations and recriminations when he refused to tell her. In short, a wife who would make his life the hell his father's had been.

No, Sally Feverel must be firmly and completely put out of his mind. He was determined to marry someone quiet, peace-loving and biddable, someone who would give him the freedom he had set his mind on. Her sister, Serafina, in fact. He was leaving Sussex the next morning and the memory of what had happened this afternoon would soon fade. By the time he saw Sally Feverel again he would have to regard her with equanimity as his future sister-in-law. He took comfort from the fact that he would probably not have to see very much of her once he was married to her sister. Whenever she came to Aldworth, he would most likely be away. In fact, it might be wiser to make sure that he was.

Serafina surprised her family when she returned home by going to her room and staying there for several hours. Angelica made an attempt to speak to her, but Serafina merely shook her head and refused to answer. When she finally came downstairs she did her best to appear normal, but this was beyond even *her* powers of dissimulation. In the days that followed she did not improve. When not actively forced into conversation by one of the others she was silent. She excused herself from the traditional afternoon outings, instead going for long walks by herself. And her performance in the Saturday play was totally lacking in the verve they had all come to expect. The Feverels were very worried. Serafina had always been the least temperamental, the most energetic, the sanest of them all. What had happened?

The climax came about two weeks after Lord Aldworth's departure when Rafe, in a misguided effort to cheer his sister up, challenged her to climb the oak tree. Serafina burst into tears and was understood to say through her sobs that she wished she had never heard of the wretched oak tree! At this piece of heresy Mrs Feverel chased the younger ones out, assured her husband that this was something only a mother could do and that she was perfectly well enough to cope with it, and invited Serafina to sit down by her sofa and talk.

'Now, Serafina, I do not intend to animadvert on past history. What is done is done, and neither tears nor temper will undo it. Is your present state of mind due to Lord Aldworth's absence in London, or to regret that you have deceived him? Or is there something else about which I have not heard?'

After some evasion and further questioning Serafina confessed to her mother that Lord Aldworth had kissed her the day before he had left for London.

'So this is what has been distressing you! I understand now. Being kissed against one's will——'

'No, Mama.'

'No?'

'I. . . . It was not against my will. I wanted him to.'

Mrs Feverel was shocked but, once she had ascertained that the matter had gone no further than a kiss, she was inclined not to treat it too seriously. 'For I understand that it is Lord Aldworth's fixed intention to offer for you when you return to London and know him a little better. He has already informed your father of this.'

'He has?' Serafina was astonished.

'He mentioned it when he was here, apparently, and has now written more formally to your father to that effect. Quite why he finds further delay necessary I am not perfectly certain, but in view of your little deception it is perhaps as well—it gives you time to tell him the truth before matters become serious between you. He has written a charming letter. Your papa showed it to me when it came this morning. Papa intended to discuss it with you, but you were so unkind to poor Rafe that I felt I had to speak to you first. . . You have not been yourself since Lord Aldworth left, and I wondered if there was something more than mere love-sickness. It seems I was right!'

'What will Papa say to Lord Aldworth?'

'I know he approves of him. But he has always felt that you should make up your own mind about your future husband. Your papa is a rare man, Serafina, as I hope you realise. Neither Lord Aldworth's riches nor his position would influence him, even though the advantages of such a match to the family are obvious. He intends to say that if Lord Aldworth can persuade you to accept him then he will give his approval. He assumes, of course, that you will have revealed your subterfuge before allowing Lord Aldworth to commit himself.'

Serafina nodded. In her present pessimistic mood it seemed most unlikely that Lord Aldworth would want to marry her when he knew how she had deceived him. Her mother continued.

'But since I assume that you will accept him, the kiss, though precipitate, was not a serious matter.'

This reminded Serafina of the true source of her unhappiness. This time there was no humour for her in the word 'precipitate' as she cried, 'But it was, Mama! When Lord Aldworth kissed me he thought I was Sally, not Serafina!'

Mrs Feverel, perplexed, regarded her daughter for a full minute. 'You know, I always regarded you as the most intelligent of my children, but I find it impossible to conceive how anyone could have put themselves into a situation where the placing of a kiss is so confused!'

'You said you weren't going to animadvert, Mama!'

'And I won't, however strong the temptation. You are being punished quite enough by the pickle you are in. What do you propose to do about this. . .misplaced kiss?'

'What can I do? But it is not very pleasant to know that Lord Aldworth had marriage to Serafina in mind before he kissed Sally!'

'Are you quite certain that he was not taking a page out of your own book? Treating you as separate people when he knew you were really one and the same?'

'No, I'm sure he doesn't suspect. He. . .he behaves quite differently to each of us. And he was very angry with himself for succumbing to the temptation. I don't quite know how that kiss happened, Mama, but now I don't know how to go on!'

'I find it quite extraordinarily difficult to advise you. Nor do I think it wise to consult your Papa. I doubt he would know how to help, and in any case I think the kiss is best kept between ourselves, Serafina. Fathers have a different way of looking at such things.' There was a silence, broken after a minute or two by Mrs Feverel.

'You will have a little time in London, I think, before Lord Aldworth makes his offer. If you have decided that you wish to accept it, you will have to use the time beforehand to attach him to you so firmly that he will accept your excuses. You can be very persuasive when you choose, my dear.'

Serafina sighed and nodded.

Mrs Feverel began to say something, stopped, looked doubtful, then took another breath and said, 'I was surprised when Angelica said you were in love. You had always seemed to me to be someone whose sentiments were admirably controlled, and I confess that I doubted what she said. But is it true, Serafina? Do you really love Lord Aldworth?'

'I don't know! I have never felt like this before, Mama.'

Mrs Feverel looked grave. 'You must be sure that you know what you are facing, Serafina. I have not met Lord Aldworth so I cannot judge him. Your father likes him, and that is a recommendation, but he of course sees him from a man's point of view. When we discussed the question of your marriage initially you seemed content to marry for material advantage, for companionship, perhaps, but not for love. I wonder if that is still the case?'

'It is still necessary. Gabriel's debts——'

'Gabriel's debts are nothing compared with your happiness, Serafina. I would persuade your papa to forbid the match if I thought you were going to be unhappy!'

'Oh, no!'

Serafina's involuntary cry was ignored by Mrs Feverel, who went on, 'What you tell me about that kiss—that it was Sally Lord Aldworth thought he was kissing—would indicate a certain lack of scruple in his approach to women. There are many such men and, as long as they are reasonably discreet and continue to show consideration to their wives, the world does not condemn them. If Lord Aldworth should indeed turn out to be such a man, it would be easier for you if. . .if you were not. . .too attached to him.'

'I understand that, Mama. I will keep it in mind.'

After Serafina had gone Mrs Feverel sighed and took out a letter from her workbox—a letter which she had no intention of mentioning to her daughter. Lady Chilham, unaware of Lord Aldworth's request to Mr Feverel, had written to warn her friend that Serafina should return to London soon.

Lord Aldworth is in town again and is constantly seen with Louisa Paget. We all thought she had returned to Vienna—she left London last month— but apparently she merely spent a few days in Paris, shopping, from the look of it, then suddenly turned round and came back here! It is my opinion that she must have learned somehow or other of Aldworth's decision to return early to England. In her anxiety to see him again Lady Paget appears to have quite forgotten that she has a husband waiting for her in Vienna. The Dowager Lady Aldworth is furious, but seems powerless to stop the affair. The sooner Serafina is here the better, I miss her, anyway. It's time she was back.

Serafina's departure from Sussex was not a joyous occasion. Her family was sad to see her go—they would all miss her. Mr Feverel, a born optimist, was sure that Aldworth would be sympathetic when his daughter confessed, but Angelica was afraid that he would refuse to listen, and was already regretting the loss of such a handsome, eligible suitor for her sister. Mrs Feverel's views were more complicated. She suspected that Serafina's feelings were more deeply engaged than even the girl herself knew, and she was torn between hope that Lord Aldworth would not make Serafina unhappy by rejecting her after her confession and fear that greater unhappiness lay ahead for her daughter if he were to marry her.

Serafina herself was sure that Lord Aldworth would not accept any excuses. She had made him ridiculous, and no man of breeding and pride would tolerate that. So it was in a mood of melancholy resignation that she joined her godmother once more in Curzon Street.

'Good heavens, Serafina, I do not know what has happened to you! There is work to be done, child, and you sit there like one of Lord Elgin's statues! You must go to see them, by the way; all the world is talking of them again. But I must tell you, dear child, that Aldworth is paying Louisa Paget the most marked attention once more. The whole town is talking of it, and it is no secret that his grandmother has sworn she will not attend any function where they will be seen together.'

Serafina suffered a momentary pang, followed by a surge of anger. 'How dare he?'

Lady Chilham looked at her in amazement. 'What do you mean? It is annoying for us, of course, but you have no claim as yet on his loyalty. And you may well never have if that woman is not stopped in her efforts to ensnare him.'

'Lord Aldworth, ma'am, has been good enough to convey to my father his intention to ask me to marry him!'

'His intention to ask. . . I have never heard of such an arrangement before. You mean he has asked your father for permission to pay his addresses to you?'

'Not exactly, ma'am. It seems there must be a short delay before he does so. He wishes to give me time to get to know him better, he says, but I think it is really because he has some unfinished business on hand. Lady Paget, perhaps?'

'It may be so,' said Lady Chilham doubtfully. 'But what an extraordinary way to be going on! I had thought better of Aldworth—if these are continental manners, then I have no wish to know more of them. But,' she continued, brightening up, 'whatever the reason for the delay, you are to be congratulated, Serafina, on capturing one of the most eligible *partis* in London. I knew you could do it!' She embraced her god-daughter warmly. 'Now, what will you wear tonight to the Granthams'? We must not be complacent—that woman is dangerous. . . I wonder if we should give you a touch of colour? You look sadly pale, child. I thought the country was supposed to be a healthy place!'

CHAPTER SEVEN

THE pleasure Serafina had formerly taken in her plot to trap Lord Aldworth had almost completely disappeared, but she was persuaded to make an effort to look her best that evening—though she strenuously resisted any effort to add colour to her cheeks. In the event she looked enchantingly ethereal in a dress of white Urling's net, worn over a pale blue satin slip and decorated round the hem with bunches of silk forget-me-nots. Lord Aldworth, who was standing in a corner conversing with Lady Paget, drew in his breath at the sight.

'What is it, Charles?' Lady Paget followed his eyes. 'Oh, the Feverel child—charming, absolutely charming.' She turned back to him. 'You know, it is really quite depressing once one is past a certain age! I spend a fortune on a Paris creation, I enjoy the services of a first-class lady's maid, who spends hours dressing me, and what happens? A child like that, in a dress which was probably made by the village dressmaker, quite outshines me!'

'Quite!' said Lord Aldworth.

'Charles!'

He looked at her with an apologetic smile. 'I'm sorry, my dear. I'm afraid I didn't hear what you said. Was it about Miss Feverel?'

Lady Paget was offended, but dared not show it. Though Charles had frequently sought her company in the past few weeks, she did not deceive herself that his

heart was in their flirtation. As she had discovered in
those early days in Vienna, and later in London, when
he chose he could make any woman feel entirely
desirable, the centre of his world, a goddess among
women. His devotion, while it lasted, was comprehen-
sive. But this feeling was noticeably absent from their
present affair. He occasionally smiled at her in the old
way, and then, in spite of herself, her heart would
quicken. But suddenly, without warning, his attention
would fade and she would feel she had lost him again.
Lady Paget was a clear-sighted, intelligent woman, but
Lord Aldworth's present behaviour was puzzling her. It
was characteristic of a man who was interested in
another quarry, and on Lord Aldworth's past record
that would not be at all surprising. Though it was
vexing. And highly inconvenient.

But who could the new object of his affections be?
She had dismissed Serafina Feverel as a possible rival
without a second thought. The chit was very lovely, but
she had nothing to offer a sophisticated man of the
world such as Charles. No, he was reluctantly obeying
the orders of his harridan of a grandmother in his
cultivation of Miss Feverel. Even though Lady Paget
had found it galling, she had understood why she had
been so suddenly dropped before Christmas. The poor
man had to set up a marriage of sorts after his brother's
death, and she had been sure that her time would come
again when Charles eventually grew tired of the girl's
simpers.

But matters had now become more serious, and more
urgent. This was not the time for Charles to lose
whatever interest he had once had in her. . . She stole a
glance at her companion. His eyes were still on Serafina

Feverel. He could not be in love with her! Men were often fools, but she would give her best Parisian bonnet to the Little Sisters of the Poor if Charles Dacre had been caught by a pretty face with nothing behind it! He wasn't even looking at her in that way—more. . . regretfully, as if he were looking at a ghost, or a shadow. How odd!

Her musings were cut short.

'Louisa, I ought to say a word to Miss Feverel. I had no idea she was coming to London quite so soon. Will you excuse me? I am sure you understand why I am not proposing that you should accompany me?' He looked at her with his familiar glinting smile.

She forced herself to say calmly, 'Of course, Charles. It is kind of you to spare me Lady Chilham's icy courtesies—I swear I shall catch cold from them one of these days! In any case, I see Denham over there, trying to catch my eye. He can amuse me while you are gone.'

'My dear, you are, as always, the perfect companion—tolerant and almost too understanding! I shall not be long.'

He walked away, a tall, confident figure. Lady Paget frowned. There had been something in his tone then—a touch of contempt? Surely not. She watched him as he crossed the room and wondered what her best plan of action would be.

Serafina had seen Lord Aldworth and his companion, of course, and she had been surprised by another sudden surge of anger. How dared he, indeed? She thought waspishly that there was no necessity to ask what sort of 'overwhelming impulses' bound him to Lady Paget. They were perfectly natural ones of the baser sort! But she looked suitably demure as he came over and spoke to Lady Chilham.

'I see you have your god-daughter back with you, Lady Chilham. You must be happy to see her again. Indeed, we are all the happier for seeing Miss Feverel in London again—and in such beauty.'

Looking somewhat sceptical, Lady Chilham assured him that she was delighted to have Serafina with her, and thanked him for his complimentary remarks. 'Though they are perhaps too extravagant. Surely in the whole of London there must be one or two who. . .do not share your pleasure, Lord Aldworth?' She allowed her eyes to rest fractionally on Lady Paget.

He had the grace to look somewhat disconcerted by this direct attack, but recovered and turned to Serafina. 'Miss Feverel, what can I say? This is an unexpected pleasure!'

Serafina was faced with an almost irresistible urge to ask him if she had been precipitate in her return, but restrained herself. It was not the moment.

'Are your family well, Miss Feverel?' he continued. 'Your parents, and brothers and sisters?'

Serafina suddenly realised that she was sitting on a keg of gunpowder! Lady Chilham was unaware of the separate existence of Sally and Serafina, and might well betray her before she was ready. She must turn the conversation away from her family without delay! For once, her air of nervous hesitation was not assumed as she replied, 'Thank you, Lord Aldworth, they are all well. I hope Lady Aldworth is not ill—I have not seen her here tonight.'

This was an unfortunate remark, as she realised the moment the words were out of her mouth. She knew

perfectly well why Lady Aldworth was not present, as
did most of London. She blushed as Lord Aldworth said
thinly, 'My grandmother is indisposed at the moment. I
am sure, however, that she would enjoy a visit from you
now that you are back. May I call on you tomorrow,
Lady Chilham? I hope to see you then, Miss Feverel.
Your servant, Lady Chilham, Miss Feverel.' With a
graceful bow and a smile that did not reach his eyes he
was gone.

'Really, Serafina, I sometimes think you have more
hair than wit! Whatever persuaded you to refer to his
grandmother? You know why she isn't here; I told you
myself only today!'

'It was a natural enough question,' Serafina said
defensively.

'But not one to please Aldworth!'

'That was not my aim——'

'Well, it should be! He hasn't come up to scratch yet,
my girl. You could still lose him.'

'That is the very thing I wanted to talk to you about,
ma'am. But it must wait until we are more private. . .'

'Serafina! What were you thinking of? Aldworth will
never forgive you for making such a fool of him,' wailed
Lady Chilham when Serafina told her of her double
identity. 'Oh, it is really too bad of you—to have
captured the interest of the most eligible bachelor in
London and then to throw it away with such wilful
idiocy. . . I hope you realise that if a word of this gets
around you will have ruined your chances with anyone
else, as well? Oh, how could you? After all my
work. . .'

Serafina's heart sank at this confirmation of her own

worst fears, but she rallied and said tentatively, 'I
thought if I waited a little before telling him he might
become sufficiently attached to overlook it, ma'am.'

'You cannot be serious! A man would have to be
besotted to do so, and Aldworth of all people would
never allow his feelings to run away with him to such an
extent.'

'In that case, ma'am, I am lost indeed, but I have
nothing to lose by trying. Will you. . .could you now
forget what I have told you, and only remember to be
silent about Sally?'

Lady Chilham looked outraged and shook her head,
but Serafina's powers of persuasion were considerable,
and she was finally prevailed upon to do as her god-
daughter requested.

The season was now showing signs of stirring, and it
promised to be a glittering one. The storm and stress of
the Napoleonic wars were over, and no effort was
spared in the pursuit of pleasure. The ladies of Society
were busy planning balls, routs, assemblies and recep-
tions, each one striving to outdo the next. Fountains of
flowers, pyramids of fruit, tents of feathers—nothing
was too extravagant for the ambitious hostess who wished
to create a stir. The Prince Regent's latest extrava-
gances—his increasing interest in Brighton and the
pavilion there, the scandalous behaviour of Lady X or
Lord Y—were the main topics of conversation. Serafina
sometimes grew impatient with this frivolous world, but
rigorously excluded any hint of such feelings from her
demeanour. She exerted herself in public to be as
beautiful and as biddable as Lord Aldworth could
possibly wish, but in the privacy of the Curzon Street

house she continued to read the newspapers and learn of the world outside England.

Not everywhere was as peaceful. Napoleon was vanquished, but the spirit of the French Revolution was far from dead. The ideals of liberty, fraternity and equality, the desire for independence, were still giving the autocratic rulers of Europe some trouble. The American colonies had been free from British domination for some time, of course, but now the South Americans were fighting fiercely for their independence from Spain. And the British Government, aware of its status as a parliamentary democracy and, more cynically, interested in the possibilities for trade, was finding itself increasingly, if unofficially, in sympathy with the rebels.

But none of this was discussed at the functions which she attended, and if it had been she would not have permitted herself to join in. She was waiting, with a mixture of hope and fear, for Lord Aldworth to make his offer. She often caught him looking at her with an expression she found difficult to define, but he made no attempt to declare himself. He too seemed to be waiting. And meanwhile he was seen in Lady Paget's company often enough for the gossip to continue. The Dowager Lady Aldworth decided that she had had enough of London, and removed to her house in Berkshire.

Before she did so she sent for Serafina. 'Well, Miss Feverel, what have you to say? Why are you standing at the side waiting for Charles to fall into the arms of that harpy?'

'Why are *you*, ma'am?'

'Because I cannot stop it, that's why! Charles seems to have lost all sense. He absolutely refuses to listen to anything I have to say. I have never known him so. . .so deaf to any advice.'

'I cannot stop it either—and it would be out of the question for me to give him advice, or even to approach him on the subject of his relationship with Lady Paget.'

'You're no fool, however. I have the impression that you could think of something if you chose. Surely the fact that my grandson is about to make you an offer gives you some influence over him?'

'Lady Aldworth, you know better than most what sort of relationship Lord Aldworth wishes to enjoy with his chosen bride. Do you really think she could have any influence whatsoever on him—especially before she is married? And he has not yet even asked me.'

'He will, he will. He has said so. He had made up his mind before Christmas—before he went to Vienna. But since his return. . .he has been so different.' She frowned. 'I don't understand him. And I don't understand why he insists on waiting before approaching you. It's that Jezebel!'

'Lord Aldworth does not appear to me to be happy in Lady Paget's company. . .'

'Nor should he be!' The Dowager shot Serafina a look. 'So you've been watching him, eh?'

'Discreetly. He goes through the form of paying her attention, but I am almost sure that his interest in her is not as straightforward as it seems. He sometimes appears to be as indifferent to her charms as he is to mine.'

'Does he indeed? I have avoided seeing them together for some time, so I cannot judge. Indifferent to Lady Paget, eh? That's more encouraging. But in that case, why. . .?' She stopped and seemed to be debating something. Finally she said slowly, 'What do you know of Charles's work, Serafina?'

Serafina had a fleeting vision of Sally's discussion with Charles in Sussex. Sally knew a little, but not Serafina. She sighed and said, 'His diplomatic work, ma'am? Almost nothing. He never discusses it with me.'

'No, he wouldn't, of course. But if it isn't his interest in Lady Paget which prevents him from making a formal offer, then it must be his work.'

Serafina was surprised. 'What do you mean, Lady Aldworth?'

The Dowager was silent for a moment. Then she said, 'I'm about to betray a confidence. I don't like doing it, but I think you should know, and I am as certain as I can be of your discretion.'

'What is it?'

'Charles sometimes does highly. . .secret work for the government. Not often now—he did a lot more some years ago in France.'

'When Napoleon was in power?'

'Yes. He speaks French like a native, of course.'

'And?'

'He is probably postponing his marriage plans until a particular assignment is over—and I have an idea that, whatever it is, it is not part of his normal diplomatic activities.'

'But why should that delay anything?'

'He says it isn't dangerous, but perhaps he thinks it might be.'

'I see. And I am. . .unworthy of his confidence. Perhaps he shares that with Lady Paget—she is, after all, part of the diplomatic world.'

Serafina must have revealed how depressed she was,

for Lady Aldworth suddenly sounded old as she leant forward and begged, 'Don't give up, Serafina! I am relying on your skills to rescue Charles from a disastrous mistake. The more I see of you, the greater is my conviction that you are the very one to make my grandson happy. Get him to offer for you, Serafina. Once he is officially betrothed he will give up any thought of Lady Paget, I am sure. The rest will follow.'

Serafina was too conscious of her own difficulties in the matter to respond positively to Lady Aldworth's plea. 'You place a heavy burden on me, ma'am,' she said sadly. 'I will do my best, but it may not be enough.'

Nevertheless Serafina thought hard about Lady Aldworth's recommendation, and eventually decided on a course of action which might help.

Lord Aldworth was not, of course, Serafina's only admirer. She seldom lacked partners at any function she attended, and her room in Curzon Street was rarely without a floral tribute of some kind. The most recent was a lavish arrangement of exotic blooms, and Serafina had cringed at the crass sentimentality of the verse which had accompanied it. Her first impulse had been to throw the card in the fire and take the first opportunity which presented itself to make it clear to the sender that such effusions were not welcome. But with Lady Aldworth's words in mind she had restrained herself, and instead placed the flowers and their message in a prominent position in Lady Chilham's salon. Here she waited for Lord Aldworth. He had taken to calling quite regularly—almost, Serafina thought resentfully, as if she were an elderly relative in need of the comfort of a daily visit.

As she sat in the salon, surrounded by the heavy scent

of the flowers, Serafina reviewed the past few weeks.
She could hardly claim to have made much progress in
her efforts to attach Lord Aldworth. Except for his
calls, which seldom lasted very long, she saw him less
frequently now than she had before Christmas. And
even when he was with her he would quite often sit in
silence for several minutes, frowning at Lady Chilham's
Aubusson carpet as if something about the design
displeased him. He occasionally invited her for a drive
or a visit to some exhibition, but he seemed strangely
reluctant to be seen in public with her. For a man who
was contemplating an offer of marriage his behaviour
was certainly odd.

Was it that he had become aware of her duplicity?
She examined the evidence for this and rejected it. The
trouble, whatever it was, did not concern her directly,
she was sure. True, she sometimes caught him looking
at her with a fleeting expression of regret in his eyes—
perhaps he was finding it more difficult than he had
thought to forget Sally? Her heartbeat quickened at the
thought, but she quickly grew calm again. Even if it was
so, that was not the chief reason for the change in him.

Serafina got up and walked about the room
impatiently. The scent from those flowers was giving her
the headache; she was finding it difficult to think! She
stopped by the long windows and rested her forehead
against the cool glass. There was nothing she could do
directly; so much was certain. At the moment he
regarded her as a stupid, doll-like creature, unworthy of
any sort of confidence. Should she confess now—this
afternoon? It took less than a moment's reflection to
discard that idea. He would pack her off to Sussex and
she would never see him again! Very well, she would

have to keep up her deception and do what she could by indirect methods. It would entail some risk, but when had she ever refused a challenge?

At this point in her musings her visitor was announced.

Lord Aldworth entered the room, elegant as ever in a blue superfine coat, a spotless cravat tied in its usual intricate folds, and pale pantaloons over gleaming top-boots. He bent over her hand in a graceful gesture, murmuring a greeting, but as he straightened again an expression of distaste marred his handsome features. He surveyed the room through his glass. 'Ah,' he said, staring at the flower arrangement.

Serafina took up her role, and looked distressed. 'You do not like the flowers! I thought they were very pretty, but perhaps I am mistaken?'

'Not at all, Miss Feverel. I am merely surprised at Lady Chilham's choice. Their—er—perfume is some-what overpowering.'

'Lady Chilham did not choose them; they are mine, Lord Aldworth. Mr Allen sent them. With such a very lovely poem.'

'The devil he did!' Serafina was pleased to see that Lord Aldworth was looking slightly affronted.

'Yes, shall I show it to you? Or. . .perhaps I should not. Mr Allen may prefer me to keep it private.'

'I am not having other gentlemen writing private love letters to you, Serafina!'

'It is a poem! I liked it as much as anything I have ever seen in Papa's books. Mr Allen is so clever——' She stopped as Lord Aldworth calmly removed the card from her hand, as she had intended he should. 'Lord Aldworth! You should not!'

'Allen wrote this. . .poem to you?'

'Yes! Is it not lovely? Of course, I am not really an angel, but don't you think it was clever to use my name like that? "Seraphic Serafina, angelically fair"?' She sighed happily. 'Papa called us all after angels, you know. Even Rafe is really Raphael.'

'What about Sally?'

Serafina held on to her happy expression with difficulty as she cursed her carelessness. 'Sally? What do you mean? Her real name is Cherubina,' she said, improvising rapidly, and blessing the day that she and Angelica had debated what her parents could possibly call another girl. 'Oh, you are asking why we call her Sally? When she grew older she hated Cherubina—though I think it is a pretty name. But Sally can be very determined when she wishes. Sarah is her second name—it is Mama's name too, of course.' She appeared to lose interest in her sister as her eyes returned to the card in his hand. 'I know I'm not nearly as beautiful as Mr Allen says, but the sentiments are expressed in such a lovely way. Pray give the poem back to me, Lord Aldworth! I am going to keep it forever!'

'I think not. I could not permit it,' he said sternly.

'But I like it!' Serafina put her hands together and looked up at her visitor with hurt reproach. The look worked its usual magic.

'I am sorry, my dear,' said Lord Aldworth more gently. 'Allen must be told that you are not free to accept such. . .missives. I am surprised that Lady Chilham allowed it!'

'I didn't know! Am I not?'

'Not what, Serafina?' he said, looking down indulgently.

'Not free?'

'Well, of course you are not! Did your father not tell you?'

'He said that you were intending to. . .intending to. . .'

'To ask you to marry me? I am.'

'But. . .' Serafina raised large, puzzled blue eyes to Lord Aldworth. '. . .you haven't yet,' she said timidly.

Lord Aldworth looked down into the blue eyes gazing into his and cleared his throat. 'Er. . .there are reasons why any announcement cannot at present be made public,' he said. He sounded pompous but Serafina could see that he was experiencing some difficulty in resisting the lure of blue eyes and red lips so close to his own.

'As you wish, Lord Aldworth,' Serafina said submissively, but with patent disappointment. She made to move away but Lord Aldworth's arm stole round her waist and he pulled her back.

'Do you wish to marry me, Serafina?' he murmured.

She was almost overwhelmed by a passionate and totally unexpected urge to wind her own arms round his neck and pull his face down to hers, to repeat the kiss they had exchanged in the garden at Blanchards. Oh, God, she thought, alarmed, he's going to kiss me and I don't know if I will be able to act my part! With a supreme effort she controlled her panic. A little agitation was surely permissible. 'I. . .I. . .Yes, I think so.'

'May I kiss you?'

Her eyes flew once again to his. There was a look of complacency about him which was her salvation. She offered her cheek.

He laughed. 'Oh, no,' he said. 'Your lips, my dear,

those lovely lips. . .' Pulling her to him, he kissed her full on the mouth. Serafina remained passive, her eyes and lips firmly shut, her feelings firmly under control. 'You may open your eyes, Serafina.' Slowly she opened her eyes and looked at him. Lord Aldworth was examining her face as if searching for a resemblance. . . He sighed, then smiled encouragingly and said, 'What a child you are! But you'll learn.'

'Are we betrothed, Lord Aldworth?'

'I think you may call me Charles, don't you?'

'Oh, I couldn't——' She smiled shyly. 'Very well, Charles.'

'Serafina, I have an odd request. I am delighted—and proud too, of course—that you have agreed to be my wife. But may I ask that you keep our engagement secret for the next month or so?'

She looked puzzled but said, 'Of course, but why?'

'I cannot explain.'

Nothing venture, nothing gain. Greatly daring, Serafina said sadly, 'It's Lady Paget. She is so much more beautiful than I.'

'No, you are wrong. That is to say, Lady Paget is part of the problem, but only a part. You need not fear that my feelings are engaged elsewhere. . .certainly not with Lady Paget, whatever the appearances. My work is complicated and sometimes not for discussion. I wish to finish a particular part of it before our marriage plans become general knowledge. Will you trust me?'

Serafina looked at him uncertainly. Could she learn any more by further questions? She rather thought not, and she dared not risk arousing any suspicion that she was less compliant than she seemed. 'Very well, Lord

Ald—Charles. Do you wish my godmother to be kept in ignorance too? I shall try, but. . .'

'I think I know enough of her to trust her discretion. But you had better leave things to me. I don't think I need say more to your parents—they are already aware of my intention to marry you.'

No suggestion that she might refuse him—only the assumption that things would go as he desired! It was a pity, thought Serafina, that this strange urge to be kissed by Lord Aldworth, this even stranger desire to share his troubles and comfort him did not blind her to his conceit and arrogance!

'Yes, Lor—Charles. Of course I will,' she murmured. 'Whatever you wish.'

Lady Chilham came in at that point, and Serafina sat quietly by while Charles gave her godmother the news and extracted a promise of secrecy from her. He left soon after.

As soon as he had gone Serafina was embraced warmly. 'So you did it! How did he take your confession?'

'I. . . I didn't tell him,' said Serafina defiantly. 'No, dear godmother, please do not scold. My reasons were sound. Firstly, he has conveniently insisted on keeping our betrothal private for the next month, so I still have time to tell him the truth before it is made public. If he then wishes to disown me he will be able to do so without a scandal. Second, being engaged to him gives me some privileges—a very few, it appears—and I wish to use these to help him. He is troubled in mind, and it has something to do with our friend Lady Paget. Not, as you are no doubt thinking, because he has formed any lasting passion for her. In fact, from the manner in which he spoke of her I should say rather the reverse. This intrigues me, and I want to find out a little more about it. I have a better chance of this the closer I am to him.'

'Why are you doing this, Serafina? It goes far beyond the bounds of a simple wish to make an advantageous marriage.'

Serafina grew scarlet as she stammered, 'I. . . I h— have always had a nose for intrigue, ma'am. I cannot resist it.'

Lady Chilham looked penetratingly at her god-daughter. 'Hmm,' she said. 'As long as you don't find Charles Dacre too intriguing. You wouldn't be the first to break her heart over him, not by any means.'

'What do you mean, ma'am? I? Fall in love with Lord Arrogance? You are sadly mistaken!'

Lady Chilham was not convinced, but allowed the matter to drop. Instead she said, 'What on earth is that smell? Good God, Serafina, what on earth are you thinking of, putting Mr Allen's flowers in the salon? What if Aldworth had noticed them?'

Serafina's eyes danced. 'Oh, but he did, ma'am! And I rather think they helped matters along enormously.'

'Oh, did they, indeed? Well, you may now have them removed. I shall tell Bates to put them in your bedchamber.'

'On no account, please! Could they perhaps be put in the hall where there is a movement of air? It might disperse their somewhat overpowering fragrance. If not, they can be thrown away. They have served their purpose.'

*   *   *

The relationship between Lord Aldworth and Serafina changed surprisingly little following his proposal. His visits continued to be frequent, though short, and though he kissed her both when he arrived and when he left his attitude remained friendly rather than lover-like. Much as she resented this calm lack of any real feeling, Serafina was on the whole glad of it. The slightest hint of passion might have caused a breach in her defences against him. As it was she often spent the minutes after his departure wishing for she knew not what and cursing the day she had learned what it was to be kissed properly, as a woman, by the real Charles Dacre. Then she would excuse herself to Lady Chilham and go for an unfashionably energetic walk in Green Park, sur-rounded by nursemaids and their charges, or she would take up her *Guide to London* and visit one of the places of interest in the capital, concentrating hard on what she saw. Lady Chilham watched her with anxious eyes but said nothing, not even to discourage her from these solitary expeditions.

It was on one such walk that Serafina caught sight of Lady Paget. Since she had no wish to indulge in one of the barbed conversations in which the lady specialised, Serafina took measures to avoid being seen. But what was such a fashion-conscious woman doing in Green Park at this hour?

She was soon to learn. A gentleman, dressed neatly but soberly in brown, came hurrying up to Lady Paget and greeted her with a decidedly foreign-looking bow. Serafina recognised him, though she did not know his name. He had been at the Granthams' in the company of the Spanish ambassador, and Serafina's curiosity had been roused because he had looked so out of place.

Later she had decided that his Excellency had thought
so too, for the man had soon disappeared. Now here he
was again, in decidedly odd circumstances. Serafina
could not imagine what sort of business could bring
Lady Paget and this unpleasant-looking little man
together at such a very unfashionable hour and in such a
very unfashionable place. It was clear that they had no
wish to be discovered for they wasted no time. A few
minutes' concentrated conversation, then the Spaniard
set off towards Piccadilly and Lady Paget hurried in the
direction of St James' Park. Serafina walked slowly back
to Curzon Street, pondering on what she had seen, but
unable to find an explanation. It had not been a lovers'
tryst, she was sure.

CHAPTER EIGHT

WHEN Lord Aldworth called the next afternoon she was still debating how she could get him to tell her more about the man she had seen in Green Park. Finally he asked her what was wrong.

'What do you mean, Charles?'

'You seem abstracted. And I have something particular that I wish to say to you.' Serafina pulled herself together and sat attentively while he went on to tell her that he might have to go away for a short while.

This must be what Lady Aldworth had talked about. 'Where. . .where are you going?'

He frowned, as if her question was too direct. 'Now, my dear, you must not become too curious. My work often takes me to strange places, and I cannot be answerable to you all the time. I shall be back within the fortnight, and then we shall set about telling the world that we plan to marry. Will you like that?'

Since it seemed to be expected of her, she looked delighted and breathed, 'Oh, yes, Charles! I would like it above anything. But I wish I knew when you were going, exactly. . .?'

He frowned again. 'I am not quite sure. Quite soon. So if I do not call on you for a little while you must not worry.' When she remained silent he said somewhat coldly, 'You look dissatisfied, Serafina. Is it not enough that I have promised to return in a very short time?'

Serafina wanted to cry, No, it isn't! If you are going

into danger I want to know about it, I want to help you! I want at least to share your worries! How dare you shut me out like this? But she restrained herself.

'I'm sorry, Charles,' she said. 'I really didn't mean to offend you. I only wanted to know if you were going before the rout at Carlton House. Gentlemen often have things they must do which they do not wish their wives to worry about. I must remember that in future. But you did promise to escort us.'

She held her breath while he looked at her closely but then he decided that she was sincere.

'When is it? The day after tomorrow? I cannot make any promises, my dear. Shall I ask Denham or one of the others to take you if I am not here?'

'That is kind of you. Godmother and I would not like to miss it. Everyone says it will be a splendid occasion.'

They talked of other things for a while, then Serafina took a breath and said, 'Charles, I saw someone at the Granthams' a little while ago, but I have forgotten his name. It would be so awkward if I met him again. Do you think you could help me?'

'I will if I can, of course. What does he look like?'

Serafina described the man she had seen in Green Park.

Charles's face was expressionless and his tone neutral as he said, 'You were introduced to him? By whom?'

Serafina said, 'I. . . I cannot remember. Oh, please tell me who he is, Charles! I have been in a quake in case I met him again! Indeed, I nearly did, the other day. He was in Green Park, but fortunately he didn't see me.'

'Miguel Barros? In Green Park?'

'That's the name! Thank you, Charles. I knew you

would help me! Now I shall know what to call him—
Sen. . . Señor Barras.'

'Barros. But if you wish to please me, Serafina, you
will forget him. He is not a man I wish you to know.'

'I don't know him, really. Only I saw Lady Paget with
him in Green Park. It seemed a strange place for them
to be. . .'

'*What*?'

Serafina was quite genuinely startled by Charles's
sharp exclamation. He said more calmly, 'You must be
mistaken. Lady Paget would sooner be seen dead than
in Green Park with the nursemaids. I am surprised you
go there.'

'It's pretty! The cows and milkmaids, and all the
children. It's very nice there. But I did see Lady Paget
with Señor Barr. . . Barros, Charles. I am sure I was
not mistaken.'

'Well, you might have done, I suppose. But I trust
you will not mention this supposed meeting to anyone
else. I wouldn't like to have you thought a scandalmon-
ger, and I still think you might have been mistaken.'
When she would have spoken he added firmly, 'Take
my word for it, Serafina. Forget the matter. Shall I call
on you tomorrow? At five o'clock? We could go for a
drive in the park if it is not too cold.'

Serafina decided on submission. 'I shall be here.'

At the door he seemed to sense that all was not well.
He stopped, took her in his arms, and smiled at her in
such a way that her heart turned over. 'I shall be glad
when I have finished my business, Serafina. We shall put
the notice of our engagement in the *Gazette*, and then it
won't be long before we are married and our life at
Aldworth can begin.'

The thought of the confession which must precede that happy situation caused Serafina to shiver. He misunderstood.

'You needn't be afraid. I shall be a most considerate husband, my dear.' He kissed her gently, and she in her anxiety allowed herself to respond, just a little. His arms tightened and he kissed her again. Though she trembled in his grasp she dared not show more feeling. He stepped back and surveyed her. Serafina refused to look at him but instead kept her eyes on the floor. He laughed. 'Lady Modesty! But I think you're learning, Serafina!'

Serafina returned from an outing with Lady Chilham the next day resolved to look her best for the drive with Lord Aldworth. It was gloriously sunny, and she had a new promenade outfit which she wished to put on. The muslin dress was simple enough, but the dark blue spencer and white bonnet edged with blue and white plaid silk which went with it were extremely flattering. Wherever Lord Aldworth was going she was determined that he should remember her!

It was disappointing, therefore, to find a note waiting for her, written in his firm, clear hand. Lord Aldworth presented his regrets, but he was unable, after all, to take her for the promised ride. He hoped she would understand. He had arranged for his friend, Lord Denham, to take Serafina and Lady Chilham to Carlton House on the following evening. He hoped she would enjoy the evening, but not so much that she would forget her most devoted admirer et cetera, et cetera.

It was more than disappointing. When Serafina thought over her conversation with Lady Aldworth she suffered some disquiet. Was the mission, whatever it was, dangerous? Surely not. Europe was now at peace, Britain's power and prestige well-established. Surely no one would dare to harm an envoy of His Britannic Majesty? She tried to dismiss her anxiety, but the niggle of doubt remained.

The following evening Lord Denham arrived in good time to take them to Carlton House. His lordship's open admiration of Serafina was sufficient explanation of his readiness to perform this service for his friend.

'Thank you, Denham,' said Lady Chilham graciously as the ladies came into the hall. 'It gets so crowded in Pall Mall, and I hate arriving late.'

'Do you know Carlton House, Lord Denham?' asked Serafina. 'I have never been there, and I am so looking forward to it.'

Lord Denham smiled down at her and confessed that he knew it well. 'Though each time one goes there one wonders what one will see, or where one will be! The Blue Velvet Room might have been changed overnight to the Yellow Salon, or the Gothic dining-room to the Roman library! The Prince Regent is notoriously. . . fickle in his tastes, I'm afraid. But the refreshments will be first-rate. The Prince never stints on entertainment. Pray, let me help you with your cloak, Miss Feverel.' Serafina's cloak was taken from the footman and placed reverently round her shoulders, much as a connoisseur of porcelain would handle a Ming vase. Serafina hid a smile, and thanked him prettily.

Serafina had heard of the marvels inside Carlton House, and in spite of Lord Denham's warning she was eager to see them. But as she and her companions filed

through one room after another she was conscious of a
sense of disappointment. The furnishings were magnificent, of that there was no doubt. But for her taste it was
too overpowering. It lacked restraint, refinement—and
the atmosphere was suffocating. The Prince Regent
received them affably, teasing Denham on his good
fortune in escorting the prettiest girl in London and
holding Miss Feverel's hand with every sign of appreci-
ation. Serafina was glad to escape—such princely attention was a trifle overwhelming.

The evening wore on, the crowds grew, the entertainment was indeed lavish and Serafina was hardly ever
without a partner, but she became more and more
dispirited. Where was Charles now? Was he in danger?
What was she doing here at this stupid party, in these
overheated rooms, among this babbling, peacock
throng? Though she made every effort to disguise it she
became more and more agitated. Lady Chilham noticed
how pale she had become and asked her if she was
feeling unwell.

'I. . . I think, if you do not mind, ma'am, I should like
to sit somewhere cool. I have a slight headache.'

She was taken at once downstairs to the conservatory,
which was a decidedly exotic affair, built in the Gothic
mode, but with classical statues and urns. Overhead the
elaborate fan vault was filled in with little bits of
coloured glass, and at the far end there was a Gothic
screen decorated in gilt, vermilion, blue and yellow. It
made her eyes ache to look at it. But the conservatory
was practically deserted and blessedly cool, scented with
banks of flowers and plants. Long windows towards one
end opened on to the garden. Here her godmother
found her a seat in a secluded alcove, saw that she was

comfortable and left her, promising to return soon with a drink of water.

Serafina sank gratefully back against the cushions and closed her eyes. Images of Charles haunted her—in London, in Sussex, talking to Serafina, talking to Sally. Where was he? And how was she ever to get out of the fix she had put herself in? She was hard put to it to stop herself from crying. This was ridiculous! What was wrong with her?

She was disturbed by the sound of voices. By some trick in the structure of this extraordinary room she could hear them quite clearly, though they must be some feet away. They were foreigners, apparently—Spaniards. She closed her eyes again and hoped that they would not disturb her. . . Then the mention of a name caused her to sit up and listen with all her attention.

'Lord Aldworth left London this afternoon.'

'Where is he going?' A soft, silky voice with a quite characteristic lisp—where had she heard it before?

'Sussex, *señor*.'

'And then to France?'

'Not immediately. The arms ship will not arrive at Newhaven for a day or two. Did Lady Paget not say that Lord Aldworth would be travelling to France with it? And that he would meet Garcia somewhere near Dieppe? But I do not know where he intends to stay until he sails, Señor Barros. I shall find it out.'

'I know it already. Lord Denham told me. Aldworth has a house down there, just a few miles from Newhaven. This begins to fit together.'

Serafina had placed the voice. It was Barros, the man who had been speaking to Lady Paget in Green Park. But. . . She grew cold as she took in what he was saying—Lady Paget? Lord Denham? What did that mean? They were Charles's friends! Or. . .were they? The other man spoke.

'The ship will be well-guarded, *señor*.'

'That is obvious. So we must attack Aldworth before he goes on board. At this Blanchards. We need more detailed information from him about the meeting place with Garcia. And there is a letter of authorisation, apparently. . .'

'Lord Aldworth won't give in easily.'

'It may take a little while, Felipe. But everyone gives in, eventually. Or they die.'

'You would kill him? An English lord?'

'I hope it won't be necessary. But we have our own boat, and the Channel is both wide and deep. . . Someone is coming. It will be the ambassador. Let me talk.'

There was a sound of footsteps coming in from the garden. They stopped by the two men.

'Good evening, Your Excellency.'

'Who is this?'

'He is not important, Excellency. He has been helping me to gather information.'

'And?'

'Lord Aldworth has left London and is now on his way to France. But I think we can intercept him.'

'Good. There must be no violence, mind! All I wish is that Aldworth and Garcia do not meet. That arms shipment must be stopped. You can pursue Garcia later.'

'It will be, Excellency. Leave it to me.'

'Then I shall go back. His Highness will be wondering

where I am. Come with me to the door, Barros. Send your fellow away.'

Serafina's heart jumped as she heard footsteps approaching. There was no escape—they were going to see her! She put her head in her hands and waited.

'Miss Feverel! Are you ill?'

She gave a start, looked up, then rose and gave a deep curtsy. 'Your Excellency! Oh, please forgive me! I didn't see you. I have such a headache. . .' She allowed her voice to trail away.

'Sit down, sit down! I hope we didn't disturb you?'

'When?' asked Serafina blankly.

'Just now. You didn't hear us talking?'

'I heard voices. . . I think. But my head was aching so. . .' Her voice trailed away again as she sank on to her seat.

'Of course. But why are you alone like this?'

'Lady Chilham has gone to find someone to bring me a drink of water. I am so ashamed of myself, Your Excellency. The Prince Regent has been so kind. . . I hope he will forgive me.'

'Who would not forgive such a very lovely young lady? I hope you will soon feel better. I'm afraid I must go back to your prince. Shall I tell him about you?'

'Oh, no! Thank you. My godmother will be here very soon. Pray do not disturb yourself on my account.'

He bowed and walked away. As they moved away Barros said rapidly in Spanish, 'Do you think she heard us, Excellency?'

'What was there to hear? In any case, we were some distance away and speaking in Spanish. I know Miss Feverel quite well. An exquisite creature, but as stupid as she is lovely. We need not worry that she understood anything. Incidentally, do you know that she came here with Denham? An intriguing situation, wouldn't you say?'

The two men laughed, then parted. Barros gave Serafina a quick glance as he passed her and went out of the doors at the end into the garden.

As soon as the two men had gone Serafina jumped up and ran to search for her godmother. She was lucky. Lady Chilham was just appearing at the door. Behind her was a footman with a glass of water in a very fine crystal goblet, but Serafina ignored him.

'I must go home at once, ma'am,' she cried. 'I . . . I feel faint!'

'But, Serafina, I have no idea where Lord Denham may be. He arranged with me that we should meet in half an hour! It would be impossible to find him in this crush.'

'I must go!' The desperation in Serafina's voice convinced her godmother.

'Very well.' She turned to the footman. 'Kindly find some transport to Curzon Street for Miss Feverel and myself. Then you will find Lord Denham and inform him that my god-daughter has been taken ill and I have taken her home. Quickly, man!'

In a very short time Serafina and her godmother were back in Curzon Street.

'Now, tell me what is wrong, Serafina!'

'Ma'am, I beg you to understand. It is very important to me that I go down to Sussex immediately!'

'But why?'

'Lord Aldworth is in danger.'

'Whatever are you talking about, Serafina?'

'The Spanish ambassador—I heard them talking. And the other men! They intend to kill him!'

Lady Chilham looked at her in horror. 'You must really be very ill, my dear. It has turned your brain! Let me feel your forehead.'

'Please, Godmother, please let me go. I must go!'

'Bed is where you must go, my girl! I shall send for Dr Hobson tomorrow——'

'No! I am not raving! The Spanish ambassador was talking with Miguel Barros in the conservatory—he doesn't want Charles killed, but they are going to!'

'What farrago is this? As if His Excellency would contemplate anything of the sort. He is a most gentlemanly creature. And who is this Barros?'

'It's because of the South American rebels!'

'What South American rebels?'

'Have you not read about them? *The Times* has had several articles on them.'

Lady Chilham looked sadly at her god-daughter. 'You poor thing. I'm sorry you miss Aldworth so much, my dear, but you must not go chasing after him, you know. I always feared you were more attached to him than you admitted. But he is perfectly safe—he will be back shortly, and then you will be married quite soon. Now, try to forget all this rubbish about South America and rebels and killing. It isn't at all suitable for a young girl. I always said no good would come of all that reading. It has gone to your head.'

'Charles is in danger, I tell you!'

'Of course, of course,' said Lady Chilham soothingly. 'I'll get Denham to look into it.'

'No, you mustn't! They mentioned him too. It

sounded as if he might be one of them! And Lady
Paget.'

'Now that is too much! Really, Serafina, I will not
tolerate any more of this nonsense. You will please me
by going to bed immediately. I shall send one of the
maids with a sleeping-powder, and Dr Hobson will see
you tomorrow. Goodnight, child.'

'But Godmother——'

'Goodnight, Serafina!'

Serafina saw that it was hopeless, and abandoned her
attempts to convince Lady Chilham. But she had not
given up. As she meekly allowed herself to be undressed
and put to bed her mind was racing. It was already half-
past four. Her resources would not stretch to a private
chaise—besides, where would she find one? But she
knew that one of the new fast coaches left Gracechurch
Street at six forty five a.m. and arrived in Brighton in
the early afternoon. Both Gabriel and her father had
used it. She could be at Blanchards not long after.
Escaping from Curzon Street presented no problems to
Sally—there was a tree just outside her bedroom
window—but getting to Gracechurch Street would be
more difficult. . . A hackney coach from Berkeley
Square? It was risky at that hour of the morning, but it
would have to be done. Somewhere in the closet was an
old cloak she had discarded. . . When the maid brought
the sleeping-powder Serafina was apparently already
asleep. Betty placed the glass on the table next to the
bed and tiptoed out.

Serafina waited a little while till the household was
quiet again. It would not be long before the lower
servants were getting up to start their day, but no one
would think of disturbing the mistress and her guest till

noon or later. She must write a note—perhaps she should simply tell her godmother that she had gone home to Feverel Place? Lady Chilham might understand that better. That done, she swiftly packed a small bundle together, put on her simplest dress, gathered up the cloak, and went to the window. . .

The streets were deserted, but there was one solitary hackney coach in Berkeley Square—it had probably delivered a customer home from some function or other. She pulled up the hood of her cloak and ran towards it. The driver took a little persuasion, but he eventually agreed to take her to Gracechurch Street.

Waiting for the coach to leave was tedious, but Serafina attached herself to an obvious countrywoman, who had spent the night at the inn and was now having a generous breakfast. When Mrs Bunniman heard that Serafina was travelling to see a sick relative she immediately took her under her capable wing. As a result, some of the problems faced by a young girl travelling alone were avoided, and the journey passed in reasonable comfort, except for the length and detail of Mrs Bunniman's stories.

In spite of the stories Serafina had time for consideration on the journey. Feverel Place lay on the direct route between Brighton and Blanchards. She would stop briefly at her home, both to get some assistance and to change into Sally's clothes. The time would be well-spent, for if Charles was alone at Blanchards he would be astonished and possibly angry at Serafina's sudden appearance, and if he was not alone—if, God help him, the Spaniard had already got there—then she would definitely need someone else with her. Michael would come, she was sure.

But after she had dismissed the chaise at Feverel Place her plans received a set-back. Her family was not there. Susan, the gardener's little daughter, came running round from the back to tell her that they were in Brighton! Mr Feverel had decided very recently that a stay in the resort would benefit Mrs Feverel, and had taken a house on the Steyne. The family had removed there the day before, together with most of the servants. Susan's father had been left in charge, but he had gone to East Bourne to look for some plants. There was no one there except herself to help Miss Feverel.

Refusing to let herself be daunted, Serafina hurried into the house, changed into her old skirt and jacket, snatched up some food from the larder and stuffed it into her pockets, then made for the stables. She was soon galloping over the hill to Blanchards. As she drew near she became more cautious. She left her horse in the field behind the house and walked discreetly round to the front.

A great deal of work had been done on the building since Serafina had last seen it. The roof had obviously been mended and the paintwork refurbished. But the shutters in the front of the house were all closed and the place looked deserted. Had Charles already left for France? Or was he not at Blanchards at all but somewhere else? She drew swiftly back into the shadows of a large beech tree as a figure came round the side of the house. But it was not Charles. Nor was it Sam Eckford. It was a stranger—a swarthy, stocky, unpleasant-looking stranger. He shouted something in Spanish and disappeared into the house. Serafina's heart was beating unevenly. This was what she had most feared. She was

too late—Barros and his men were already at
Blanchards! But where was Charles?

She slipped between the bushes and shrubs, making
her way to the back of the house again. She had spent so
much time in her youth exploring Blanchards and its
grounds that she knew every path, every gate, every
wall. It was not difficult for her to remain unobserved,
even had anyone been looking. In the courtyard at the
back stood a travelling coach—an old-fashioned, cum-
bersome affair—which looked exactly like the one her
grandfather had used when he had come visiting. Many
a time she had played in just such a coach, for it was full
of little nooks and crannies, fascinating to children.
There were horses in the stables, too—five or six. As
she watched, a roughly dressed character, looking more
like a gypsy than a nobleman's servant, came out of the
stables leading one of the horses. It was saddled, and
after a minute the first man she had seen came out of the
house and mounted.

'I shall not be long, Aitken,' he shouted. He was
speaking in English, but it was clearly not his native
tongue. 'I have some business at the inn but it won't
take long. See if Barros wants help inside.'

'I'm paid to look after the horses, not people,' was
Aitken's surly reply.

'You won't be paid at all if you don't do as you're
told. Get inside! They're upstairs.' The Spaniard rode
off, and Aitken looked up at one of the windows which
was slightly open, cursed at it, and went in.

There was no question in Serafina's mind that she
should now go back to summon help, but the temptation
to find out exactly what was happening first was too
strong, her anxiety for Charles too great. Tucking her

skirts up, she ran lightly across to the creeper which covered the wall at this point. It was an old friend—she and Michael had never been able to get into Blanchards, but that particular window had a most conveniently placed twist of branches immediately below it. She started to climb.

When she got to the point where she could see into the room she was hard put to it not to betray herself with a gasp of dismay. Charles was facing the window, his arms and legs tightly bound and a bandage over his eyes. He was speaking to someone out of sight—Miguel Barros, presumably. Serafina ducked and listened intently.

'Curse you, I've told you till I am tired! I don't know what you're talking about. How dare you keep me here like this? I demand that you release me!'

'You may go with our goodwill when you have given us the letter and the information you carry in your head. If you continue to deny their existence, Lord Aldworth, you will continue to be kept prisoner.' The voice was the same soft, lisping voice that she had heard in the conservatory at Carlton House. Charles started to protest, but Barros cut him short.

'Forgive me, but I am really quite tired of this! If you will not tell us, then you must allow me to tell you. We know that England plans to aid the enemies of Spain by providing arms for the rebels in South America. No doubt your government would deny this as strenuously as you have been denying it. But we have known of the existence of such a plan for some time.'

There was a silence. Then Charles said calmly, 'You must be mad! Castlereagh would have to be unbelievably stupid to defy the wishes of the rest of the Allies in such a way. I cannot imagine he would countenance such a thing. But in any case, what has this to do with me? What the hell do you think you are doing here, treating me like this? Even if such a ridiculous plan did in fact exist, why should you think that I have anything to do with it?'

'Lady Paget has been most helpful——'

'Ah, now I see.' Charles's voice was full of amused scorn. 'You are a fool, sir. I am surprised that you have allowed yourself to be so duped.'

'Duped?'

'Perhaps you do not know the lady very well? Then I must tell you that she is an attractive woman with an overgrown sense of drama. She likes to be at the centre of attention, and I have recently been neglecting her. No doubt she thinks to revenge herself by this outrageous farce.'

'Farce? This is no farce, milord.'

'What else would you call the machinations of an unbalanced woman? I hope you haven't paid her, or promised her anything?'

'She will receive a share of the emeralds.'

'It gets better! What emeralds?'

'Stop pretending!' Barros's voice rose, but he took a breath and continued quietly, 'The plan was drawn up by you and Sir Robert Paget. You met a man called Pedro de Garcia last January in Vienna—the inn was called the Zum Goldenen Topf. You made the arrangements then, and since that time you have been waiting for him to return with payment, in the form of emeralds from New Granada, for the arms your perfidious government has agreed to release. You, Lord Aldworth, are now on your way to France in order to meet him. The shipment of arms is due off Newhaven within the next forty-eight hours. Do you need more?'

Charles was still calm, but a note of tension had crept into his voice. 'How very detailed! Where did you hear this. . .farrago?'

'Initially from Lady Paget.'

'Not Sir Robert?'

'Aha! So you have been suspecting your old friend? Is that why you have so assiduously courted his wife?'

'I courted Sir Robert's wife because, before she grew tiresome, she was a damned attractive woman—and—er—very willing. Barros, think carefully about what you are doing. For no reason at all, as far as I can see, you have chosen to believe the unsupported word of a jealous woman. You are in grave danger of making a fool of yourself, to say nothing of causing a very unpleasant diplomatic incident. His Excellency, who is a man of honour, will not thank you for this. Now release me before the affair gets out of hand.'

'You are a brave man, milord, but a foolish one. You will not persuade me that it is nonsense—we have had the story checked and rechecked. Lady Paget may be a discontented woman tied to an elderly husband, and she is certainly a greedy one, but she is no fool. And I believe her to be very fond of you still. She was most concerned that you should come to no harm. Now, before we are forced to disappoint her and try. . .less agreeable methods of persuasion on you, will you admit to the truth of the story? Then, if you will tell us where you have hidden the letter of authorisation and give us the rest of the necessary information, we shall let you go free—subject to certain conditions.'

'I would certainly not agree to any conditions whatsoever with vermin such as you.' The bored contempt in his prisoner's voice roused Barros to anger. There was the sound of a sharp slap. 'You do see what I mean?' The contempt and boredom were still there. 'My hands and feet are tied, and I am blindfolded. A worthy target for vermin, wouldn't you agree?' said Charles.

Barros said unpleasantly, 'You are right, of course. My employers may be gentlemen, but I am not. I work for Spain, but I am also as greedy as Lady Paget. I too have been promised a share of the emeralds, and to succeed I would do almost anything. Do not deceive yourself, milord. If you continue to refuse to tell me then I shall kill you. Or wait! Perhaps I have a better idea! Would you like me to have Miss Feverel brought from London to join you here? I could have her delivered by tomorrow evening—in plenty of time to take her to France with us. It could be an enjoyable experience—she is very lovely.'

'You would not dare!'

'But I would. It would not even be difficult. Miss Feverel would be an easy target—she is beautiful, but not very clever, I think. Shall I ask the men to bring her?'

The silence was longer this time. Then Charles finally spoke. 'There is no letter, whatever Lady Paget might have told you. And there is no password. I alone am the key. Garcia will reveal himself only to me, and only I can make him known to the captain of the ship. In return Garcia will hand over the emeralds. To me. No one else will do. So if you kill me you will have nothing. Why don't you give up? You cannot succeed. I might be able to arrange for you to have your share of the jewels if you do as I suggest.'

'You forget, milord. I may covet the jewels, but I am also a patriot. Let me think.' There was yet another silence, after which Barros said, 'I am inclined to believe that there isn't a letter. We have searched you, your baggage and the coach extremely thoroughly. For the rest—you might be telling the truth, though I doubt it. But it appears that we have to take you with us if we wish to see either the jewels or the arms.'

'You will never succeed in taking over the ship!'

'I do not intend to. We shall take you to France ourselves. The arms are less important to us than Bolivar's agent. And the emeralds. So—you will come to France, Lord Aldworth. But if, as I suspect, you are thinking of playing any tricks, you will be the first to die, I assure you.'

There was a knock. Footsteps could be heard moving away towards the door and Serafina risked a look through the window. She saw that Barros had gone out to talk to someone on the other side, leaving the door almost closed. Charles was trying vainly to loosen his bonds. She ducked down again quickly as the door started to open and Barros came back.

'Felipe has returned. Our vessel is ready and waiting, and by the time we reach the port the tide will be high. We shall go immediately. What is this? Surely you haven't been trying to release yourself, Lord Aldworth? A foolish and useless endeavour! But just as a precaution. . . Aitken! Aitken! Fetch my bag from the next room, if you please.' A moment or two passed, then Aitken returned. There was the sound of a struggle and a chair turned over. 'Hold him down!' Barros said curtly. Serafina was filled with horror. What were they doing to Charles? A faint, sweetish smell came drifting out, and when she stole a quick glance into the room she saw that Charles was lying quite still on the floor.

'That should keep him quiet for a while. Long enough to get him to Newhaven. But we'll leave him tied up, just in case. . .'

CHAPTER NINE

SERAFINA decided that she could do no good where she
was. She must race home and send to Newhaven to alert
the coastguards. She was sure that a man on a good
horse could overtake that heavy coach. Cautiously she
climbed down and looked around. It was still quite light,
and she had no idea where Aitken was—she would have
to risk it. She had not got very far when Aitken
appeared at the back door, but fortunately she was
hidden from him by the carriage. She froze. Then to her
horror a horse and rider came into the courtyard, and
started to make for the stables. Serafina was in a panic.
If she was discovered now there would be no possibility
of help for Charles or anyone else—herself included!
But just when discovery seemed inevitable there was a
call from the house and the rider dismounted and went
over to the door, where he stood discussing something
with Aitken. Now was her opportunity to hide—but
where? She looked round and noticed that the door of
the travelling coach was slightly, but invitingly open.
Without a second thought she slipped inside and
crouched down on the floor. She was just in time. The
men walked past within inches of where she had been
standing seconds before, and went into the stable.

Serafina forced herself to think calmly. There was no
chance of escape from the coach while Aitken and the
other man were anywhere in the yard. She was effec-
tively trapped inside. Even now one of them was passing

again on his way into the house. But what would happen if she could not escape before they all drove to Newhaven? Her blood ran cold at the thought of discovery—she must find some sort of hiding place, she must! Her grandfather's coach which, as far as she could see, had been exactly like this one, had been intended for long journeys during which the traveller might wish to sleep in his own coach. The seats had been like these—broad and deep. And underneath there had been. . . Ah! Yes—there it was! A leather flap under the seat which pulled down and held more valuable luggage in behind it. It had been perfect for hide-and-seek in the past, but would she fit in there now? She wriggled and squirmed and discovered that she could—just. She pulled the flap down in front of her and lay there trying to regain her breath. It would not do if they heard her, and someone was approaching! Two men, carrying a heavy burden, got into the coach. There was a thump as they dumped something on to the seat opposite, then they sat down themselves over her head. The coach set off. . .

Afterwards Serafina remembered the hour that followed as one of the worst, most excruciatingly uncomfortable experiences of her life. If the road to Newhaven had been any longer she would have betrayed herself by being sick! She dared not relax, for a pothole or even a steep slope might have sent her rolling forward into view. She clung to the strut at one side and held her foot against the other as the coach swayed and jolted along, and wondered why Charles had chosen to travel in such an antique when he had a perfectly comfortable chaise. Unless. . . If the coach really was the twin of her grandfather's then it had a

small cache in which to hide jewellery and money from
the greed of highwaymen. Was there, in fact, a letter,
though Charles had denied it? Was he playing some
deep game of his own? And had he hidden it where no
one who did not know the secret could possibly discover
it? Perhaps. There was no way of finding out at the
moment.

At last the nightmare came to an end. The coach
came to a halt and Serafina could smell the sea and hear
the sound of the waves crashing on to the shore. They
must be at Newhaven. She tensed as the men got out,
but they were apparently engrossed in extracting their
unconscious prisoner and carrying him away. She must
be patient. It would be some time before the ship could
set sail, and the coach could not be under observation
all the time. She would wait inside a little longer—they
would come back for the luggage. Daylight was fading
but there was still a little light inside the coach. While
she was waiting this might be the time to test her theory.
She lifted the flap cautiously and peered under the
forward seat. On one side was a small piece of wood—a
flaw in the panelling, one would have said. So far, so
good. Gently she eased it out with her fingernail. Under
it was a tiny knob, which she pressed, quickly putting
her hand over the piece of panelling before it made a
noise as it fell out. She had been right! Behind it was a
small recess in which lay a letter and a bag full of money.

The bag was heavy, and when she peered inside she
could see a large number of gold and silver French
coins. Charles must have had it ready for his journey.
Thanking heaven that she was wearing her old jacket,
Serafina put the bag and the letter into one of her

pockets and then, hearing the sound of returning footsteps, she slipped back into her hiding place.

'Take the luggage on board as quickly as you can, Aitken. We're sailing in a quarter of an hour! Hurry! The longer we stay here, the more dangerous it gets, and the tide is perfect. You take the coach back to the house. Make sure you put it in the coach-house, and see to the horses. We don't want any questions. You have your story ready?'

'Course I do!' muttered Aitken. 'Where's my money?'

'You'll get it when the luggage is on board, not before. Get on with it! I'll just make sure that his lordship is. . .comfortable in his quarters. He should wake up soon.'

Grumbling and cursing, Aitken untied the boxes and started carting them towards the ship. Now was her moment! Serafina slid cautiously forward, then lifted herself up to see out. Aitken was bent double under a large box, making his way slowly to a fishing boat moored alongside. By screwing up her eyes she could make out its name—*Maria Cristina*. Barros was just going on board. At some point or other Serafina must have made up her mind, for now, without any hesitation, she got out of the coach on the landward side, almost falling as the money bag pulled her over to one side and her stiffened limbs refused to take the weight. She paused for an agonising moment or two, then sidled round and, taking a deep breath, darted to the shelter of a pile of boxes near the edge of the quay. Here she crouched until she saw her opportunity. Aitken was back at the coach, Barros had gone below, and the crew was occupied forward. She slipped like a shadow onto

the ship, and made for the stern, where she had seen
huge piles of fishing nets. Hoping to heaven that the
captain and crew were too concerned with their human
cargo to do any fishing, she burrowed her way between
the nets, made herself comfortable as best she could,
and lay down. Whatever happened now she could do no
more. Soon the orders to the sailors increased, there
was much scurrying to and fro, and the *Maria Cristina*
started to move. The strain of the past twenty-four
hours took its toll, and Serafina. . .fell asleep.

Shouts and cries, the mewing of seagulls, the noise of
wheels on cobblestones—Serafina gradually became
aware of all of these. She had been cold in the night, but
now she was warm—almost too warm. A vast expanse
of blue sky met her eyes as she slowly opened them. She
lay there for a moment as memory returned—memory
and the scent of danger. There was also a strong smell of
fish all round her. Cautiously she lifted her head,
thankful that she was still wearing her beloved woolly
cap. She had found it in her pocket when she had woken
briefly in the middle of the night, and had put it on. The
Maria Cristina was just edging alongside a stone wall.
Serafina ducked down again as a sailor came past,
whistling. He leapt up on to the wall and busied himself
pulling the boat by means of thick ropes which he
wound round capstans on the quay. He was watching
the animated scene on the quayside as he did so—much
to Serafina's relief, for he would certainly have seen her
otherwise. He finished what he was doing and stepped
away out of her sight. There was the sound of a woman's
voice and laughter.

'Manuel! Come down here and finish your work!'

shouted a voice of authority in Spanish. Manuel reappeared, swaggering along the quay towards the other end. Serafina breathed again. But she must get off the boat as soon as possible. Over there were a couple of rungs up the side of the wall, but how could she get up them without being seen? Perhaps Manuel would be as interested in the ladies at the other end? She peered over the nets. Yes, his back was towards her and he was flanked by two buxom fisherwomen. He had an arm round each, and was clearly flirting with them. Several other members of the crew came to join him, laughing raucously, and there was soon a crowd on the quay at the far end of the boat. A man who was clearly in charge came hurrying down towards them all, waving his arms and shouting. Now, if ever, was her chance. She ran to the side, scrambled up the rungs, and was on dry land in a trice. Quickly she merged with the moving throng on the quayside.

Wherever she was, she was in France, and it was quite clearly market day. Stalls of fish, fruit and vegetables, cheeses of all kinds, household goods and a few clothes lined the streets. Women in voluminous skirts, sabots, and heavily starched white bonnets walked along them, sampling this, feeling that, bargaining with the shop-keepers. Booths selling wine and cider were ranged along the front by the boats, their customers sitting on barrels and bollards, quaffing from huge tankards. It was a noisy, lively, colourful scene.

Serafina eyed the stalls and felt faint with hunger. She had woken in the night and consumed the pathetic remnants of the food she had stuffed into her pockets at home. It had been something, but not nearly enough, and now the smell of freshly baked bread was reminding her of how little she had eaten for two days. Her fingers curled round the bag of money that she had found in the coach and, without taking it out of her pocket, she extracted several coins. They were silver francs. Even one was too much for bread—she must buy something else first. A change of clothing wouldn't be a bad idea, for her clothes reeked of fish. As she watched the girls walking so gracefully in their swinging skirts and aprons, pretty caps or stiff white bonnets on their heads, baskets on their arms, the glimmering of an idea came to her.

She wandered away from the main shopping area and sought out a quieter street in which were a number of shops with various items of clothing for sale. She spent a little time examining the wares laid out in front, becoming conscious of the stares and significant sniffs as she walked along. She smiled ruefully at a pleasant-looking woman who was standing at the door of one of the smaller places.

'I've had an accident, *madame*,' she said, affecting a strong Spanish accent—the women would know that a Spanish vessel was in port. 'On my brother's boat. I think my clothes are ruined—all of them, including the ones in my bags. He's given me some money to dress myself, but I don't know if it will be enough.' She held out a few of the francs.

'My poor little cabbage! I'll find something for you. Come in. I think you will need a wash, too, *hein*?' The shopkeeper went along the shelves and selected some garments. Then she beckoned to Serafina and showed her into a tiny room at the back. She fetched a bowl of water and a cloth, and left the new clothes on the chair by the door. 'Call me if you want anything else,' she said. 'And there's a privy outside where you can throw the water when you've finished.'

It wasn't long before Serafina was once again sweet-smelling, and dressed in a full skirt, a white blouse and a large apron. She hid the precious letter in her bodice and, after taking out a few more coins and putting them in her pocket, she tied the bag of money on a piece of cord round her waist and hid it under her skirt.

'*Ooh, la—la*!' said the woman when she reappeared. 'Why can't I look as pretty as that in the clothes I make? But you'll need stockings and sabots. And perhaps a cap? Would your brother pay for a cap, *chérie*? I've a very pretty one here, quite cheap.' When Serafina finally left the shop a prettier serving maid would have been difficult to find. With regret she abandoned her own outer clothes in the dustbin by the privy. They were quite ruined. Smiling her thanks, she paid the woman, and set off to look for food. A roll and some cheese washed down with a cup of fresh milk made her feel better straight away. Then she went in search of other necessities, the first of which was a large basket, rolls and cheese to fill it, and a starched napkin to cover it.

Then she went back to the quayside. Here she bargained for a wicked-looking knife which was used for cutting fish, and put it under the rolls. She was almost ready. Out of the corner of her eye she saw that Miguel Barros and the other Spaniard—Felipe?—were striding purposefully to the hostelry at the end of the quay. It was a post-house—it looked as if they were going to hire some horses. After a few minutes they rode out of the yard and down the main street with the air of people who were going some distance.

Serafina took a deep breath and walked swiftly up to the inn.

'And what might a pretty little ladybird like you want?'

The innkeeper was smiling, but definitely curious.

'I. . . I was looking for Señor Barros. He asked me to meet him here,' she said.

'The Spanish gentleman? He's gone off to Bourg-Dun. He won't be back for a few hours. Was there something. . .special you wanted?' The look in his eye suggested that he might be willing to provide it.

'No, no,' she said hastily. 'I'll wait for him on the boat. But I'll take something to drink for the others.'

She bought a bottle of wine, which she put in her basket, and a jug of cider, and started off down the quay.

She had to run the gauntlet of cries and cheers from the fishermen drinking at the booths, but managed quite well until one, slightly drunker than the rest, actually tried to stop her by putting his arm round her. Serafina, hampered as she was by her basket and the jug, was helpless, but the burly owner of the booth pushed the man aside. 'Let her be, Jules! Can't you see she's on her way to someone else? Now, sit down and stop making a fool of yourself.'

The fisherman subsided and Serafina thanked the stallholder and went on to the *Maria Cristina*.

'*Bonjour*!' she called. She wasn't sure what dialect was used in this part of France, but she was equally certain that the Spaniard wouldn't know either. Nor would he notice any accent.

'*Señorita*!' He nodded and smiled, but stepped forward and barred her way as she came down the plank.

'I have food for the prisoner—a Monsieur Barros ordered it from the inn over there, before he set off to Bourg-Dun.' She turned and pointed to the posting inn. The burly stallholder was still staring at them. 'Don't worry about him,' she said. 'That's just my father. He likes to keep an eye on me. Well? Are you going to let me pass?'

'Señor Barros said we weren't to let anyone on board. . .'

'That's strange. His instructions to me were very clear, and he paid for all of this! The wine and food for the prisoner, and the cider for you. . . Oh, well, I'll take it away again. I hope he won't want his money back, though.'

'Wait! He must have meant strangers, not serving girls—at least, not pretty ones like you.'

Serafina dimpled. 'I hope there aren't too many of you left on board—it's not a very generous amount of cider. . . Pedro?'

'The others have gone off into the town. And my name's Juan. But I prefer wine, anyway,' he said, eyeing the bottle.

'The cider is better than the wine, I assure you, Juan. Monsieur Barros said that the wine was for the criminal, and that's about all it's fit for! Is he. . .is he very dangerous?'

'He's well-watched. There are two of us here and we both have weapons. He won't get loose.'

Serafina gave a realistic shudder. 'Just two? You are both so brave! I shall leave the cider with you, yes? And take the prisoner's breakfast in.' She smiled entrancingly again and offered him the jug. He put his weapon down and took it, standing aside as he did so.

'Leave some for your friend!' she said with a roguish look as she went round to the cabin.

In the gangway outside the cabin was another sailor. He was armed with a large pistol, and an even larger knife was in his waistband.

'*Oh, mon Dieu*!' cried Serafina. 'What a terrible sight! A pistol and a knife! But I suppose with only two of you to guard the whole boat you need such dreadful weapons. *Ooh, la-la*!' She eyed the cabin door. . . .

Inside the cabin, Lord Aldworth was experiencing difficulty in not giving in to something close to despair. For the hundredth time since being surprised at Blanchards by Barros he cursed the careless tongues at the Foreign Office. Louisa Paget he had known to be an informer, and had used her, carefully feeding her false information about the time and place of his rendezvous in France. That had been useful this morning when he had sent Barros and the other man off on a wild-goose chase to Bourg-Dun. But someone must have gossiped about Blanchards. He hadn't told her of that, and he hadn't thought it necessary to be on his guard there, either.

What was going to happen when Barros returned? His chances of survival, never very great from the moment Barros had overwhelmed him, were now extremely slim—non-existent, in fact. He had lied to Barros about the letter and the arrangements for the exchange in order to gain time, but once the Spaniard realised that he was not going to give them any information of value his end was inevitable, and probably painful. Barros had been too cunning and too cautious. They had trussed him up so carefully that it was impossible to escape, as he had hoped. His limbs were aching, tied as they were with hands together and legs bound by the ankles to the bed. And this wretched blindfold prevented him from judging distance or anything else! They had released him for a short while last night and this morning—but two of them had waited in the cabin with their pistols ready. He had been able to do nothing. Then he straightened his shoulders. He must not give in! While there was life there was always hope—a little. He could hear voices now, and someone was coming towards the cabin. . .

'*Oh, mon Dieu*! What a terrible sight! A pistol and a knife! But I suppose with only two of you to guard the whole boat you need such dreadful weapons. *Ooh, lala!*'

He must be mad or dreaming! That voice! He dismissed the thought for the fantasy it was. Sally Feverel could not possibly be anywhere near. It was an illusion—a similarity of timbre and quality, though it was speaking French. He strained his ears all the same as the door opened.

'Do not leave me alone with this villain, I beg you! Oh, how I wish Monsieur Barros had gone somewhere else to buy his food!'

The French, though nearly perfect, had a slight accent.

'You'll be perfectly safe, *señorita*. I shall stand by the door with my pistol ready. Just make sure you do not get between it and the prisoner.'

'You mean I am to feed him! To approach him? Never!'

'He can feed himself.'

'How? He cannot see, and he has no hands.'

'I suppose you'd better take the blindfold off his eyes,' said the guard reluctantly.

'What about the rope round his wrists? I'm not going near him when his hands are free!'

'Don't be afraid, *señorita*. Just remember what I said about not shielding him.'

A pair of hands held Charles and gave him a warning squeeze. The knots were undone and the kerchief removed. He turned his head and met Sally's eyes. He tried to speak, but Sally forestalled him. 'He doesn't look such a desperado, does he? In fact I feel a bit sorry for him. I shall give him some wine first.' She poured some wine into the glass on the table and held it out to him. He raised his bound hands mutely.

Sally knelt down in front of him, and the guard said immediately, 'Move, *señorita*! I would not wish to shoot you.'

Sally gave a scream and jumped up. She said angrily, 'Then you must free his hands yourself. I cannot undo knots from the side, me. It is impossible!'

Charles could see that the guard was perplexed. To get too near the prisoner would be dangerous, especially if his hands were released. At last he said slowly, 'Take my knife and cut them. I will stay here.'

'He will not hurt me?'

'I give you my word, *mademoiselle*,' said Charles in perfect French.

'*Oh, mon Dieu*, the villain speaks French!' she exclaimed. She looked uncertainly at him and then turned to the guard, who nodded and levelled his pistol purposefully. Serafina took the knife, moved gingerly to Charles's side and cut the rope round his hands. She jumped quickly away and put the knife on the table.

Then she picked up her basket and, having rearranged
the food a little, she put it on the bed beside him.

'Bread and cheese, *monsieur*.'

Charles looked down. The handle of a knife could be
seen under the napkin. Sally moved away and went over
to the guard.

'There! That's a relief. I was afraid he would grab me.
But then you were here, were you not? You would have
saved me. . . Pedro?' She looked up at the unfortunate
man with melting blue eyes.

He gazed down bemused, and murmured, 'My name
is Luis.'

Sally dropped her voice a little and said, 'Your friend
on deck—Juan—said you would be free this evening
perhaps. If you are not already engaged would you have
time for a little French girl and her sister? We sometimes like a change from the French boys. . .'

'Your sister? Is she as pretty as you?'

'Much prettier. With black hair and. . .and. . .'
Sally's hands were much more expressive than anything
she could have said. 'Would you like to see her? She's
on the quay. Come—you can see her from this
porthole.'

The guard cast an uneasy glance in Charles's direction, but saw that he was munching stolidly.

'Come! He won't trouble you. What do you expect
him to do, tied to the bedpost as he is? Leap on you
from behind? I hope you're not going to disappoint
Arlette and me. She likes her men brave and strong—as
well as handsome.'

The guard allowed himself to be led over to the
porthole. 'Now, that's my father—you see that burly
fellow up there? But he is going out himself tonight.

And next to him is Arlette. . . . Oh, she isn't there! Wait,
I think she's just behind him. Can you see her? Black
hair and a white blouse cut low in the front. Maman says
she has no shame, that one! You'll have to crane your
neck. . . .'

The guard was clearly enjoying the sensation of
holding Sally while they both attempted to peer out at
the same time. He was a pathetically easy target.
Charles jerked him back then hit him hard. He went
down without a murmur.

'Quick, the rope and the kerchief!' But Sally already
had them ready. Luis was soon on the bed, trussed up
and gagged.

'This isn't the moment to ask how or why you're
here—there isn't time. But thank God you are,' he said.

'Now for number two,' she said, grinning up at him.
'Don't forget Luis's pistol. I have his knife.' She picked
up the basket again and tripped out. 'Thank you, thank
you, *monsieur*!' she trilled. 'I'll see what your friend
Juan says.'

When Serafina went on deck she found that Juan had
been finding the cider quite to his taste. The jug was
empty, and Juan had a slightly foolish grin on his face.

'Ah, *señorita*. . .'

'Oh, Juan,' cried Serafina reproachfully. 'You've
finished it all! Never mind, you shall have some more
tonight. Luis says you will both be free. He'd like to
spend the evening with me and my sister. Will you come
too?'

'Wha' time?'

'*Zut*! I forgot to ask! I'll wait here while you go and
ask him.'

'Gorra stay here. On duty.'

'Oh, but you can just pop down for a second, can't you? I dare not. Papa is still looking this way—he'll start to wonder if I go below again. He's very strict——' she lowered her voice '—but he'll be out tonight.'

Juan cast an eye at the burly stallholder. 'All ri'.'

He stumbled round the corner. There was a thump, and the sound of something falling. Serafina went back and helped to gag Juan and tie him up before he was taken to join his friend. Charles shrugged on his coat, which was looking decidedly the worse for wear, then he locked the door and they walked unhurriedly off the boat, dropping the cabin key over the side as they went. Once in the crowd, however, they left the quayside as quickly as possible.

'We'll carry on talking French, if you don't mind. You're good enough to fool most people, and I don't want to draw attention to us.'

'In that case you'd better get some other clothes! You're a touch conspicuous in those!'

Charles laughed as he looked down. 'I must remind you of the occasion in the greenhouse at Blanchards! Decidedly dirty.'

'But still handsome,' said Serafina involuntarily. 'I remember thinking how handsome you were.'

He stopped and looked down at her. 'Really?' he murmured with a glint in his eye.

'Yes, but don't let it go to your head. It needs to be clear at the moment. And I've. . . I'm——' She stopped and swallowed. Reaction was setting in and she was feeling distinctly strange.

'Sally! Don't give way now! You've been such a heroine. Wait! We'll sit here in the shade for a moment.'

They sat in silence for a little while, then Serafina

said, 'I feel better now. I'm sorry, Charles. What a poor
thing I am! I don't even know what happened. When we
got off the boat I was feeling very cheerful, and then
suddenly I wanted to sit down and howl my eyes out.'

Charles looked at her, his eyes warm and sympathetic. 'I've had the same sort of thing happen to me in the
past, Sally. It's nothing to be ashamed of. You were
quite superb on that boat. If I hadn't known who you
were I'd have sworn you were a minx who had never left
her father's tavern in Dieppe. And. . . I owe you my
life.'

'Rubbish! You'd have got out somehow.'

'We'll never know. But we're not out of the wood yet.
We need money and transport. I have some English
money, but it won't be nearly enough. The rest was left
in England, and at the moment I don't know where or
how to get any more.'

'Will this do?' Serafina turned away from him, lifted
up her skirt and removed the bag of money.

'Where the devil did you get that?' He examined it.
'It's mine!' Charles gave her a penetrating look. 'Just
what have you been up to, Sally? Are you a witch?'

'I'll explain, but it will take quite a time. Shouldn't we
be moving on?'

'You're right. Well, this solves the problem of our
finances—there's enough here and more. We can buy
all we need. As you say, I really need some other
clothing. A smock? And a beret? And then when I have
those I could perhaps purchase a horse and cart.'

'We need something faster than that! A chaise or a
curricle, surely?'

'I can afford to buy a horse and cart. I'd have to hire a

chaise. If you were Barros what would you do when you found I had escaped?'

'I'd go after you—oh, I see. I'd enquire at all the post-inns, of course!'

'And when you found someone who answered to my description, you and some of your band would ride after him. Quite. I don't want to face Barros until I am better equipped to.'

'But how far is it to——? Where are you going, Charles?'

'Paris.'

'Paris! But that must be a hundred miles! Why?'

'It's the place Garcia and I arranged to meet if either of us didn't turn up at the rendezvous. He'll be there waiting for me. But the most urgent problem at the moment is getting away from Barros. Sally, we have a lot to discuss, including what I'm going to do with you. And I'd like to know by what miracle you came to be here, too. But there isn't time. We have to get out of Dieppe before Barros returns.'

'It's better if I go and buy clothes. I can say they're for my father. Stay here!'

CHAPTER TEN

HALF an hour later Charles and Serafina were driving at a slow but steady pace along the road to Paris. Their cart was shabby but in good repair and, besides a small load of hay, it carried some provisions and a few extra clothes. Charles, smoking a long pipe and wearing a dun-coloured smock and a shapeless hat, no longer looked quite so distinguished. In fact, thought Serafina with a certain degree of satisfaction, he was the picture of a respectable, though not very rich farmer, returning home from market. She herself now sported a stiffly starched white cap and a flat straw hat with a wide brim which shaded her face. A bright blue fichu covered her shoulders. She looked the epitome of a respectable farmer's wife.

After all the activity of the morning Serafina was content to sit in something of a daze for the first part of the journey, watching the Norman countryside roll by and letting its peaceful beauty restore her. Charles was quiet too, apparently sensing her need for peace, and perhaps himself needing time to recover from his experiences. His night must have been, if anything, even more uncomfortable than hers. As time went on, however, she began to think again—Barros would surely soon return to Dieppe from Bourg-Dun. What would he do? How long would it be before he decided to search the road to Paris? She became uneasy. It was a relief to hear Charles say comfortingly, 'You can stop looking behind us, Sally. It will be an hour or so yet before Barros could catch up with us, and I'm leaving the high road before that. In fact. . .here's the turning.'

'Why are we leaving the Paris road?'

'We aren't. Trust me—I know the country between Dieppe and Paris like the back of my hand. I ought to. This is a very pleasant alternative road along the other side of the forest, and it's cooler here, too. We can relax a little.' They travelled on in silence for a short while until the high road was well behind them. Then, 'I think explanation time has come, don't you?' said Charles.

'Tell me first what this is all about. I thought you were a diplomat.'

'I am. But sometimes I. . .do other things. Not often now—I did more during the war. As you know, my grandmother is French, and I speak the language fluently. So do you, I notice. Tell me where you learned it.'

'My father invited the widow of a French emigré to live with us until she was able to go back to France in 1816. She spent a year with us, and we all spoke to her in her own language. I still correspond with her.'

'Could you go to her now? It might be a solution to one of our problems,' asked Charles sharply.

'I'm afraid not. She lives in the Auvergne.'

'I see.' He thought for a moment. 'Well, it seems as if I shall have to take you to Paris with me. I can't leave you on your own in the wilds of Normandy, and you'll be safer with me than with anyone else. Safer from Barros, anyway.' He smiled at her with a glint in his eye.

She said hastily, 'You were going to tell me about your work.'

He nodded. 'I think you deserve to be told. But it's not for general consumption, Sally.'

'Oh! You disappoint me. I was about to stop the next peasant we see to discuss it with him!'

He smiled at her remark but then grew sober again. 'I meant even after we get back to England. At present what I am doing for the government is highly unofficial, and, if questioned, my superiors would deny all knowledge of my activities. They concern a man called Bolivar. Do you know who he is?'

'The Venezuelan who is leading a rebellion against Spain in South America? Yes, of course.'

He looked at her with a smile in his eyes. 'Of course,' he murmured. 'Most of the people in England have never heard the name, but Sally Feverel knows him.'

'With a father like mine it would be difficult not to. Carry on.'

'Bolivar has access to some of the most valuable emerald mines in the world in New Granada. He has the wherewithal to purchase arms to carry on his struggle — more than enough. But except for a few hundred rifles from the United States he can't find anywhere else to buy them. The major countries of Europe wouldn't dream of supplying him, because he's rebelling against one of their allies.'

'And we are? Supplying them, I mean?'

'That's where I come in. We aren't—officially. But when Richard Rush, the American ambassador, approached us a little while ago we. . .listened, shall I say? A colleague of mine — Robert Paget — '

'Ah, yes,' murmured Serafina. 'Lady Paget's husband.'

'Yes,' he said curtly. 'Yes, well, Robert arranged a

meeting in Vienna between Bolivar's agent and ourselves. The terms were agreed and now the arms are
ready and my job is to carry out the exchange—
emeralds for arms. Barros's task is to stop it.'

'What will happen now? The ship carrying the arms
was due in Newhaven soon, wasn't it? Where will it go
now?'

'Are there no secrets left? Where did you learn that?'

'I'll tell you later. What happens to it when you aren't
there to board it?'

'It will go back to Portsmouth and wait for further
orders.'

'I see. So Sir Robert Paget was. . .is a colleague in all
this? Er. . . Where does Lady Paget come in? I
thought. . . We thought you were. . .'

Charles looked down at Serafina broodingly. 'For a
short while I was—if you are asking whether I was in
love with her. She was never my mistress. But then I
discovered that she was dishonest—a cheat and a liar. It
killed any feeling I had for her. Since Christmas I have
been using her to deceive Barros.'

'Your feelings about deception seem to be somewhat
illogical, Charles. Surely you have indulged in a little
double-dealing yourself in the past? In Vienna, for
example?'

'I take it you're referring to my affairs again. I told
you once before, Sally—they are not important. Fidelity
in marriage doesn't seem to count for very much in
Vienna. I respected very few of the people I knew there.
I liked them—they were witty, informed, polished—but
there were very few whose integrity I trusted. Sir Robert
was one, which is why I. . .never quite lost my head

over Louisa Paget. I don't deceive people I respect, Sally. I would not, for example, lie to you.'

A cold finger touched Serafina's heart. She said slowly, 'And integrity is important to you. . . Would you be as unsympathetic as you sound if I lied to you, Charles? Or if Serafina lied to you?'

'I can't imagine either of you doing so, especially not Serafina. But yes, I would. How could you respect or trust anyone who lied to you? Why? Are you about to lie to me?'

'No, I am not about to lie to you. Sally Feverel is always herself with you, Charles.'

'Well, then, tell me how you came to turn up on Barros's fishing boat in time to rescue me.'

Serafina's mind was made up. She had considered making her confession here on the road to Paris, for Charles was grateful to her, and the time had seemed more propitious than any other. But what he had just said made it impossible. How could they continue in each other's company all the weary way to Paris after a revelation such as hers? It would be impossible. No, she would keep her confession for a better occasion. There would be one. She said slowly, 'I heard you were at Blanchards. I. . . I wanted to apologise to you because I hadn't been very polite the last time we had seen each other. But then I saw the strangers, and I became suspicious. . .'

From there on it was easy. She told Charles everything that had happened between her arrival at Blanchards and their meeting on the boat, finishing by saying, 'I've given you the money. This was in the cache as well.' She handed him the letter.

Charles looked at it and grasped her in his arms. 'You

wonderful girl! You can't imagine how much trouble this is going to save me when we get to Paris. I. . . I'm overwhelmed, Sally.' He kissed her. Then he kissed her again. And again, and that kiss continued until a whinny from the horse as he felt the reins drop caused them to draw back from one another.

Serafina's nerves were again stretched to their limit. Not only had she just come through a harrowing forty-eight hours, she was now being subjected to the greatest temptation in her life. This man, she knew in her soul, was probably the only man she would ever love, and as soon as he knew the truth about her there was a strong possibility that he would never wish to see her again. The temptation to seduce him during their journey to Paris, to bind him to her with chains he could not in all decency break, was almost overwhelming. But some inner sense of honour held her back. She was committed to the original deception, but she would not make it impossible for him to cry off from their engagement.

She was trembling, but she pushed him firmly away as she said, 'Charles, you must not. I know you mean nothing by it, but it isn't fair—either to me or to Serafina. And we have a long road to Paris.'

He took the reins again, but didn't move the cart on. Looking at her with a puzzled frown, he said slowly, 'Each time I kiss you, Sally. . .it means a little more.'

'It mustn't!'

'No, I know. I'm sorry. Oh, devil take it, Sally, I'm always saying that to you. I don't know what it is about you. . . Look, I swear I mean you no harm, and I intend to keep my word to Serafina. I know I mustn't make love to you, or even kiss you. But somehow, when you're there. . . I kissed you just now without even

considering whether I should or not—I was so delighted
to see that letter. Then one kiss didn't seem enough. . .
Oh, God damn it, I know I mustn't seduce you! That
would mean breaking my promise to Serafina and
marrying you instead. . .' He looked at her for a
moment. 'No, it would be an impossible situation. And
a marriage between us wouldn't work either!'

'I think you're right, Charles. It would be an impossible situation. But. . .why do you say that a marriage
between us wouldn't work?'

He said carefully, 'If you married me, we should have
two choices. Either you would take Serafina's place in
my life and stay most of the time alone at Aldworth with
our children while I travelled abroad. I cannot imagine
that you would tolerate that, nor would I wish to subject
you to it.'

'Or?'

'You would travel with me. And you would soon find
that my life as a diplomat would suit you no better. It's
never normally as adventurous as this. It usually consists
of what you would hate most—what you would call
stuffy people at stuffy dinners, exchanging gossip.
London, Paris, Vienna, Berlin—they're all the same.
Protocol, precedence, formality and gossip—you
wouldn't be happy. I should imagine you would find it
very difficult, if not impossible, to conform. And. . .my
work is important to me, Sally.'

'No,' she agreed quietly. 'I shouldn't be happy.' She
heaved a sigh, then grinned at him bravely. 'Well, now
that we have cleared the air, let's be friends on this
adventure. I shall regard you as I do Gabriel, and you
shall overcome this strange desire you have to kiss
me. Done?'

Charles looked a little grim, but he said with resolute cheerfulness, 'Done!'

And so it was for the rest of that day, and for the two days that followed. They ambled steadily through the French countryside, stopping at remote inns, buying provisions as they needed them, and never once catching a glimpse of Barros and his men. Charles's manner, which was at first somewhat restrained, slowly relaxed, and the time passed pleasantly in animated conversation or companionable silence. Their minds were in perfect harmony and, if anything, the secret, silken threads which bound them grew stronger by the hour. But Charles treated 'Sally' as she had asked—as Gabriel or Michael would have treated her.

On the third day they had to make a considerable detour to ford one of the numerous small streams which flowed into the river Epte. They had intended to stay at Gisors but found themselves late in the evening with a good few miles still to go. The horse was visibly flagging, and though they went on for a little way, hoping to find somewhere to stay, it was in vain. Finally they decided to spend the night outdoors in a wayside clearing. It would not be much more uncomfortable than one of the inns—they had hay in the cart, and the night was warm. Charles saw to the horse, and made a bed in the cart for Serafina. Then he gathered up his thick woollen cloak and spread it on the ground near by. In answer to Serafina's look of enquiry he said, 'There are limits to my resolve, Sally. I don't intend to find out where they are. I'll be more comfortable down here.'

Serafina nodded mutely. They had managed not to share a room at the two inns where they had stayed—to share the narrow confines of a cart would be even more dangerous. She went to the nearby stream and rinsed the dust and sweat of the day from her face, then returned to the cart. Here she lay down. The hay felt rough to her face, so she took off her fichu and spread it under her head. Charles made his own preparations for bed, then they lay down and talked for a while until daylight faded, the moon came out, and the world was asleep around them. Then their talk became more desultory and finally stopped. Serafina lay gazing at the stars in silence until she, too, slept.

Charles woke with a start to find the rays of the sun on his face and a blackbird singing in his ear. He had slept more soundly than he would have imagined. He sat up and surveyed the clearing. The horse was munching some grass near the tree to which it was tethered—perhaps that was what had woken him. The cart was close by, and he could just see Sally's foot hanging over the edge. He got up and made his way softly to the stream.

Sally was still asleep when he came back. He stood by the cart, unable to take his eyes off her. She was lying on her back; her wonderful hair, released from its confining cap, was spread out over the blue fichu—pale, molten gold on a ground of azure. He had always thought her a pretty girl, but now that her face was in repose he could see how classically pure her features were. She was quite extraordinarily lovely—a perfect model for *Beauty Discover'd Sleeping*, an unconscious but none the less almost irresistible invitation to a kiss. One hand cradled her cheek, the other was flung out over the hay. Her right leg was bent, but the other lay straight, so that her foot overhung the end of the cart,

and he noticed with a smile that her boot had fallen off.
For a moment, Charles Dacre, the connoisseur of
beautiful women, took over. How often in the past had
he contemplated a sleeping woman, traced the line of her
nose, her throat, her bosom. . .? He caught his breath
as he saw that Sally, unused to the restriction of a laced
bodice, had loosened its strings for greater comfort, and
her blouse—a peasant woman's blouse, large and gen-
erously cut—had fallen away to reveal more than a hint
of the exquisite curves of her breast. . . He was seized
with a desire greater than any he had ever before
experienced, and he had taken a step forward before he
knew it. Then he stopped short with a groan. This was
Sally, and he must not! He groaned again at the irony—
never before had he felt so strongly moved, and never
before had he suffered the slightest scruple about taking
what he desired. But this was Sally. He must not ruin
her life, as he knew he could. He stood for a moment
while this strange emotion, this new and curiously
tender wish to protect her, battled with the most
powerful feelings of desire he had ever felt.

'Charles!' Sally had opened her eyes. 'Oh, Charles!'
She was looking at him sleepily, but with such joyous
delight that he forgot all resolution, all restraint. As she
sat up he grasped her in his arms and lifted her bodily
out of the cart, holding her against him and covering her
face with kisses. She gave a little cry and leant back,
gasping in ecstasy as his mouth roamed over her face,
her throat, her bosom. Then, feverishly returning his
kisses, she slowly put her arms round his neck, and
together they sank down to the ground. . .

'Them's nice goings-on, I must say!'

Charles was suddenly still. He turned and looked up.

Over his shoulder Serafina saw a vast figure with a red,
bucolic face looking at them in patent disapproval. Next
to him was a boy who, in contrast to his father, was
gazing at them in open delight. He moved a little in an
attempt to get a better view of Serafina, staring at them
all the while.

'Stop staring, Martin, do!' The older man gave Martin
a shove, and Martin staggered and yelled in fright as his
foot went down a rabbit hole.

'What do you do that for, Pa?' he shouted. 'I only
wanted a look. She's pretty.'

'That's as may be, but how many times do I tell you
not to stare? There was that bearded woman at the
Martinmas fair—she wasn't all that pretty, but you
couldn't take your eyes off her either. . .' The two
argued for a minute, and this gave Charles the opportunity to get up, stretch over for Serafina's fichu, and
pass it to her. Refusing to show any shame, she turned
to face the cart and then calmly put herself in order,
ending by twisting her hair up and putting her cap on.
The straw hat followed. She turned back to the men and
looked at them. Martin was now subdued and his father
back in control again.

'What's your business here, friend?' he asked.

'It's private,' said Charles curtly, keeping himself in
front of Serafina.

'Well, it may look as if it did ought to be, but it ain't—
not on the public highway, it ain't. I've a good mind to
let the magistrate know 'bout you two. Vagrants, that's
what you be—vagrants!'

'We are not vagrants. We are on our way to. . .
Magny.'

Father looked sceptical, but made no attempt to

challenge this, perhaps because Charles had sounded decidedly aggressive.

'I think you'd better be gettin' on, then. Before I do let 'im know, like. Good mornin' to you, friend. I don't suppose I'll see you on my way back. Come on, Martin.'

Father set off purposefully, and after a moment Martin followed. As he went he could be heard saying, 'I think she's prettier than the bearded lady, Pa. . .'

Charles let out a breath. 'That was close,' he said. 'If they had tried to take us to the magistrate, we'd have been sunk. God, Sally, I'm sorry! I must be mad. To fall on you like that. . .'

'You didn't,' she replied, not looking at him. 'I invited it. It seems I'm as bad as you at remembering.'

'But I'm older. I should know better.'

'Oh, for heaven's sake, Charles, don't let's argue about who is more to blame!' exclaimed Serafina. 'We must just make sure it doesn't happen again. Unfortunately we have to stay together until we reach Paris, otherwise I would suggest we part company. But that is impossible.' She stared at him angrily. Then her lips started to twitch. 'Martin had never seen such a spectacle in his life. . . His face. . .' She started to laugh.

Charles joined in. 'At least he has taste. He thought you were prettier than the bearded lady.' They went into paroxysms of laughter, and the tension between them eased. 'I think you're prettier than a bearded lady, too, Sally,' gasped Charles. 'Though I haven't seen her, of course, so I can't really judge. . .'

After a moment or two they grew serious again. 'All the same, Sally, all the same. . . If those two hadn't turned up. . .'

'Well, they did, and I'm glad they did. Don't let us repine over what might have happened but didn't.'

'I take it as a useful warning. No more nights under the stars, my girl. In any case, after Gisors I think we shall have to stick to the high road. The others are not so good, and I'm running out of time. Come on—we'll pack up the cart and go. Luckily I have a friend in the town who will give us a good breakfast.'

Halfway through the morning they drove into Gisors, past the huge château-fort which dominated the town, and wound their way through the narrow streets until they reached a quiet inn on the other side. Here Charles got down and, saying briefly, 'I shan't be long,' went in through the low door. He was as good as his word. Hardly a minute had passed before he emerged with another man—thick-set and swarthy.

'This is Jean-Marie Loubet, Sally. He'll provide us with a good breakfast, and news of the town.'

Serafina smiled at Jean-Marie, but said, 'News?'

'I think Barros might have been here. It would be natural. He would guess that we are making for Paris, and Gisors is an obvious place to stop. But come in. We can talk over breakfast—or nuncheon, if you prefer.'

They were able to repair some of the damages of the journey in that small but surprisingly comfortable inn. Jean-Marie disappeared soon after they arrived, but his wife looked after them well.

'I've asked Jean-Marie to find some faster transport for us. The horse and cart have served us well, but time is passing and I must be in Paris now as soon as possible. He's finding out if Barros has been here, too.'

A little while later Jean-Marie returned. He brought with him news, and a curious assortment of clothes.

'The word is in the market-place that good money will be paid for news of an Englishman who speaks French like a native, who may or may not have a blonde woman with him.' He glanced at Serafina. 'Forgive me, *mademoiselle*. I merely quote what is being asked. And Pierre Douleaux was boasting that he'd be rich before nightfall.'

'Pierre Douleaux?'

'It seems,' said Jean-Marie carefully, 'that he came across a suspicious-looking couple on the road to St Eloi.'

Serafina blushed scarlet and, not looking at her, Jean-Marie went on, 'The—er—lady had blonde hair.'

Charles muttered something which, on the whole, Serafina was glad she could not hear. 'So Barros and his agents are looking for us. And if this Douleaux person tells them that he saw us near Gisors they'll be on the watch at the gates on the Paris road.'

'Yes, but. . .' Jean-Marie paused for effect '. . .they may not recognise you.' Charles started to speak, but Jean-Marie interrupted him. 'Look!'

He held up a set of clothing—the black breeches and dark upper clothes of a notary, complete with flat hat.

'They'll still look for the "blonde woman", Jean-Marie!'

'Of course. But she will not exist. Look!'

Once again Jean-Marie held up some clothes—a boy's suit, again with a flat hat, from which hung a fringe of coarse, dark hair.

'You're a genius!' exclaimed Serafina.

'You don't mind?'

'Of course not, Charles. Unless you think modesty is more important than our lives?'

'Since you put it like that. . . And it might be better at that. . .' His significant look was not lost on Serafina, and she grew scarlet once more.

Charles grinned and took a quick glance at Jean-Marie, who was preoccupied with sorting out the clothes. 'The temptation will be considerably less, Sally,' he said in a soft voice.

'And I have a gig for you, with a good horse, and other horses booked on the way. I'll give you the names of the inns to call at. Barros won't find you,' said Jean-Marie.

After a day and a half they reached Argenteuil, just outside Paris. Charles drew up before they entered the small town and said, 'This is where we stop, Sally. I'm going to leave you here with some friends of mine.'

'You can't! I'm coming to the embassy with you.'

'Oh, no! Think for a moment—you've been travelling more or less in my company for more than five days. What would that do to your reputation if it were known? I've been considering how to get round the problem ever since we left Dieppe, and this is what I've decided. I have some good friends here, and I think they would agree to take you in. If anyone ever asked, they would claim that you had been with them since you left England. Please, Sally.'

Serafina saw the justice of what he said. Charles was notorious for his affairs. Her name would be irreparably damaged if it got out that she had spent so long unchaperoned in his company. No one would believe the truth. Trying not to sound as depressed as she felt, she said, 'Very well. I'll do as you say.'

'Good girl! Er. . .the only thing is. . .' Charles looked highly uneasy and Serafina wondered what on earth could cause this self-possessed man such embarrassment. He cleared his throat. 'My friends, I am sure, will help us all they can, but it would make their position much easier if. . .'

'Yes?'

'If they believed you were my fiancée—if they thought you were Serafina!' He went on rapidly before she could say anything, 'I know that deception is abhorrent to you, but our position—even to good friends like the Brecys—is somewhat equivocal. Madame la Comtesse especially would be uncomfortable. She is a very conventional creature at heart. Naturally your parents and Serafina will have to know the truth later, but until we get back to England I really think it would be advisable. I promise not to abuse my position,' he added wryly.

Serafina stared at him. She could hardly believe it! The irony of the situation was almost too much to bear. She started laughing, but the trouble was that once she had started she couldn't stop. The tears started to roll down her cheeks and, without her quite knowing how, she was suddenly crying as if her heart would break.

'Sally! Oh, God, Sally, I'm sorry. I'm a clumsy fool. If you hate the idea so much we'll forget it.'

'It. . .it's not that,' she sobbed through her tears. 'I think you're right—it would be better. I think I must be overwrought.'

He smiled at her. 'There's an inn over there. I'll take you there and bespeak a private parlour, where you can recover a little. Perhaps the landlord has something to restore your spirits. Come.'

Serafina allowed herself to be led into the inn. The innkeeper was sympathetic when told that young Etienne was feeling unwell, and bustled about fetching a more comfortable chair and opening the window for more air. He saw the 'boy' seated in a cool private parlour with a tisane and a glass of weak brandy and water in front of him. He waited for further orders, but when Charles nodded he went out, closing the door quietly behind him. After a while Serafina was quite calm again, and better equipped to deal with the topsy-turvy situation in which she found herself.

Charles said softly, 'I really ought not to delay things much longer. If I didn't meet Garcia at Dieppe as planned, the arrangement was that he would make his own way to Paris, taking a roundabout route. He should be there tomorrow. I'd like to see you safely installed with Armand and Giselle de Brecy, but I must see them first. Will you wait here while I call on them?' Serafina nodded. He sighed and lifted her chin. 'You'll like them.'

When she still didn't speak he went on, 'The business about the engagement. . .it has a great deal to commend it, you know. It isn't as if many people would be involved—just the Brecys, in fact. My only thought is to protect you, Sally. The thing is, I'm not quite sure how they would regard you if you weren't. . .engaged to me. It might be embarrassing for them and for you.' He paused. When she refused to look at him he said, 'But if you really cannot bear the thought of it, I'll abandon the idea.'

'I'll agree to anything you say, Charles.'

'Good. I'm sure it's best. You will have to put your skirts on, of course, before Giselle sees you, but we have our other clothes in the baggage, and there's a wood just before the château where you can change. It would be too strange to do it here. The landlord is puzzled enough.' She looked at him enquiringly. 'Your hat! I'll have to think of some reason why you can't remove it. The blonde hair might come as a bit of a shock on top of that black fringe.' He fetched the landlord and explained that he was about to see the Comte de Brecy, and would prefer to ask the Comte's permission before taking his son to the château. He asked if he might leave the boy in the parlour.

'Of course. Mind you, the Comte is a kind man, and I am sure there would be no difficulty. . . But there, it is perhaps better not to take things for granted. And your son does look very pale—he has been crying, is that not so. . .? Has he been upset?'

Charles looked stern and said repressively that his son was not always as obedient as he would wish. The landlord looked at him doubtfully, then said, 'Well, he will soon recover from his headache here, *monsieur*. Argenteuil is a quiet town and he will not be disturbed. Now that the abbey has gone there isn't much to bring the crowds. . . Should he perhaps remove that heavy hat?'

Charles said solemnly, 'That was the very cause of Etienne's distress. It is absolutely forbidden for him to remove his hat in the daytime for the whole of this month, my good fellow, a fact which Etienne sometimes ignores. Our sect is strict in these matters, and he must learn. With suffering comes patience and ultimate joy— remember that, Etienne!' Then, promising to be back within the hour, he left. Serafina had some difficulty in keeping her face sober. Charles was outrageous!

She was quietly sipping her tisane when she heard the sound of two horses drawing up. Their riders dismounted and came into the inn. She heard the innkeeper exclaiming and apologising. A hatefully familiar voice said, 'Never mind, never mind! We arranged to meet some friends on our way to Paris and we appear to have missed them. I don't suppose an English gentleman has stopped here, has he? Perhaps in the company of a fair-haired lady?'

CHAPTER ELEVEN

SERAFINA'S heart leapt into her mouth. It was Barros!
Oh, God! What if he came in? She jumped up, but flight
was impossible. Then she calmed down again. The last
person he would expect to see in France was Serafina
Feverel—even if she were recognisable, which she
wasn't. She seated herself again, further way from the
light, and pulled her hat down over her features.

The innkeeper seemed to think that it was his fault
that no such person had called at the inn. He was even
more apologetic when Barros asked to be served with
some wine in his parlour.

'I'm sorry, *monsieur*. So very sorry. It is already
occupied. A sick boy—travel sickness. He's very pale,
and I think he's been crying. . . His father left him here
for a while. *Monsieur*!'

Barros had flung open the door and was staring in. He
ignored Serafina, sitting in a dark corner with her head
in her hands. His eyes raked the room, then he went out
again.

'I just wanted to make sure,' he said curtly.

The innkeeper was affronted. He said coldly, 'Perhaps *monsieur* would prefer to drink some wine elsewhere? There is a very adequate hostelry on the other
side of the town. *Monsieur*?'

'Another inn, you say? Where?'

Within seconds Barros was on his way. Serafina wiped
the sweat off her face and breathed again. But then a

thought occurred to her and she jumped up and ran to the innkeeper. 'Can you tell me where the Château des Colombes is, sir? In which direction? It isn't on the other side of the town, is it?'

'No, no, boy. It is a step or two back the way you have come. It isn't far. Is your father seeking work with Monsieur le Comte?'

'I. . . I don't know,' faltered Serafina. 'My father doesn't tell me much. . .'

'Such a strictness,' marvelled the innkeeper. 'Come, you must go back into the parlour. Your father might return at any minute and he will be angry again. Have you still some tisane left? Look, you haven't finished the brandy, either.' Serafina smiled timidly and sat down again. She sipped the brandy. The innkeeper went on, 'Mind you, my boy, it's better to have some discipline than none at all—look at that fellow who came in here just now. There's manners for you! A foreigner, he was—Spanish by the looks of him. He didn't frighten you, did he?' He tutted, then smiled. 'I hope he likes the Trois Corbeaux. It's a hole!'

Charles came back soon after and Serafina flew out to meet him.

'Barros!' she whispered urgently. 'He was here.'

'There, there, Etienne,' said Charles, with one eye on the innkeeper, who was staring. 'You needn't worry about a thing. Monsieur le Comte would be pleased to receive you tonight. He is a kind man and sympathetic to our cause, I think.'

He paid the innkeeper and they got in the cart and drove off.

'Charles, I'm worried. Barros was asking for you. He is determined to track you down.'

'I'll be at the embassy before he finds me. Besides, he won't catch me out again. I'll be on my guard this time— and I am armed.' He took out the pistol. 'Meanwhile you'll be safe with Armand. There's really nothing to be afraid of.'

'That's why you want me to stay here, isn't it? Because of Barros. Whatever you say, you know there's danger.'

'I want you to keep out of sight of any English people who might talk about you! Even as my fiancée you would still be exposed to some gossip. There is a slight— a very slight—risk that Barros will try again. But the odds are small. Please, Sally, don't make things more difficult than they are. I hate leaving you, you know that.'

A little way down the road they turned off into a wood where Serafina changed into a girl again. She discarded her hat with relief, laughing again at Charles's ingenious tale. Then they drove through some iron gates and up a long drive, stopping eventually with a bit of a flourish in front of a small château.

'Well done!' cried an exquisitely dressed gentleman at the top of the steps. 'The horse is not exactly the purest Arab strain, and the phaeton is a touch rustic, but the style. . . Ah, that was perfect!' His voice changed as he came round to assist Serafina. 'And *mademoiselle* is enchanting! Charles, you have the luck of the devil. I congratulate you. Your servant, Miss Feverel.'

'My dear, this is Armand de Brecy. In spite of his foppish appearance he is a good friend of mine.'

'I shall call him out—you will see it, *mademoiselle*. One day he will go too far, and then. . . Come—my wife will be ready now to meet you. She is inside.'

Giselle de Brecy had a charming smile, but Serafina could see why Charles had wanted to make their story as respectable as possible. The Comtesse might be kind-hearted and ready to help her husband's friend, but she would not tolerate anything really irregular. Her loyalty and sympathy were stretched to the full as it was. The Comte had been a colleague of Charles in the old days, and he was eager to discuss them, but Charles was impatient to be gone. It was important to meet Garcia, especially as he now knew that Barros was also descending on Paris.

'You'll be careful, Charles?' asked Serafina, unable to hide her anxiety. They were alone on the drive for a few minutes before Charles set off for Paris. Armand de Brecy had found some clothes for his friend and, though the fit was not perfect, Charles looked his familiar handsome self again. The Comtesse de Brecy had found similarly suitable clothes for Serafina.

'Of course! There's no real danger now.'

'How can you say so, when you know——?' Serafina bit her lip. This would never do. Charles had to go to the embassy, she knew that. It was not sensible to make a fuss. 'Good luck, then.'

He looked to where the Comtesse was framed in the doorway, then bent forward and kissed Serafina's brow. 'Don't go far, my dear—it would be advisable not to leave the grounds of the château. I ought to be back within the week.'

'Goodbye, Charles.' In spite of her best efforts Serafina's voice wavered.

'Oh, to hell with propriety!' Charles ground out. He seized her in his arms and kissed her hard. Then he left without another look.

As she went in again, Serafina was conscious that her hostess was looking at her with a slight air of disapproval. But when the Comtesse saw how unhappy she was she softened, embraced her warmly, and suggested a walk in the pleasure garden. Listening to the soft voice talking about the flowers in the beds all around, Serafina slowly recovered.

Charles sent a note every day, and after two days he told them in guarded terms that he had found 'the man he sought' and that their business had been conducted satisfactorily. He would soon be with them again. Serafina rejoiced and the Brecys made plans for a celebration—a *fête-champêtre* for the four of them in the forest of Laye, near St Germain. The servants were set to making all sorts of savouries and sweetmeats, and the wine was put to cool in the icehouse in the grounds of the château. The Comtesse arranged for her dressmaker to make up some pretty muslins, which were simple but perfect for the warm, sunny weather.

So it was that Charles returned to an excited household determined to celebrate the success of his mission. The Brecys persuaded him that no harm could come of the expedition—St Germain-en-Laye was seldom visited by Paris society in May, for the Bois de Boulogne was so much more convenient.

The day was brilliant, the procession truly impressive. An open barouche carried the Comte de Brecy, his wife, and their two guests. The ladies looked enchanting in their thin muslins—the Comtesse in pink, Serafina in blue. They wore villager straw hats with ribbons to match their dresses, and were carrying dainty parasols— all to protect their complexion. The gentlemen were in the first stare of fashion, Charles having equipped himself in Paris. Behind the barouche was another, larger coach containing the servants and all the refreshments, and everything else that was necessary for their comfort. The drive took over an hour, for they had to cross the Seine, but it seemed to pass in a flash.

Serafina was determined to enjoy herself. Since the Brecys had no notion of how Charles's fiancée had behaved in London, and Charles thought of her as Sally, she decided to be her natural self. But, in fact, the weeks in London had taught her a lot, and the Serafina on the way to St Germain was no longer the Sally of the old days. She had always been graceful, but now, though she was not conscious of it, her movements had more natural elegance. Sally's exuberance had been toned down and, though she had lost none of her spontaneity, she had acquired polish and refinement. Her discussions with Charles on the journey from Dieppe to Argenteuil had not only taught her a great deal about the world he lived in, she had learned a lot about the art of conversation, too. She no longer interrupted impulsively, nor was she quite so eager to make her point at the expense of others. The conversation in the barouche flowed easily and naturally, with a great deal of amusement and polished wit. She was secretly entertained at the look on Charles's face when he realised that hoyden Sally was more than holding her own with his fashionable friends!

The picnic was a great success, the food excellent and the wines exquisite. After it was over, the Comte announced that he and his wife were proposing to enjoy the fresh air and sunshine without moving from the spot. He added with a knowing look that he expected

Charles and his fiancée would like to wander through the trees. . . The Comtesse looked doubtful, then approved of a walk—as long as it did not take too long, and they did not wander too far.

'They seem to be even more strict in France than they are in England,' said Serafina as she and Charles strolled through the glades and clearings.

'It's even worse in Spain,' said Charles. 'Until they are actually married young men and women never see each other without a duenna present.'

'Charles, tell me about Barros.'

'He seems to have dropped out of sight. I saw Garcia at the embassy and, once the letter and the emeralds had been exchanged, we thought it wise for someone different to escort him to Portsmouth. The arms ship will be waiting for him there now, and I shall see him when we get back. If Barros is still in Paris he will be watching *my* movements, not those of anyone else.'

'So you are still in danger?'

'He won't make a move unless he sees Garcia with me. And now that can't happen. Garcia has left Paris.'

'What a relief! So our troubles are over.'

'They won't be completely over until I see you safely back in England with your parents. I sent a message, by the way, both to Sussex and to Serafina in London. It didn't say much—even the diplomatic couriers are not completely discreet—but I said you were staying with friends near Paris and I asked Serafina to arrange to visit Feverel Place straight away. That will keep her out of London for the moment. Then I can deliver you to your home on my way to Portsmouth.'

Serafina pushed away the thought of the confusion which would be created both in Curzon Street and in

Sussex. And her family would probably still be in Brighton!

'You are taking a great deal of trouble on my behalf, Charles.'

'You took more than a great deal on mine, Sally. I can never repay you for what you did.'

Serafina looked up at him and smiled wistfully. He murmured something and took her roughly into his arms. When her ridiculous hat got in the way he pushed it back, so that it hung by its ribbons while he kissed her. Then he groaned in despair and buried his face in her hair.

'What am I to do, Sally? I can hardly bear the thought of losing you. In spite of the danger, in spite of the discomfort, the week with you was the happiest in my life, and the moments in that clearing—I sometimes think I shall go mad if they are never to be repeated. You were seldom out of my mind all the time I was in Paris, and I couldn't wait to come back to you.' He kissed her desperately again, then put her from him and turned away. 'But it won't do!' he said with angry emphasis. 'I can't subject you to the sort of life I must lead. I dare not! You would die under all the petty restraints and artificialities, the criticism you would face for being yourself. The girl I love would disappear. All that enthusiasm for living, that lovely spontaneity would vanish, buried under the demands of a diplomatic career. Louisa Paget, for all her faults, had the same zest for life before she married Sir Robert. Look at her now—a bitterly disappointed woman, seeking satisfaction in her intrigue and the quest for wealth.'

'I hope you do not compare me with Lady Paget, Charles?'

'Of course not. Your honesty, your integrity place you beyond comparison with her.'

Serafina was silenced. Then she said carefully, 'And Serafina? Are you going to marry her, feeling as you do?'

Charles hesitated, then said, 'I don't know. I am committed to her, you know that. It would be difficult to betray that commitment. And. . . Serafina is different. She would be content with so much less than you—her children, her home. I could make Serafina happy, I think.'

'I see. . .' Serafina gave an unladylike sniff, and a tear rolled down her cheek.

'Oh, Sally, Sally!' Charles pulled out a handkerchief and wiped her eyes. Then once again he held her to him, tightly, painfully. . .

'Well, Charles! So this is why you were so anxious to get away this weekend! An idyll in St Germain, eh?'

Charles released Serafina and whirled round, sheltering her from the speaker. This was an elegantly dressed woman, not in the first flush of youth, but still lovely. She was standing at the edge of the clearing next to a distinguished-looking gentleman of about forty, and there were several other well-dressed ladies and gentlemen behind them. They were all regarding Charles and Serafina with some amusement.

'I don't blame you in the slightest, my dear. Such a very pretty little companion! Why have we never seen her in Paris—or Vienna? Or is she a new. . . acquisition?'

'Don't tease him, Lady Harcombe. Can't you see he's embarrassed? It must be for the first time,' said the gentleman, openly smiling. 'I'm sorry to have inter-rupted you, Charles. Come everyone!'

'No, wait! Ambassador!' The gentleman turned back in surprise at Charles's peremptory tone. 'You misun-derstand the situation completely, Ambassador.' Charles drew Serafina foward. 'Miss Feverel is my fiancée. May I present her to you, sir?'

'Indeed?' Sir Charles Stewart, British ambassador to France, spoke in a neutral tone, but his companions were openly sceptical.

Charles grew pale with anger, but restrained himself and said with careful courtesy, 'Miss Feverel is at present a guest of the Comte and Comtesse de Brecy at Argenteuil, sir. They invited us to a picnic in the forest here to celebrate the completion of my mission, and Miss Feverel and I were taking a walk while our host and hostess rested. I believe you know Armand de Brecy?'

The ambassador looked highly embarrassed himself. 'Charles! My dear fellow! What can I say? If you can bear to introduce me I shall give Miss Feverel our deepest apologies for our unworthy thoughts about her—and for any distress we've caused her.'

Serafina, conscious of what Sir Charles had observed, was having no difficulty in looking suitably distressed. Charles was still cool as he made the introductions.

The ambassador said, 'Lucius Feverel's daughter? I met him at Oxford many years ago. A brilliant man, though some of his articles on international affairs have been a thorn in our flesh! Miss Feverel, once again I cannot tell you how vexed I am that our careless tongues have upset you. Please forgive us. Though since we had no inkling that you were in France. . .'

'Miss Feverel is here on a private visit, sir.'

'Let Miss Feverel speak to me herself, Charles—if she will.'

Serafina said, 'I'm afraid it was my fault that you were not informed of my visit, Ambassador. Charles would have been pleased to announce it, but I have too much pride! I did not wish the world to know what a silly creature I am. I'm sorry to have to admit it, but I persauded the Comte de Brecy and his wife to invite me to stay with them. I was so anxious for his safety that I practically followed Charles to France! Perhaps I do deserve some censure.'

Sir Charles looked amused at this graceful way of relieving him of some blame. 'Not at all! But you are not at all silly, Miss Feverel. And now I know why Charles was so determined in his refusal of our invitation to the ball tomorrow night in honour of Prince Yurievski and the rest! You must change your mind and bring Miss Feverel with you, Charles. I will not allow you to say no. And if the Comte de Brecy and his wife will agree to come also, Miss Feverel will not need any other chaperon.'

'Sir, we couldn't possibly impose on the Brecys in this way. Tomorrow night is surely too short a notice?'

'In a moment, Charles, you will have me believing that you are ashamed of Miss Feverel! You seem very reluctant to let her be seen. . .?'

'Not at all! I am very proud of her. But. . .'

'We shall go to find the Brecys. I cannot imagine that Armand will refuse.' He offered Serafina his arm and she curtsied and took it. Together they went back to the Comte and Comtesse, followed by Charles and the others. Compliments were exchanged, the ambassador used his considerable skill to present his invitation tactfully, and when it was accepted he added, 'Perhaps you would all join us at dinner beforehand? If Miss Feverel is about to be a diplomat's wife—for which, I may say, she seems eminently suited—she ought to experience the full rigours of a diplomatic occasion!'

To Serafina's surprise the Brecys were pleased about the invitation. 'My dear, it will be a splendid affair,' said the Comtesse. 'What a baptism of fire!'

'That is exactly what it will be,' said Charles grimly. 'A baptism of fire. The poor girl will be exposed to some of the most critical eyes in Europe.'

The Comtesse looked surprised. 'But your fiancée will manage beautifully, Charles! She is absolutely *comme il faut*. You can have no doubts that she will cope!'

Serafina could see that Charles had grave doubts of Sally's ability to cope with some of the greatest sticklers for etiquette in Europe but, in the circumstances, he was unable to express them. However, a more urgent problem was exercising her own mind.

'What shall I wear?' she asked. '*Madame* has been kind enough to give me these muslins, but a ball. . . They will hardly do. I cannot go, Charles.'

'Of course you must!' The Comtesse hesitated briefly, then said, 'I have a ball-dress that I have worn only once, and that was last year when Armand and I were in Madrid. No one here has seen it, for we live rather quietly at the moment. It is just right for the occasion and I think, with a very slight alteration, that it would fit you. Come, *mademoiselle*, I will show it to you.'

Serafina was persuaded to try the dress on. It was the

most beautiful dress she had ever seen—Parisian to the
last bow. There was a slip of white satin, finished at the
bottom with three narrow pipings of blue silk, looped
and twisted. Inside each loop was a fleur-de-lis made of
tiny pearls and crystals. Over the slip was a layer of
white lace, caught up to one side and looped with bows
of the same blue silk. The bodice was plainly cut, made
of white satin under a delicate net richly embroidered
with shimmering crystals and gleaming pearls. It was
held under the bust with a rouleau of blue. Serafina
looked like someone quite different in it—as ethereal as
the London Serafina, but. . .more sophisticated, more
self-assured. Her three admirers were unanimous that
she should wear it.

'And when Hortense has dealt with your hair you will
be a sensation, even in Paris,' said the Comtesse
ecstatically.

'But surely you will wear this yourself, *madame*?'

'You flatter me! Since the birth of little Thierry I am
far too. . .generously built! But do not worry. I have a
perfectly adequate dress to wear, *mademoiselle*.'

The alterations were soon effected. The Comtesse
sent for her jewel cases and selected a necklace in the
form of a *collier* of crystals and pearls, and a delicate
crescent of the same crystals and pearls which would
hold Serafina's pale gold curls in place on top of her
head.

The following evening Serafina, in her borrowed
plumes, looked as if she had spent her life in the courts
of Europe. Charles handed her a bouquet of small white
roses and deep blue ribbons, and assisted her into the de
Brecy carriage. The Comtesse de Brecy, looking
extremely handsome in a poppy-red dress and dia-

monds, was already inside. The Comte joined them and they rolled away.

'Are you nervous, Serafina?' said Charles with a smile.

'No, not really. I'm looking forward to it, I think. Are you?'

'I have seldom been more nervous in my life. And it is all on your behalf.'

'My behalf?'

'I. . . .' He looked at her smiling face. 'I want you to enjoy it.'

Serafina was certain that Charles had changed what he had been going to say. And she had a fair idea what his original thought had been, for it had already been expressed earlier in the day by the Comtesse. She had asked *madame* to tell her something of the people she was likely to meet that evening and the things she might need to know.

'I should not like to disgrace Charles,' she had said. 'And things are different here in France.'

The Comtesse had been very pleased to help, and they had spent a profitable hour. But before they had gone down to join the gentlemen again the Comtesse had said, 'I shall be there to help you, but you need have no fear, *mademoiselle*. I cannot imagine why Charles is so nervous—for he is, you know. I find it rather touching, don't you? It seems to me that you have everything in your favour—youth, beauty, and a great deal of spirit.'

She had thought for a moment, then said, 'You lack experience, I suppose, and Charles knows, as I do, that diplomatic circles can be very cruel, with little sympathy for anyone who is guilty of a solecism. There will be some who will regard you with envy, and their eyes will be all the more critical because of it. I confess, I do not like it, this world—that is why we use the excuse of little Thierry to spend most of our time here at Argenteuil on our estate. But I do not fear for you, and you must have no fears for yourself, or for Charles's reputation. He will be the envy of all the gentlemen, that is certain! You must enjoy it!'

'Then I will! Indeed, I would be a poor creature if I didn't after all your kindness—this lovely dress, the jewels and all the other things, your maid's attentions. . .and the help and encouragement you have given me. Thank you, *madame*.'

And now Charles was having doubts again. Serafina put up her chin and resolved that she would not fail—or at least if she did she would go down with all flags flying. No one was going to dare to be ashamed of her!

The journey took about an hour and on the way she quizzed all of them again on the protocol for the evening, and the personalities of the guests who would be there. It was treated in a light-hearted manner, with a great many scandalous anecdotes, especially from the Comte de Brecy, but Serafina learned a lot. And since she had a very good memory she had mastered most of it by the time they reached the embassy.

The ambassador's dinner party was a large affair, with over thirty guests. Serafina's first ordeal was waiting in line on the stairs to be announced. Word had got round that Aldworth—who was well-known for his jaundiced view of marriage!—had now shackled himself to a dream of a girl, a real diamond. Naturally everyone was anxious to see the beauty, and Serafina had to put up with a large number of well-bred stares and whispers. Charles grew a little restive, but Serafina smiled at him calmly and ignored the rest. The Brecys were a great help. They talked on unexceptionable topics during what seemed to be an interminable wait. At last they reached the top, where the ambassador was waiting.

The major-domo announced them. 'Lord Aldworth, the Comte and Comtesse de Brecy, Miss Feverel.' Sir Charles, who had been elegantly but informally dressed at St Germain, was imposing in full regalia—black silk knee-breeches, decorations and all. His manner was still as charming, though with a line of guests extending down the stairs, foreign nobility among them, he had little time to spend on a comparatively unknown English girl, however beautiful she was. Serafina went along the line of dignitaries, curtsying correctly wherever necessary, and eventually entered a beautiful room lined with mirrors and with a splendid chandelier in the centre. A vast table was laden with crystal, silver-gilt cutlery and candelabra, white napery, and flowers. When the Comtesse de Brecy took her to the list of guests to find her place, Serafina, who naturally came low on the scale of precedence, found herself placed some distance from Charles, who was to sit on the opposite side of the table nearer the ambassador and his guest of honour.

'Hmm, you've been put next to young Ashleigh,' said Charles. 'A rising star, it's said.'

'And the Vicomte de Vaubois is on her other side,' said the Comtesse. 'Oh, Charles, you will have to take care! You might lose Mademoiselle Feverel if you are not careful. The Vicomte is a charmer, too!'

At that moment a young man who was almost as tall as Charles, but slighter, with a thin, clever face, came up and asked if Charles would introduce him. This was Mr Ashleigh. They all chatted for a moment, then the Comtesse's partner, the Comte de Guions, came up and bore her off. Mr Ashleigh and Charles grinned at one another.

'You have to give the ambassador his due,' said Mr Ashleigh.

'Indeed,' Charles replied. 'Giselle de Brecy is one of the few women in Paris who is placid enough to keep our friend under control.' He saw that Serafina was puzzled. 'Surely Armand told you about Philippe de Guions?'

'I don't think so.'

'The Guions are an old Gascon family, Miss Feverel. They are notorious for being hot-tempered, and Philippe is worse than most. His father was the same.'

'Surely you've heard of the battles he and Philippe had when they lived in London during the wars, my dear?' said Charles. 'They were famous.'

'I think I must have been too young.'

Mr Ashleigh laughed. 'I would have liked to have been there when Papa de Guions yelled that all sons were ungrateful, unmannerly wretches and the Prince Regent took it personally.'

'Old Guions was never made welcome at Carlton House after that, it's true. It was a pity, though. He was always accusing Philippe of unfilial behaviour, but they were really very fond of one another. It was just that *monsieur* didn't allow his son any independence, and Philippe resented it!'

A stir at the door indicated that the guests of honour—Prince Yurievski and his wife—had arrived. Everyone bowed and curtsied as the ambassador led

Prince and Princess Yurievski to the table. The rest of
the guests followed suit. Mr Ashleigh took Serafina off
to her place with an air of a man who knew he had the
prize. Charles looked at them with a mixture of apprehension and amusement, then collected his own dinner
partner, the wife of an Austrian diplomat, from the
group who had just come in.

Charles's manners were usually effortless. But,
though she could not possibly have guessed it from his
behaviour, he had to work hard that evening to pay his
partner the attention he owed her. Several times he
found his eyes straying to where Sally was sitting.
Whenever he looked the conversation was always flour-
ishing, sometimes with young Ashleigh, sometimes with
Vaubois—never exclusively with either, and never with
anyone else. At least she had remembered something of
company manners! But did she have to look so. . .so
happy? As if she was enjoying every minute of what
ought to be an ordeal! As for the two young men. . .
they were quite clearly fascinated. Ashleigh knew his
manners well enough to give the lady on his other side a
fair share of his attention. But Vaubois! An arrogant
young cub, if ever he saw one! And Sally was looking
positively fascinated by him. Both Ashleigh and
Vaubois were nearer Sally in age than he was, of course.
Charles turned to Madame von Logau.

CHAPTER TWELVE

ON THE international scene it was admitted that cracks were appearing in the Grand Alliance—cracks which the British Government's attitude to South America was not helping to cure. Word of Charles's latest mission to help Bolivar had seeped out in the way those things did and the Austrians, to say nothing of the Russians, were not altogether pleased. But all difficulties were put aside on the evening of the ball held in the British embassy for the Tsar's delegation. It was afterwards generally agreed that it was one of the season's successes. There were several stars at the ball—not least Prince Yurievski——but the unknown Miss Feverel was certainly another. She danced through the night with hardly a break, and her partners spoke afterwards of her charm, her wit and her poise. Not even the sourest dowagers could find a genuine cause for criticism—unless it was that she seemed to have an unfair share of all the most interesting gentlemen!

Serafina enjoyed it all—what girl would not be flattered by the attentions of half of Paris society? But the man she really wished to impress was Charles himself, and nothing in his manner suggested that she had succeeded. He could hardly have failed to notice how popular she was, but she wanted him to acknowledge that he had been wrong to dismiss her as unsuitable for sharing his life, to see that she was more than capable of coping with whatever demands were made on her. He

had danced with her once, but had seemed somewhat
distant. Charming, but distant. As the evening wore on
she waited impatiently for him to ask her again. When
the invitation came she was surrounded by admirers and
he had to make his way through to her.

'I hardly dare take you away,' he said a little coolly.

'Quite right, Aldworth! Leave her here!' cried
Vaubois.

'Oh, no, Vicomte! I am betrothed to Lord Aldworth.
I must do as he wishes,' said Serafina, with a bewitching
smile at the Vicomte. She put her hand on Charles's
arm, and allowed herself to be led into the ballroom.

'No one could deny that you are a success, Sally. Are
you enjoying it?'

'Of course!'

'What were you were talking about so eagerly at the
dinner-table! Ashleigh could hardly take his eyes off
you, and Vaubois didn't even try.'

She looked at him with a hint of mischief in her eye.
'Do you really wish to know?'

'Only if you wish to tell me.'

'Well, the Vicomte and I talked about the Vicomte.
Then we talked a little—a very little—about me, then
we talked about the Vicomte again. Mr Ashleigh and I
talked about the new translation of Shakespeare into
German. Then we talked about you.'

'About me?' Charles was startled.

'He admires you enormously—much more than he
does me. I was quite cast down,' Serafina said mourn-
fully, gazing at him over her fan.

'You are a minx, Sally. Ashleigh is smitten along with
all the rest.'

'Yes, but only for tonight. And I encouraged him to

talk about you. I must say, Charles, I found it fascinating.'

'What did he say?' asked Charles, somewhat uneasily.

'Oh, nothing to compromise you. Mr Ashleigh is an extremely discreet young man. He didn't tell me about Lady Harcombe. . . You mustn't stand still in the middle of a waltz, Charles.'

Charles, thus admonished, started dancing again. 'Who did?' he asked grimly, after a pause.

'I can't remember—one of the tabbies.'

'It all happened long ago, Sally.'

'It really doesn't concern me, Charles. Nor do any of the others. After all, you had to do something before you met——' Serafina stopped short. She had been going to say, Before you met the girl you fell in love with. For a moment, under the influence of this evening, intoxicated by this waltz with Charles, the signs of jealousy she saw in him, Serafina had deceived herself into believing their own myth: Charles did love her, whatever name he called her. He had asked her to marry him because he could not imagine life without her. They were going to live happily ever after in Aldworth, London or even in Europe—it didn't matter to either of them, as long as they were together. But suddenly the bubble was burst, and cruel reality showed through. She rather thought that she was never going to marry Charles—not as Sally, not as Serafina, let alone all the rest. So she said instead, 'Before your brother died and you needed an heir.'

'Sally——'

'Heavens, Charles, don't sound so serious! I shall begin to think you don't know how to behave!'

He smiled in spite of himself, but then grew serious

and said softly, 'We cannot talk here, Sally. But I promise you that we shall have a proper discussion before long. It's a pity that this affair came along. It meant that we had to postpone leaving for England.'

'But I wouldn't have missed it for the world! I love it!'

The dance came eventually to an end, but Charles kept hold of Serafina and led her over to a group in the next room which included the ambassador.

The talk there seemed to be more serious than the occasion warranted. The discussion had apparently turned to the question of South America, and in spite of His Excellency's efforts it was getting heated. The Vicomte de Vaubois was hotly defending the colonials' right to self-determination, and this was being disputed by the Gascon, the Comte de Guions, and the Austrian, Graf von Logau. Disaster loomed, and Serafina saw the ambassador give a discreet nod to Mr Ashleigh to fetch the Comtesse de Brecy. It looked as if her peacemaking efforts were going to be needed.

'*Monsieur,*' said Graf von Logau, civilly enough, 'consider these Spanish colonists for a moment—they have no idea how to run a country. Spain has looked after their interests for so long.'

'Ah, Charles, there you are,' said His Excellency gratefully. 'And Miss Feverel, too. What do you think of the orchestra?'

Serafina assured the ambassador that the whole evening was perfect. Charles asked if Prince Yurievski was staying long in Paris.

'I believe he returns on Friday to St Petersburg,' said the ambassador. 'A beautiful city—but cold in winter. Have you been there, Graf von Logau?'

Graf von Logau was not to be distracted. 'Not yet,

Excellency. But the Tsar will not be any more pleased than Metternich at this encouragement your government is giving to Bolivar and his ilk. I tell you, the Spanish colonials are not yet fit to govern themselves.'

'The colonials have every right to do so——' began Vaubois.

'Be silent, young man! I have listened long enough to your radical maunderings!' said the Comte de Guions, growing redder. 'Colonies are like children. They have to be kept under control until they are fit to look after themselves! I was very disappointed to hear that Lord Aldworth had taken part in some escapade to deliver arms to the rebels. Very disappointed.'

'Children have a habit of growing up, sir,' said Charles mildly. 'The British Government was forced to let our colonies in North America go their own way some time back. But I believe we are now on the way to building up a good relationship with them once more—this time based on trade and equality. Should Spain not do the same for her "children"?'

'Bah!' The Comte de Guions suddenly turned on Serafina. 'What do you think of it all, Miss Feverel? Do you approve of what Lord Aldworth is doing?' He put it into a woman's terms for her. 'Do you agree with setting up children to defy their own parents?'

The attack on an inexperienced young lady was unfair—everyone except Guions felt it. Charles and the ambassador spoke together.

'Really, Comte——'

'Miss Feverel can hardly be expected to have formed a view. . .'

But Serafina was not disturbed. 'Well, *monsieur*, I would not dream of disagreeing with anything Charles did—not in public, anyway.' She gave him one of her enchanting smiles. 'But, forgive me—as I listened to you I was wondering what you would have said twenty years ago? When your father was alive?'

Since the Guions' family battles were well-known to most of the people there, the group dissolved into laughter. Even Guions himself smiled. Some good-natured teasing followed and the atmosphere changed. With a sigh of relief the ambassador called for more wine for the gentlemen and led Charles and Serafina away.

'Brilliant, my dear. Quite brilliant. Charles, this young lady will be wasted as your wife—we ought to have her on the strength.'

'I can't spare her, sir.'

The ambassador smiled as he saw the look Charles gave Serafina. 'I understand,' he said. 'I understand perfectly. Take good care of her, Charles.'

Soon the evening was over. When the four drove back to Argenteuil dawn was breaking over the roofs of Paris. Serafina was exhausted. So much was happening—and so much more was still to come, most of it not pleasant. She resolved there and then never to regret the past week, but to remember it when she was an old, old lady—a maiden great-aunt, telling tales to the Feverel grandchildren.

Soon it was time for Serafina and Charles to leave the Château des Colombes. Giselle and Armand pressed them to come again soon, after they were married. Serafina was hard put to it not to show how unlikely she thought that would be. The hired post-chaise was brought round, and their slender amount of luggage strapped on. An elderly lady, a certain Madame Houblon, had been engaged to chaperon Serafina for the journey. She would join her daughter and son-in-law in London when her duty was done. Charles produced a fourth member of their party—a tough-looking individual, John Derby, who was a member of the embassy household, and who would apparently serve as Charles's valet.

At the last minute Giselle de Brecy handed Serafina a dressmaker's box. 'It is for you,' she said. 'I could not possibly wear it again, even if it fitted me. I shall always remember how lovely you looked in it at the embassy ball.' Serafina embraced her impulsively, and placid, correct Giselle held her tightly. 'Come back, Serafina,' she whispered. 'Please come back.'

With much waving and some tears on Giselle's part, the coach moved off on the way to Calais and England.

They drove along comfortably enough—the roads were quite good and the weather favourable. In contrast to their journey from Dieppe the pace was brisk, as Charles wanted to reach Portsmouth as soon as possible. Garcia would wait as long as he could, but the arms were already overdue. So they pressed on, intending to be in Calais in time to get the packet boat to Dover in three days' time.

Madame Houblon was a pleasant enough woman, but her presence hindered any real conversation. Serafina was not altogether sorry—time enough for revelations when Charles returned to Feverel Place after seeing Garcia. But they soon discovered that the chaperon was not a good traveller, and some time had to be spent in occasional stops for her to have 'a breath of fresh air'.

Charles chafed at the delay, but there was nothing he could do about it, except pay a little more at the post-houses for first-class horses which would make up the time. In spite of their delays, they kept up to schedule, and found themselves on the road through the Forest of Crecy to Montreuil, their last stop before Calais, with a little time to spare. It was late afternoon on a very sunny day, and the carriage had become very hot. The forest looked invitingly cool, and when Madame Houblon requested them to stop Charles gave the order willingly enough.

'You don't want to stop here, sir,' said the post 'boy', a wizened, elderly man, who rode on the leader. 'It's a bit isolated here.'

'Oh, please!' exclaimed Madam Houblon. 'I am so very hot!'

'Just for a short while, perhaps, Charles?' said Serafina. 'Madam Houblon is very flushed—and I too find the carriage stifling.'

'Three minutes,' said Charles. 'But don't go far.'

The ladies descended and went a little way into the forest. Charles turned to the post boy. 'What is wrong?'

'Well, I could be mistaken, but I disliked the looks of a certain cove what was asking about an Englishman and his party this morning. Before you stopped at our place. Foreign, he was.'

Charles nodded, then took out his pistols and went to speak to John Derby, who had been travelling on the box. When he turned round again Sally and Madame Houblon were vanishing into the trees. 'Sally! Come back! I said not to go too far.' There was a wavering cry and then a yell. Sally's yell. Charles leapt through the undergrowth in the direction of the sound. As he ran he heard an exclamation and some loud swearing, followed by a sharp smack. He burst into a clearing and stopped short. Barros was standing there, holding Sally in front of him like a shield. His face was bleeding. At his side were two others, one clutching a half-fainting Madame Houblon, the other pointing a cocked pistol in Charles's direction. Sally was struggling valiantly, but Barros had a very firm grip of her, and even as Charles watched he twisted her arm up behind her. She gave a little cry and was still.

'Half a loaf is better than nothing, milord Aldworth. Garcia, I hear, left Calais some days ago. The arms are probably already on their way to South America. But there are still the emeralds. Where are they?'

'Release Miss Feverel and Madame Houblon and I will tell you.'

'Oh, no! I've been tricked once before by that sort of arrangement. The emeralds! Or first the old lady then the fiancée will die.'

'Who is going to kill them? Your henchmen? They don't look as if they relish the idea of killing defenceless women in cold blood.'

'Your fiancée is not a defenceless woman, milord. You see my cheek? I think I could kill her myself with pleasure. But the men will do as I order them. And if they will not I shall kill them too. Fetch the emeralds.'

'If you harm either of the ladies any further I swear you will die, Barros,' said Charles.

'Much as I would like to teach Miss Feverel a lesson, I would prefer to live, and enjoy the advantages the emeralds will bring. It will be a complete and painless exchange—the emeralds for the ladies, I assure you. Why are you hesitating? I am not a gentleman, so my word is not valid, eh? But I am a realist, milord. I am not as anxious to shed blood as Miss Feverel, and I am more likely to escape if it is merely a matter of theft.'

'The emeralds are in the carriage. I will fetch them if I can take Madam Houblon and one of your men back with me.'

Barros thought for a moment. 'Very well. Luis—you go.'

The man holding Madame Houblon put one arm round her and supported her as she tottered back to the carriage, followed by Charles. Here she subsided on to the seat. Charles said to the driver of the carriage and the post boy, 'Wait here. We shall be back to go to Calais as planned in a short while.' Then he said to the valet, 'Follow me at a distance. If anything goes wrong, shoot to kill—first Luis here, then Barros.'

Having thus ensured that at least one of Barros's men would be eager to see that things went well, Charles opened a small case on the seat, took out a leather bag, and walked back to the clearing. He held it up. 'The emeralds.'

Barros said, 'Take the girl, Juan!' Then he turned to Charles. 'Bring them to me.'

Glancing at Luis, Charles said to the valet, 'Remember what I said!' Then he walked up to Barros and handed him the bag. Barros up-ended it and tipped a couple of the stones out on to his hand. He smiled. 'Good! Come, Juan! Come, Luis!' Juan threw Sally to the ground and while Charles knelt down to rescue her the three Spaniards ran to their horses and galloped off.

'You must go after them!' Sally struggled to get up, but Charles put a restraining hand on her.

'Let them go! We must make all speed to Calais.'

'But, Charles——'

'Do as I say, my love.' Ignoring her protests, he lifted her up in his arms and carried her to the carriage. Here he put her carefully down, signalled to the coachman to drive off, and pulled the door shut behind him. The driver needed no urging to hurry to the next stage—he was as anxious as they to reach it. He wanted no further truck with all these foreigners.

'You're hurt!' Charles took Sally's chin in his hand and looked with concern at the abrasion on her cheek.

'He hit me. . .back,' she murmured. 'But my arm is more important. May I borrow your handkerchief?'

'What happened?' asked Charles, looking in concern at the long, deep scratch which was still welling blood.

'Juan's knife. He must have got a new one. It was stuck in his belt, and as he threw me down it caught on my arm. It's not serious, but it makes a mess. Ow!'

Charles had taken off his cravat and was binding it tightly round the wound. 'That ought to do till we get to Montreuil. But let me know if it hurts any worse.'

'Worse than what?' she asked, pulling a face. But as time went on she settled down and even slept for a little.

They spent the night at Montreuil and set off the next day for the last stage. Madame Houblon was very nervous, but Charles assured her that all would be well, that the devils had got what they had come for. A certain tone in his voice caused Serafina to look at him sharply. Her suspicions were further raised when Charles insisted on an extra guard and the inn's fastest horses, even though they were well up to time.

'To set Madam Houblon's mind at rest,' he said, when he saw Serafina looking at him. She nodded, but was not totally convinced.

They reached Calais early in the evening, and were able to go on board almost immediately. John Derby accompanied them and stationed himself outside the cabin Serafina was sharing with Madame Houblon. The only incident to disturb them was a scuffle on the quayside about half an hour before the packet sailed, when a trio of foreigners were turned away, somewhat roughly, from the gangplank.

The crossing to England was not very comfortable. A most unseasonable storm blew up, and in the end the eight leagues from Calais to Dover seemed more like twenty—and took longer. Madame Houblon, of course, felt sick almost as soon as they left the harbour, so Serafina left her to the good offices of the steward and went on deck. Huge storm-clouds were banked above, but there was still a glimmer of light in the sky to the west, and she could see Charles up at the bows. She made her way through the various bits of rope and cargo and joined him.

'You shouldn't be here. It's going to be rough, I'm afraid. Where's Madame Houblon?'

'Already succumbing. In the cabin. Charles, I must ask you. Why did you let Barros have those emeralds so easily?'

'Easily? He was threatening your life!'

'You gave in too quickly.'

He looked at her with a little smile on his face. 'I'm glad Barros didn't think so.'

'He doesn't know you as well as I do.'

'He might know me better now.'

Serafina looked at him sharply. 'The emeralds weren't real ones? But Barros looked at them! He examined them!'

'Only a couple, which you might say—rolled out to order. Fairly small ones, too.'

'What a risk! What if one of the others had come out?'

'The others were carefully restrained by a fine but very loosely tied net.'

'What were they? Glass?'

'Very good glass. The best.'

Serafina was silent for a moment, then she grew indignant. 'All the same, what would have happened to me if Barros had found out? The ambassador told you to take very good care of me! Did he know?'

'No one knew except myself, John Derby and Armand. And you were well looked after, Sally—at least, you were all the time you stayed near the coach. But you strayed away—I only took my eyes off you for a few seconds. . .'

'It was that wretched woman. She insisted on being private. . . Where are the real ones?'

'I'll tell you later. When it's all over. How's your arm? I see you have a nice black eye.'

'Black eye? Oh, never say so!' she wailed.

'Well, it's nearly a black eye, but it'll fade quite soon. Pull your hat down over it,' he said reassuringly. 'The arm is more worrying.'

'It itches, but the salve you put on it when we got to Montreuil seems to be working.'

'You'll have a scar for a bit. But it's not permanent.'

'A scar, a black eye, an abduction, my life threatened. . .and you were the one who dared to tell me that an acquaintance with *me* led to complications! But I dare say you've forgotten that.'

He grew very still. 'I think I remember everything

you've ever told me.' His fist came down on the rail. 'I wish to heaven I could see my way out of the coil I'm in,' he said violently. 'I've been such a fool. I never realised, you see. . .'

'What, Charles?'

'That I would fall in love. Really fall in love, with someone who would share. . .everything.'

Serafina almost told him then. But a desire to wait, to postpone what was bound to be a difficult scene until they were in the privacy of her home, held her back. She put her hand over his. 'It might turn out all right,' she said.

'How? How can I make Serafina so unhappy? It would be better to give both of you up.' He swore under his breath, then as a gust of wind sent the boat heeling over to one side he said, 'You'd better go in, Sally. It's dangerous. And in any case you mustn't stay out here with me any longer.'

She went to go. He drew her back and held her against him for a long moment. 'Oh, Sally, Sally!' he groaned. Then he turned her round, kissed her very gently, and then released her.

They got into Dover very late. It had always been unlikely that they could get to Hardington in one day, but the delay made it impossible. Charles was taciturn, wrapped in his own thoughts, and Madame Houblon still felt queasy. The time spent in driving along poor roads through Hythe and Winchelsea to Hastings seemed endless. They spent the night there and went on the next day to Hardington, arriving at Feverel Place in the early afternoon. Serafina was relieved to see the house full of activity—her family was back from Brighton.

'Sally! Sally! Where have you been? What's wrong with your face?' The children came running out to greet her, full of questions which the travellers ignored for the moment. They got out stiffly and Serafina helped Madame Houblon up the steps. Mr Feverel was in the hall. In contrast to the children, he appeared to be neither surprised nor delighted to see them.

Charles was businesslike. He checked that Mr Feverel had received his message, and said that he was in a desperate hurry to get to Portsmouth. Serafina introduced Madame Houblon, and said that she was on her way to London. The children's eyes were growing rounder by the minute, until their father sent them away. 'Lord Aldworth——'

'Sir, I am deeply conscious that I owe you all sorts of explanations. And I intend to satisfy you. But I have a very urgent commission in Portsmouth which cannot be delayed. Sally will explain. It will take three days only. On the third day I shall be here again, when I shall be pleased to answer all your questions. May I ask your kindness for Madame Houblon? She is very tired after our long journey and needs rest, otherwise I would have taken her with me to Brighton now. May I——dare I ask your help in getting her there tomorrow for the London Mail? She has done some service to your daughter.'

'I shall be pleased to help *madame*,' said Mr Feverel with a brief smile for the lady. Then he added somewhat grimly, 'And I shall expect you in three days' time.'

Charles said goodbye to Serafina at the door of the chaise. Their parting was necessarily brief and unemotional.

'I have left some salve for your arm with your other luggage. Keep using it. And the bruise on your face is fading. I'm sorry, Sally—for everything. At the moment I have no idea what to do and, to tell you the truth, I am glad not to have seen your sister, though it is surprising. She was not expecting us, of course.'

'I. . . She is possibly out somewhere. Our arrival was, as you say, unexpected. I am sure she will be here waiting for you when you return.'

His face shadowed over. 'Yes. Goodbye, Sally. I shan't forget these past days—ever.'

'You must go. Goodbye, Charles.'

When the chaise disappeared from sight, Serafina felt desolate. The family crowded round her again, demanding to know of her adventures, but all she could think was that Charles had gone. The idyll—for it had been an idyll—was over. Never again would she and Charles share their laughter, exchange their thoughts with such perfect freedom. She would never again experience the passion which had been aroused in her by his kisses, never know its fulfilment. When Charles returned in three days' time she could no longer postpone telling him the truth.

'Serafina!' It was her father. 'Your mother wishes to speak to you. But first I should like a word, if you please. In the small study.' Serafina did not remember when he had last used such a tone to her. Though Mr Feverel had been civil enough during the arrival and departure of Lord Aldworth, his manner had been cold. He was clearly holding fire until he could have a full explanation from his daughter's fiancé on his return from Portsmouth. But now it became evident that he was, in fact, very angry, and it was an ominous sign that the interview was to take place in the study, and not in the library. Mr Feverel's library was a place for reading, repose and discussion—never for anything unpleasant.

'We shall be brief, Serafina. Your mother is waiting to see you, and I do not wish to keep her in suspense for much longer. But first I should like an explanation of these.' He handed her three pieces of paper. Two were on official embassy notepaper, the other was from Lady Chilham. Serafina read them. The two official ones were as Charles had said. He explained that Sally was with him and safe, and in the one to London he asked Serafina to go down to Feverel Place immediately. Lady Chilham had sent it, unopened, together with a letter of her own. Presumably Charles's letter to Serafina had been opened and read by her father.

'Your mother has not seen these. Fortunately, since we have ourselves only just come back from Brighton, we did not receive them immediately—they were waiting for us here. I cannot imagine how your mother would have felt if she had known earlier that you were not safe with Lady Chilham as we thought, but had disappeared into the blue. Lady Chilham herself, as you will see from her letter, was very distressed. You had told her you were coming home here, and she had assumed that was the case. She had written to us, and was waiting to hear, when this letter arrived from the embassy in Paris. I have already written to Lady Chilham to set her mind at rest.' There was a pause. Then he said, 'What does it all mean, Serafina? And why is Lord Aldworth still of the belief that there are two of you?'

Serafina was forced yet again to confess that she had still not disabused Lord Aldworth.

'But the matter is getting out of all bounds! Now you have involved the embassy and heaven knows who else in your ridiculous masquerade! I shall have things to say to Lord Aldworth myself when I see him again, but before I do you will meet him here and tell him, without prevarication, what you have been doing. How you have managed to sustain the deception I cannot imagine. Lord Aldworth seemed to me to be a sensible man when I met him here. He is apparently not only dishonourable, but a fool as well.'

'He is far from dishonourable, Papa! The whole thing was my fault!' And Serafina gave her father a necessarily brief outline of the reasons both for her actions and those of Lord Aldworth.

Her father listened intently, then said slowly, 'I don't understand all of this—you must tell me again. But now you must see your mother. Remember that she knows nothing of these letters.'

'But what shall I say?'

'That is for you to decide, Serafina,' said her father, becoming angry again. 'You are the clever one in inventing half-truths. See if you can satisfy your mother with them. And don't upset her! And don't tell her any lies, either!'

'But Papa——'

'Save your breath for your mother! And put something on your face to hide that bruise!' He went out.

Serafina was relieved that her father's instruction gave her an excuse to go to her room. She would have a moment or two to recover some of her spirits—in her present state, her mother would have the whole story out of her in two minutes. The loss of her father's regard was a bitter blow. When the full explanation was made

to him he would see reason about her escapade in
France, particularly as it had been for a noble cause. He
would think better of Charles, too, when he learned
how much Charles had done to protect her good name.
But when that was all finished her father would still
condemn her for her unforgiveable omission to tell
Charles the truth.

When Serafina finally plucked up her courage and
sought her mother out she was pleased, even in her
distress, to see that the sojourn in Brighton appeared to
have done her a great deal of good. She was sitting by
the window, entertaining Madame Houblon. The two
were talking animatedly as Serafina entered.

'My dear!' Mrs Feverel embraced Serafina warmly,
and made her sit down on the stool in front of her.
'Madame Houblon has been telling me such a tale! I
gather you were the toast of Paris! But how is this,
Serafina? Paris? And what about the villains who
threatened your lives?'

Serafina saw that her father's warnings had been
unnecessary. Before she had had a chance to prevaricate
to her mother, Madame Houblon had revealed enough
to make it impossible. But, instead of frightening Mrs
Feverel, the news seemed to have excited and interested
her. With a look at Madame Houblon, Serafina said,
'Mama, I will tell you everything—and I have the
loveliest dress you have ever seen to show you. But
Madame Houblon must be tired, and I think we should
see her comfortably installed in her room, don't you?'

Madame Houblon was shepherded away and Serafina
was left alone with her mother.

'I think you are suffering from the journey too, my

love. I think it would be as well if we left all these explanations till tomorrow, after our guest has gone. I shall tell the others that you are to rest for now. But tell me, Serafina—is all well with you?'

SERAFINA

CHAPTER THIRTEEN

WHEN Serafina remained silent Mrs Feverel said
anxiously, 'It is not, I can see. What is wrong, Serafina?'

Serafina hesitated, then said, 'I expect I am tired,
Mama.'

'Ah, my child, don't! Don't shut me out!'

'But I promised Papa! And he is angry enough with
me!'

Mrs Feverel smiled lovingly and said, 'We both know
that your papa cossets me far too much. I am really
feeling very well at the moment. And if you were to hide
the truth from me, purely out of consideration for my
health, that would upset me more than almost anything
you could tell me. We shall leave the account of your
adventures till tomorrow. Tell me for now why you are
so unhappy.'

The tears came then. 'Oh, Mama!' sobbed Serafina. 'I
have been deceitful and sly, I know. But the punishment
is so very hard! First Charles, and now Papa.'

Slowly Mrs Feverel pieced together Serafina's somewhat incoherent confession. 'So you still haven't told
Lord Aldworth about Sally-Serafina and, though you
believe him to be as much in love with you as you are
with him, you're sure he will repudiate you when he
hears the truth. Is that it? And you are upset because
Papa is angry with you too?' When Serafina nodded
mutely she went on, 'He has some reason, my love. You

have put him in an impossible position with Lord
Aldworth.'

Serafina stared at her mother with tear-drenched
eyes. 'I hadn't thought of that! Oh, Mama, what shall I
do?'

'I think I can mend the rift between you and Papa.
But Lord Aldworth. . .the case is not absolutely hopeless, but I fear it will need time. You are right—he will
probably be hurt and very angry with you at first. But
don't despair—gentlemen need time to forget damage
to their pride, but if he truly loves you he will come
round eventually. Now, I think you should go to your
room, and I shall tell Hetty to bring you something on a
tray for tonight. Tomorrow is another day, my dear.'

Mrs Feverel had obviously done some sterling work on
her husband. After Madame Houblon had said her
farewells and departed in the Feverel coach for Brighton
the children were dispatched on a walk, much to
Angelica's disgust, and Serafina and her parents sat
together in Mrs Feverel's room. In the clear morning
light her mother could see the remains of the bruise on
her cheek, and demanded to know how it had been
caused. Serafina gave both of them a full account of her
adventures, trying as she did so to explain how impossible she had always found it to tell Lord Aldworth the
truth.

Her father listened intently, then said, 'Well, Sally, I
confess I was angry with you—and I am still not pleased
with your continued deception. But I will say that I am
proud of your courage. And invention.'

'I am full of admiration and gratitude, too,' said Mrs

Feverel, 'for the care Lord Aldworth seems to have taken for Serafina's reputation.'

'Sally's reputation,' said Mr Feverel somewhat grimly.

'It was unfortunate that the ambassador found you both at St Germain, but what a triumph it led to!' said Mrs Feverel. Then her lips twitched and she started to laugh. 'But. . .but tell me, my dear Machiavellian daughter, how did you feel when Lord Aldworth asked you to pretend to be Serafina?'

Mr Feverel started chuckling too, and at the end he embraced Serafina and said, 'I have to forgive you, Sally. The situation must have been worthy of the best Greek farces. But. . .' he grew serious again '. . .I don't envy your having to confess to Aldworth after that episode. He will feel that you made a complete fool of him.'

Behind Serafina's back Mrs Feverel was shaking her head at her tactless husband. Then she said swiftly, 'We must decide how much to tell the children. They would enjoy a somewhat expurgated version—the villains for Rafe and Michael, and the ball for Angelica. Where is the famous dress?'

Serafina jumped up and ran to fetch it, but came back a few minutes later with a downcast face. 'The box isn't with the things I brought from France! Yet I know it was in the chaise. . . Charles must have taken it with him! I'm sorry, Mama—you will have to wait till he. . .till he comes back.'

The next day Serafina was in a fever of apprehension. Charles would be here before the day was out. Her feelings were not helped by her father, who invited her to his library to discuss what she was going to say.

'I shall see Aldworth first, Sally. And I have decided to tell him that, as far as I am concerned, he is to act as he sees fit.'

'You're going to tell him about me?'

'No, I think you must do that, though, if you wish, I shall stay with you while you do. But I cannot in all honour hold him to his word to marry you. If he still wishes to do so I shall be delighted, of course.' Her father's tone did not show any great optimism.

'I shall see him alone, Papa,' Serafina said unhappily.

Lord Aldworth was prompt. He came back to Feverel Place in the late afternoon and, though he must have been travelling for a major part of the three days since they had seen him last, he looked as immaculate as ever. Serafina watched him through the window of the small parlour which adjoined the library. He was carrying her dress-box. After a moment she heard his voice in the hall, refusing refreshment, explaining that he had called in at Blanchards before coming. Then the library door shut. Serafina waited in dread for it to open again.

It seemed an age before Charles was shown into the parlour, by which time Serafina's delicate lace handkerchief was torn to shreds. When he came in she was standing with her back to the window, in the shadow of the heavy velvet curtains.

'Serafina,' he said gravely, and came over to kiss her hand.

Serafina's throat was so dry that her reply was lost. She curtsied in silence. Charles took a step back and said, 'Serafina, I have concluded from what your father has just said to me that he does not hold me to my promise to you—that your sister has already told you of. . .of what happened between us in France. I can't express to you how ashamed that made me feel.'

He stopped and Serafina said, 'Charles, I——' But he interrupted her.

'I would have given anything in the world not to have hurt you, but I believe it would hurt you much more to be married to a man who is fond of you, but. . .who is in love with someone else. Your own sister, in fact. It would be a damnable situation, and you are worthy of better than that. The same applies to Sally. Though I. . . Though my feelings towards her won't change, I don't intend to ask her to marry me either. She is young—she will no doubt forget me in time—and I. . . I will not allow myself to be a cause for distress and disharmony in such a close-knit family as yours.' A sob escaped Serafina. He said desperately, 'Oh, my dear, don't! I am not worth it! You will find someone else, I swear—someone who will love you as you deserve.'

'Charles, listen to me——' She put her hand on his arm and the Paisley shawl she was wearing fell back, revealing the long scar made by Juan's knife. He stared at it.

'What the devil. . .?' He took her chin in his hand and examined her face. 'Sally!' There was a dreadful silence. Then he said in a voice trembling with anger, 'What the hell do you think you are doing? This is not a matter for tricks and play-acting. Not for me! How dare you, Sally? How could you?'

She must tell him now—she must. Serafina opened her mouth but the words simply would not come. She shuddered and hid her face in her hands. Another sob escaped her.

'Oh, my darling, don't!' He held her to him and hugged her close. 'Can't you see the situation is impossible? I've thought about this till I was almost out of my mind, but I can't marry you after rejecting Serafina. You would have to live estranged from your family for the rest of your life. You could never be really happy again, even if we were together. But Sally——' He gently removed his hands from her face and lifted her chin. 'Sally, I can't imagine not loving you. Whatever happens you've become part of me, and it will be the hardest thing I've ever done in my life to leave you.' His eyes were on her mouth again. Her heart lurched and the world went spinning round as he kissed her. She gave a little cry and threw her arms round his neck, pressing close to him, seeking comfort, raining little kisses on his face, trying to reassure herself that if they loved each other as much as this he would—he must— forgive her. And all the time tears rolled down her cheeks.

'Sally, oh, Sally!' Charles practically lifted her off her feet as he kissed her again with desperate passion. 'If you knew how I've longed to do this! If you knew how much I adore you, how damnable it will be to part from you!' He held her tightly, then gradually his passion faded and his grasp was more gentle. Slowly he released her. 'This is doing neither of us any good. Let me think for a moment. If Serafina were to find someone else, I suppose then. . . But it might be years. Would you wait? I have no right to ask you that. And I must see your sister before I say more. My darling, lovely girl, I must see your sister. Will you fetch her?'

This was the moment. No evasion, no escape. She
swallowed and said quietly, 'My sister is here, Charles. I
am Serafina.' There was a silence while he looked at her
blankly, almost as if he suspected her of another trick.
'And I am Sally too. We are one person—we always
were.'

The silence this time was longer and even more
dreadful. Then he said, 'Oh, my God!' and walked away
from her to the other side of the little room. He stood
with his back towards her for a moment or two, then he
turned and said, 'All the time. . . Oh, God! What a fool
I've been! All that heart-searching, all the sleepless
nights. . .the agonies. That ridiculous speech I've just
made. . . You heartless, lying little jade; you were
laughing at me all that time!'

'I wasn't!'

'Of course you were!' His anger grew. 'Enjoying the
power you had over me, hugging your secret knowledge
to yourself, watching every sign of self-reproach, self-
recrimination. . . Oh, my God, I even had to persuade
you to pretend you were Serafina in France! Hell's
teeth, how you must have laughed to yourself then.
You. . . Jezebel!'

'Please, Charles——'

'Don't talk to me! Don't say one word!' His voice
trembled with the intensity of his feelings. 'You could
not persuade me to think differently, whatever you said.
Why, Louisa Paget is an innocent in comparison to you!'

'Charles!'

'Why did you do it? For some unimaginably cruel
prank?'

'No! It started because you came back early from

Vienna and caught me in that tree. I had to pretend I wasn't Serafina.'

'Ah, yes! Of course. The rich Lord Aldworth was too great a prize to risk losing?'

'Yes,' said Serafina, and could not think of another word to say. This was no time to talk of love. He was angry, so his words were harsh, but the substance of what he said was no less than the truth. She deserved his anger. He came back to her and she winced as he took her chin in a cruel grip and his eyes blazed into hers.

'Oh, that look of melting reproach! You had me fooled with that one—you were very convincing. And Sally's nobility in defence of Serafina—how did it go?' His voice mimicked hers in cruel mockery. '"Charles, you must not. . . It isn't fair—either to me or to Serafina. And we have a long road to Paris." Damn you, exercising self-control on the long road to Paris almost killed me! Did you not know that? Did it please you?' He thrust her away from him. 'Of course not—you were disappointed. Now I understand the affecting scene in the clearing, the artless disarray, the carefully dishevelled clothing. You must have been furious with those peasants! If you had succeeded in getting yourself compromised I would have no choice now but to marry you! But, thank God, though you had me so enchanted that I didn't know what day of the week it was, I was lucky.' He stood for a moment, his jaw working. 'Your father knew, didn't he? I see now why he released me from my promise. He at least has some vestiges of honour.'

'Vestige? How dare you? My father has always insisted that I should tell you. Mine was the fault, not his! Take that back, Lord Aldworth.'

'Or what? You'll break off our engagement? You are

too late—it's broken, irretrievably broken, Serafina. Or do you prefer to be called Sally? Whichever it is, it doesn't really matter—I shall not be using either again. Indeed, I hope never to see you again.' He strode towards the door.

'Charles!' He stopped, his back towards her, and she took a step towards him. 'I did love you, Charles.'

His voice was icy as he said, 'You don't know the meaning of the word. If you had loved me, you would have told me the truth long ago. Goodbye, Miss Feverel!'

He turned on his heel and walked out of the room. Serafina was fixed to the spot. She could neither call after him nor follow him. She stood there, listening to the sounds of his departure—the curt excuses, her father uttering conventional words of farewell, the sound of his horse on the drive—then silence. Her heart was filled with that silence. It spread chillingly throughout her body till she was shivering. She was still standing there, still shivering, when her father came back into the parlour.

In the weeks that followed Serafina showed true courage—not the impulsive, headlong courage which had launched her into her foreign adventures, but steady, dogged, determined courage. She devoted her time and energy to her family—accompanying the children on their walks, helping her mother wherever she could, and working with her father in his library. She sat late into the night, studying mathematics and logic and puzzling over problems of philosophy, though she never opened any of the books of literature and poetry of which she had been so fond. Her family grew to dread Serafina's determinedly cheerful conversation at mealtimes, to wince at the heartbreaking artificiality of her laughter, and to avoid comment on the pitifully small amount she ate. Mr and Mrs Feverel had many private discussions about her, but Mr Feverel deferred to his wife's judgement in the matter and was patient. Something would turn up. It had to, before his beloved daughter faded away completely.

What turned up eventually was a visitor, in the form of Lady Chilham. Mrs Feverel had succeeded in making her invitation so persuasive that Serafina's godmother had agreed to overlook the manner in which she had been treated, and had come down to give her goddaughter the chance to apologise. Which Serafina did, soberly and sincerely.

'I see what you meant, Sarah,' said Lady Chilham when Serafina left them. 'The child will soon vanish altogether. And those eyes! We must do something.'

'Is Lord Aldworth in London?'

'At the moment he is in Berkshire, but Lady Aldworth says he is coming to London soon.'

'You still see Lady Aldworth?'

'Oh, yes! She is as anxious as ever to see Aldworth married. To Serafina, too. But—I have to say it, if I die for it—I cannot see that happening.'

'Would you. . .could you invite Serafina to stay with you for a little? I know it is almost impertinent of me to ask, knowing how angry you were with her, but. . .'

'Now that you have told me more of the story I see that what she did was pardonable in the circumstances, I suppose. In any case, I would have to be an inhuman monster not to wish to help her now. But would she come?'

'I think I could persuade her. Could she return with you?'

'Of course. I'll leave it to you to ask her, then. I'll do anything you recommend.'

'What do you intend to do with the rest of your life, my dear?'

Serafina and her mother were sitting on the terrace outside Mrs Feverel's room. Lady Chilham had gone for the day to Brighton, taking Angelica with her, to see the Prince Regent's seaside pavilion.

'I. . . I don't know, Mama. I thought I would stay here with you.'

'That's a dull life for a beautiful young girl. Have you totally abandoned the thought of saving the family fortunes?'

'I cannot marry—ever!'

'For a sensible, rational girl, such as you have always claimed you are, that seems to me to be a most irrational statement. Forgive me if I give you pain, but since you have obviously given up the idea of any reconciliation with Lord Aldworth——'

'What makes you say so?' said Serafina, startled.

'You are not making the slightest push to meet him again.'

'He will refuse to meet me.'

'How can he change his mind about you while you remain in Sussex and he is eighty miles away in Berkshire? I doubt he will come to Blanchards again— not for some time anyway.'

'I couldn't face him, Mama!' said Serafina desperately.

'In that case, why not see if there is in London

another gentleman who is more like the ideal you described once—a rational, sensible man of reasonable means? Perhaps you might eventually find it possible to marry him? Believe me, it is not comfortable being a spinster without an establishment of one's own. Love is not necessary; look for respect, interests in common— all the things you mentioned once before. And if Lord Aldworth should see you. . .who knows?'

'I could not go to London, even supposing that Lady Chilham would entertain the idea, if I thought that Charles was to be there.'

Mrs Feverel bent her head over her embroidery. 'Your godmother tells me he is in Berkshire. And. . . she would like you to stay with her again, Serafina.'

So it was that Serafina came to stay once again in the house in Curzon Street.

The London season was now in full swing. Parties, balls, routs, drums, *fêtes-champêtres*—nothing was lacking. The débutantes which Lady Aldworth had once decided she could not wait for were there in force, hoping to make a suitable match—even an advantageous one. But in spite of her unhappiness Serafina still outclassed them all. Her pallor, her fragility aroused a strong desire in the hearts of the gentlemen who met her to cherish her, to protect her against the slightest breeze. And, though she no longer adopted any false poses and was her natural self, she was sufficiently subdued not to arouse comment on changes in her manner. Miss Feverel might not be the sensation of the season she had promised fair to be earlier in the year, but she was soon an accredited beauty.

She had seen nothing of Charles, nor anything of

Lady Paget. When she enquired about the latter she was told that Lady Paget had rejoined her husband, and was not expected to be back in England before the following year, when Sir Robert was due to retire from public life. The former she did not mention. Slowly a little of her heartache disappeared. She found herself taking more of an interest in the world around her, even paying visits, now quite openly, to the sights she had wanted to see. She began to believe herself cured—or curable, at least.

She met several men—young and old—who seemed interested in forming a closer relationship with the lovely Miss Feverel, and she did not reject them out of hand, as she secretly wished to do. She accepted invitations to exhibitions, balls, and all the rest, but not one of her partners could claim that he was favoured more than his rivals. Lady Chilham began to despair.

'You must not let Lord Aldworth ruin your life, child!'

'You mistake that matter, Godmother. I have very nearly forgotten him!'

'Then why don't you accept Blake? He's rich, eligible—and very attentive. What more do you want?'

'He hasn't asked me!'

'You could have him do so with a snap of your fingers! Don't think you can put me off, Serafina.'

'But I don't want to be tied down yet—I enjoy the fuss everyone makes of me. I promise to think about it—later.'

Then one evening, when Serafina was changing, Lady Chilham came into her bedroom looking distinctly anxious. 'I. . . I have to tell you, my love, that Aldworth is in London. He's been working at the Foreign Office for the past week, though no one has seen him socially. Now Laura Clifton tells me he will very likely be at Home House tonight. Do you wish to cry off?'

Serafina had grown pale but she looked calmly enough at her godmother. 'I don't think so. I have to see him again some time, I suppose. Don't worry, Godmother. I shan't create a scene.'

'I never thought that for one moment! You may have had shortcomings in the past, but lack of breeding was never one of them. Put your prettiest dress on.'

Serafina smiled wryly. Her prettiest dress would never be worn again. It was here in London because her mother had insisted on her bringing it. But it would stay in its Parisian box. With a sigh she called the maid and continued with her preparations. She did, however, put on an extremely becoming white dress with flounces of net trimmed with Chinese roses. Looking her best would give her courage. And she broke her rule and allowed Martha to put the merest whisper of colour in her cheeks. . .

Lady Chilham seemed almost more nervous than she was. 'Remember, there is no need for you to be more than conventionally polite to him, should you meet. To ignore him altogether would rouse comment. . .'

Serafina hardly heard her. Her heart was racing, and her mother's words were ringing in her ears—'How can he change his mind about you while you remain in Sussex and he is eighty miles away in Berkshire?' Well, Charles was now less than a mile away. Perhaps her mother was right. Perhaps this evening might be the beginning of a reconciliation.

Events at Home House were always well-attended—the Countess was a generous and popular hostess—and

tonight was no exception. As usual, Serafina was soon
surrounded, but all the same she caught a glimpse of a
familiar face in the crowd making his way purposefully
towards her. What was Mr Ashleigh doing in London?
When he reached her he made a charming bow, and in
the teeth of all her admirers asked her to dance with
him. To their chagrin, she awarded his audacity with a
delightful smile and went with him. As they made their
way to the ballroom he said, 'This is a real pleasure
seeing you here, Miss Feverel. But where is Charles?'

Behind her a voice said, 'Here, David. So you're in
London again!' Serafina jumped and dropped her fan.
Both men bent to retrieve it, but Lord Aldworth
stepped back immediately and left it to Mr Ashleigh to
return it. Then, looking at her with all the warmth of an
Arctic sea, he said, 'Good evening, Miss Feverel.'

She was unforgiven. David Ashleigh was looking
puzzled and embarrassed. 'Er—I don't quite. . .'

'Understand?' said Serafina with a bright smile.
'Haven't you heard, Mr Ashleigh? Lord Aldworth and I
have decided that we should not suit after all. Pray don't
let us miss the beginning of the set! Lord Aldworth.' She
nodded and walked gracefully away. With another
puzzled look at Charles Mr Ashleigh followed her.

Charles followed them with his eyes. That damned
woman still had the power to stir his heart in a manner
no other could. But he would master the feeling, if it
killed him. She was a lying cheat, and he was better off
without her. Look at her now—flirting with young
Ashleigh, who was looking as besotted as he himself had
been. Well, Ashleigh would cope—he was not likely to

be as great an idiot as Charles Dacre. No man was likely to be as great an idiot! He turned away in disgust, and left Home House shortly after.

Serafina danced gaily to the end of the set, and accepted with gratitude her partner's offer to fetch her a cool drink. He escorted her to a table in one of the ante-rooms, and disappeared. Serafina sank back with a shuddering sigh and closed her eyes. On the way to being cured? What a foolish, foolish illusion. The pain was as great as ever.

'Good evening, Miss Feverel.' That soft voice with its silky overtones. . . Her eyes flew open—Barros was standing before her.

'Señor Barros,' she said coldly. 'It should be unnecessary for me to tell you that I do not wish to speak to you. Please leave me.'

'I will—but I thought I should tell you first. . .' He switched to rapid Spanish. 'I have been making enquiries about Miss Serafina Feverel—and her sister, Miss Sally.'

'How dare you?'

'Oh, I have little to lose, *señorita*. My career is already finished. About these enquiries—do you wish to know what I discovered? I will tell you anyway. I now have a very clear picture of what happened at Carlton House and on the quay at Dieppe—though what happened between the two is still somewhat obscure——'

'The quay at Dieppe? Whatever do you mean?'

'You were there.'

'You are talking nonsense, *señor*, and I refuse to hear any more. If you will not leave me, then I must leave you.' She rose to go.

'How is your sister, Miss Feverel. Not the non-existent Sally, but the equally non-existent Arlette? I hate to remind you of the unfortunate occurrences in the Forest of Crecy, but Juan saw you there and was certain that he had seen you before. So was Luis. It seemed impossible, of course, but once we started making enquiries in Dieppe we found it was not so impossible to establish the facts.'

Serafina saw Mr Ashleigh making his way towards them through the crowds. She said disdainfully, 'I suppose you are thinking to blackmail me with these lies.'

Barros looked at her sombrely. 'I am a Spaniard, *señorita*. You have ruined me with your tricks. Now you will pay—but not in money.' He walked swiftly away, slipping with ease through the throng.

'Are you all right?' Mr Ashleigh was regarding her with concern.

'I. . .yes, thank you. Of course. The heat. . .'

'I'm sorry I was so long. There's a frightful crowd here.'

'There always is.'

He handed her a glass of lemonade. 'I thought you would prefer this to champagne. But if you would like something stronger. . .'

'No, no, this is delicious.' Serafina made an effort to pull herself together. 'How long are you expecting to be in London, Mr Ashleigh?'

'I'll be working at the Foreign Office for a month or so. I'm fortunate—I've come bang in the middle of the season.' He hesitated and said, 'I should like to call on you tomorrow, if I may? But for now I think I should find Lady Chilham and take you home. Forgive me for saying so, but you do not look at all the thing, Miss Feverel.'

'Nonsense,' she cried. 'It's only the heat. Pray do not make a fuss, Mr Ashleigh—my godmother will take me home soon, I promise you.' With that he had to be content, and it was soon evident that Serafina intended to enjoy the rest of the evening to the full. But Mr Ashleigh was no fool. As he watched her dancing, laughing and, it had to be admitted, delicately flirting, he contrasted what he saw with the girl at the ball in Paris. That girl had been totally, delightfully relaxed and natural. The London Miss Feverel was as brittle as fine glass—one breath and she would shatter.

Mr Ashleigh called the next day with a handsome bouquet, and the determination to have some private words with Miss Feverel. He persuaded her to come for a drive with him, and in no time they were bowling through the streets towards Hyde Park. In Paris they had discovered a mutual interest in books and they chatted on this topic for some minutes. Then he said carefully, 'I've been working with Charles this past week.'

'Really?' said Serafina. 'Do look at those children, Mr Ashleigh—are they not delightful?'

'He is rapidly acquiring the reputation of being the hardest taskmaster in London. And the least civil.'

'Charles?' Serafina was startled out of her pose of indifference. 'I find that hard to believe. He was always the epitome of courtesy.' Except when roused to anger with her, she thought.

'There are some who say he has been disappointed in love.'

'Mr Ashleigh,' said Serafina rapidly, 'please go no further. Lord Aldworth's feelings are no longer my concern.' Then she spoilt everything by saying wistfully, 'Is he really unhappy, would you say?'

'Very. Oh, I am aware that it is none of my business, but I have always had such admiration for Charles's work. He was very kind to me, too, when I first started. He. . .he is the best of fellows, Miss Feverel. . .'

'I know,' said Serafina, and looked at him with such misery in her eyes that he drew his breath in. 'But you cannot possibly understand—or mend—the situation between us.'

'Forgive me,' he said. 'It was an unwarrantable intrusion.'

After that he took pains to make light conversation until they returned to Lady Chilham's.

Lady Chilham's maids did not know of Serafina's determination to leave the dress she had worn in Paris undisturbed in its box, and one day one of them took it out to be pressed, so that it would be ready for use when needed. Serafina was shortly afterwards confronted in her bedroom by a weeping maidservant, who was holding the dress over her arm and something in her hand.

'I'm ever so sorry, miss. I handled it ever so gentle—but this here bead come off. And now I can't see where to put it back on! Nowhere looks right to me.' She held the bead out.

'It's all right, Martha. That didn't come off this dress at all. It's green. Give it to me and take the dress back. I'll see if I can think where it comes from.' Martha curtsied and went away, much relieved. Serafina, puzzled, examined the bead. After a moment she lifted her head and sat thinking. Then she went in search of Lady Chilham.

'Godmother, I should like you to examine this. To see if it is what I think.'

Lady Chilham got out her glass and looked carefully at the object Serafina had handed to her. 'Where on earth did you get this?' she asked. 'It's a very fine emerald!'

'I thought as much. They must have hidden the emeralds in my dress-box. That's why the box was missing when he went to Portsmouth. I must send this back to him.'

'Who, Serafina?' asked Lady Chilham patiently. 'What? I don't understand a word you are saying.'

'The emerald doesn't belong to me, ma'am. I must send it back to Lord Aldworth.'

Serafina hurried back to her room, her heart beating excitedly. From what Mr Ashleigh had said Charles was as unhappy as she. Perhaps there was hope for them after all? And returning the emerald was a heaven-sent opportunity to communicate with him. She wrapped the jewel, and penned a short note—one which was formal, rather than friendly, but which left room for him to reply kindly if he chose. The two were dispatched with a messenger to Berkeley Square.

CHAPTER FOURTEEN

THE next day Serafina waited with eagerness for Lord Aldworth's reply. When it came she ran to her room and tore open the letter. A small package fell out. Stunned, she read:

Lord Aldworth presents his compliments to Miss Feverel. He thanks her for the emerald, but is returning it herewith. He is sure that the British Government would not wish her efforts towards the success of his recent mission to go unrewarded.

The note was simply signed 'Aldworth'.

Fuming with rage, Serafina dashed off another note, equally brief:

Miss Feverel thanks Lord Aldworth for his charming letter. However, service to one's country is its own reward. She regrets that she could not possibly keep anything which reminds her of an episode in her life she would far rather forget. The emerald is returned.

After that she found it easier to move about in Society, undeterred by the fear of meeting Lord Aldworth. She had torn him out of her heart, and his place was occupied by a rage which sustained her through all their meetings. She scorned to avoid him or ignore him. She was as coldly polite as he was himself. She heard no more from Barros, and had indeed totally forgotten about him, consumed as she was by her fury at Lord Aldworth.

But Barros had not forgotten her. He had already set in motion the wheels of his revenge.

The first whispers about Miss Feverel floated through Society and were ignored. Then someone in the French embassy confirmed that Miss Feverel had indeed been in France with Lord Aldworth, apparently engaged to him. The scandalmongers did not have long to enjoy that snippet before they were disappointed to hear that Miss Feverel had, quite properly, been a guest of the Comte de Brecy and his wife, and that, though she had travelled back to England in Lord Aldworth's company, a connection of the Brecys had chaperoned her on the journey.

Quite where the next bit came from no one ever learned. But soon all London seemed to know that the Brecy story was only half true—a fabrication, invented in an attempt to protect Miss Feverel's good name. In fact—and everyone had this on good authority—she had been jaunting through France with Aldworth, unattended. A whole week, said the gossips with scandalised delight, completely alone with one of Europe's most dangerous charmers! That she had clearly failed to hold him to any promises he might have made to her was obvious—you only had to look to see that he hardly exchanged the time of day with her now. Poor, poor Miss Feverel! She was completely ruined, of course, unless Aldworth made an honest woman of her, and that, in view of his past history, seemed unlikely.

Although most of Society's disapproval was directed towards Miss Feverel, Lord Aldworth did not entirely escape blame. Until now the objects of his gallantries had all been mature women of the world, and always already married. Society had not altogether condemned him for enjoying the favours of ladies who were so obviously able to take care of themselves. But in this case it was generally felt that he had taken advantage of someone who was young, inexperienced and, not to put too fine a point on it, not very clever.

The victims of scurrilous rumours were often the last to become aware of them, and Serafina was no exception to this rule. The first she heard was when Lady Aldworth called at Curzon Street and asked to have a private talk with her. She was happy to meet the Dowager again, for she had enjoyed their exchanges in the past, but she was also surprised. Surely Lady Aldworth could not still be cherishing the hope that her grandson would marry her? It was now obvious to all London that any attentions Lord Aldworth might have paid to Miss Feverel in the past were over, and that the pair were completely indifferent to each other! Still, she received Lady Aldworth cordially, and was puzzled to find that her visitor's manner was distinctly chilly.

'How may I serve you, Lady Aldworth?' she asked when they were seated.

'You can tell me if there is any truth in what they are saying about you and my grandson,' said Lady Aldworth bluntly.

Serafina said cautiously, 'I am not sure I understand what you mean, ma'am.'

'Of course you do—don't prevaricate with me, miss! Is it true that the pair of you attended a ball at the British embassy in Paris claiming to be officially engaged?'

'Er. . .yes,' said Serafina.

'Why was I not informed of this "official" engagement?'

'The circumstances. . .'

'Is it true that you stayed for nearly two weeks with Armand de Brecy and his wife?'

Serafina said carefully, 'I stayed with Monsieur and Madame de Brecy before the ball, yes.'

'For nearly two weeks, Miss Feverel?'

There was a pause. Then Serafina said, 'Before I answer any more questions I should like to know why you are asking them, ma'am. They seem a little point-less in view of the fact that Lord Aldworth and I no longer think of marrying.'

'You left London soon after Charles—the day after the reception at Carlton House, in fact. You were next seen at the embassy in Paris, about twelve days later. It is being said in London's clubs and drawing-rooms that you spent a major part of the time in between with Charles—alone. The world thinks you were indulging in a little romantic idyll with him, Miss Feverel,' said Lady Aldworth.

Serafina could not disguise her shock. The colour left her cheeks and she drew in a deep breath.

Lady Aldworth regarded her for a moment, then said, 'You don't deny it?'

'I. . . I will tell you nothing.'

'So it's true! I would never have believed it. . .' She got up and said with undisguised contempt, 'You're a fool, girl. That's not the way to win my grandson—he can enjoy that sort of liaison any time he wishes, and has frequently done so in the past.' As she walked to the door she added, 'I thought you cleverer than that. It seems I was mistaken in your brains as well as in your character. Good morning!'

Serafina felt both frightened and angry. 'I suppose you would agree that I have a right to defend myself?'

'What can you possibly say? The world has no time for excuses. If the rumour is well-founded, you are ruined, Miss Feverel, whatever the excuse. You would only be redeemed if Charles were to marry you as soon as possible. Even if, as I suspect, you had become embroiled in Charles's mission, and the time spent in France was not your fault—even then, the world would still not forgive you. As I have already told you, I think you have been a fool.' She paused. 'I will do my best with Charles, however. He ought to do something for you.' Then she went out without waiting for any more.

Lady Chilham, who had been out when the Dowager arrived, now came hurrying in. 'Serafina! Oh, my poor girl! You must send for Aldworth immediately! Indeed, I am surprised he has not already called.'

'Why, Godmother?'

'Somehow or other what happened in France has become public knowledge—Lady Clifton was saying——'

'I already know what they are saying. Lady Aldworth was here just now, and was. . .kind enough to tell me everything. She did not trouble to hide her disapproval.'

'How dared she? If she knew what you had done for her beloved grandson. . .'

'It would make little difference. She told me I had been a fool. I think she condemns me more for that than for any possible misdemeanour in France,' Serafina said wearily.

'Serafina, this is not the time for self-pity. I shall write to your father immediately, of course. Aldworth will be here very soon, I am sure, to offer you the protection of his name—he is, after all a man of honour—but it is as well to be prepared.'

'You believe Lord Aldworth will ask me to marry him? When he thinks so little of me?'

'That has nothing to do with it. He must!'

'And if I do not wish to?'

Lady Chilham was scandalised. 'Don't be so ridiculous! It does not come into question. You must!'

'It seems that Lord Aldworth and I are about to be driven into a marriage whether we wish it or not,' said Serafina, half humorously, half in despair, as she left the room.

She went upstairs and sat at the window of her bedroom, staring at the tree outside. But she didn't see the sparrows busy among the leaves, nor the garden below, nor the sky above. She was thinking of what marriage to Lord Aldworth would be like, and contrasting it with what it could have been. Most of the time her face was sad, but a fugitive thought occasionally made her eyes glow, and a tremulous smile appear on her lips. What if. . .? What if this wretched business caused Charles to change his mind about her? If they could rediscover their lost love? Then seconds later she would frown in self-disgust. She was a mindless doll, after all! This was not the time to discover that she still loved him, would marry him with joy if he truly wished her to be his wife. Lord Aldworth had made it only too clear that such miracles did not happen.

When Lady Chilham came bustling into her room in excitement, to tell her that Aldworth was below and wished to see her, she was suddenly in a panic. This was

too soon—she had not yet decided what she should do!
She said agitatedly, 'I cannot receive him. Tell him to
come another time!'

'Serafina! Must I remind you of your predicament?
You cannot afford such luxuries. Now, make yourself
pretty and come downstairs. I shall talk to him until you
are back.'

But when Serafina entered the salon a quarter of an
hour later the two people already there did not appear
to be finding a great deal to say to each other. Lady
Chilham sat by the fireplace looking grave, and Lord
Aldworth was staring out of the window. He turned as
Serafina came into the room and gave her a small bow.
There was no warmth in his expression.

'Well,' said Lady Chilham a touch nervously, 'I am
sure you will wish to discuss this matter between
yourselves. I shall be in the next room, Serafina.'

She went out, and there was silence. Then Serafina
said, 'May I offer you a seat, Lord Aldworth?'

'Thank you, I prefer to stand.'

'As you wish—you will forgive me if I sit down.'

He began abruptly, 'Miss Feverel, I am here to ask
you to marry me.'

'Oh? Why?'

'I think you know very well. As we are both now
aware, you are far from stupid.'

'But—forgive me if I appear to criticise—you do not
sound like a man who wishes to marry me.'

'I do not. But circumstances have made it imperative.
It would be unthinkable to allow you to suffer further
censure without my taking measures to end it. I am not
unmindful of the fact that I owe you my life.' Serafina

had forgotten this completely, and it now seemed slightly irrelevant.

'Pray do not allow that trifle to influence you, Lord Aldworth.'

'It must.' He paused, then said, 'Quite why these rumours are spreading through London with such circumstantial detail I have no idea—perhaps you can enlighten me? But whatever their source I must silence them.'

'Perhaps you think I started them,' said Serafina, twin flags of anger appearing in her cheeks.

'It would be a dangerously risky stratagem. But then—you have never lacked courage.'

'I suppose it does not occur to you that I might not wish to marry you?'

'Oh, come!' he said, a sardonic smile on his lips. 'It was your aim from the beginning. Why else did you try all those tricks? And now there is every reason for you to marry as soon as you can. I recognise my obligation.'

Serafina felt as if her heart was being squeezed. The pain was intense. She said desperately, 'Charles——'

'Oh, no! No tender protestations, I beg you. I am offering marriage, not. . .not love.'

'You did love me—you said so.'

He paused, then went to the window again. Looking out, he said, 'I loved a figment of my imagination. A girl —a wonderful, laughing girl—called Sally. She doesn't exist.' He turned back. 'But Serafina Feverel exists, and is in need of my name. She can have it—on the same terms my grandmother offered at the beginning. You see, we have no need of subterfuge now. I know what you want. You know what I am offering. We shall have a plain, open bargain, with no hidden devices.'

'What is this bargain?'

'I am offering marriage and a very handsome settlement. You will provide me with an heir or two.'

'And while you may not have quite the biddable wife you were seeking, you intend to claim the freedom to live your own life otherwise. Am I right?'

'Exactly. We shouldn't need to see a great deal of each other at all, especially after the children are born. Now, have I your leave to send a notice to the *Gazette*? It should be done without delay.'

'I will not marry you!'

'What did you say?'

'I said I will not marry you. Not on those terms. Not now, and not ever!' He looked astounded, then a flush appeared on his cheeks and he started to stride towards the door. Serafina leapt up and stood in front of him. 'You will do me the courtesy of hearing me out!' She waited until he went to the window again and sat down there, leaning back and crossing his legs with an air of detached patience.

'A short while ago you adopted such a high moral tone with me, Lord Aldworth—accused me of lies and deceit, called me a jade and a. . .Jezebel. And then you removed yourself from my life in the cruellest possible fashion.'

'Forgive me for being plain with you—you deserved it!'

Serafina ignored this interruption and went on, 'At the time I had nothing with which to defend myself—even the love I had for you then could not excuse me. I *had* deceived you, I *had* lied—if not directly, then certainly by implication. In fact, though I wanted to explain why I had acted as I did, my love for you silenced me, because I felt your pain as much as my own—perhaps more. But that is over!' She stopped and swallowed. 'It is over,' she said.

He stood up and bowed. 'Bravo! This performance is worthy of a bigger audience, Miss Feverel——'

'The only audience I want is one man, Lord Aldworth. If you have any sense of justice left, you will hear me out.'

He shrugged and sat down again.

'Just now,' said Serafina, 'you as good as accused me of deliberately plotting my own downfall in order to entrap you. You have not taken the trouble to disguise the contempt you still feel for me. And yet you ask me to marry you!' She paused, then, her voice trembling with scorn, she said, 'And what a travesty of marriage you are offering!'

She now had his full attention. He looked outraged at her words. 'Travesty or not, how does it differ from the one you were so eager to enter into in the spring?'

'When I first heard of you I thought you arrogant and selfish. I told your grandmother so. But I was prepared to put up with that, to be something like the wife you required, and did my best to learn how. If. . . Sally had never materialised, I would have kept my part of the bargain, though it wouldn't have been easy.'

'Then why is the thought of it so intolerable now?'

'Because last spring I had never known what it was to be in love.'

'Oh, come——'

'And as far as I can judge nor had you. Not the kind of love which Sally and Charles once had for each other.' Serafina's voice faltered and she turned away. But she soon turned back to him and said clearly, 'This is why I reject your marriage and, indeed, despise you for offering it to me. And why I would rather leave London and retire to Sussex. Now that I know what love can be I will refuse anything less, and if I cannot have the glory, then I will not make do with the dross. The love I had for you may be over, but unless I feel that same unity of spirit with someone else I will die a spinster. Anything less would be a betrayal.'

Lord Aldworth's eyes had not left Serafina's face during this last speech. He got up, started to say something, then stopped. Then he said harshly, 'Beautifully expressed. I still think you deserve a bigger audience. But if you are sincere—I say if—I will tell you that you are fortunate to have that choice, together with the luxury of despising me. I have other obligations. If you persist in refusing to marry me, then sooner or later I will seek and find someone else. I must.'

'I will not change my mind.'

'Your family?'

'They will understand my reasons. You need not fear my father,' she added, curling her lip.

He stiffened. 'I respect your father, whatever I feel for his daughter. If you should find that Sussex is not so ready to accept you, my offer of marriage is still open. But in spite of your attempts to influence me otherwise the bargain remains the same. I too remember the glory. But Serafina has none for me.'

'You mistake me. I have no desire to revive any feelings between us. As I said before, it is over, Lord Aldworth. And I will. . .not. . .marry. . .you!'

'In that case there is no more to be said. I will see myself out, Miss Feverel. Good day.'

* * *

Lord Aldworth strode impatiently along Curzon Street towards Berkeley Square. He could hardly escape fast enough from yet another occasion when he had been made to look a fool. How dared Serafina Feverel reject him? His acquaintance with that wretched girl had been disastrous from first to last, and the sooner he was rid of all thought of her the better. He dismissed a sudden, idiotic fear that her image would never stop haunting him, destroying his sleep and making the rest of the world seem grey and valueless — as it did at the moment, dammit!

David Ashleigh was waiting for him when he got in. 'I've been doing as you asked, Charles. I've had some of our people looking into the source of those rumours about yourself and. . .and Miss Feverel.'

'You needn't be so delicate about mentioning the lady's name,' said Charles brusquely. Then, because Ashleigh had been doing him a favour, he made an effort to sound more amiable. 'Have you found anything? You must have, or you wouldn't be here.'

'There's a Spaniard — Barros. He's been poking about in France — in particular the roads from Dieppe to Paris. He has some sort of network over there. You did well to escape from them yourself.'

A sudden vision of Sally in that ridiculous straw hat, sitting on the cart beside him, her face alive with laughter, made him wince and turn away from his visitor. 'I couldn't have done it alone.'

'No. Quite.' Mr Ashleigh cleared his throat. 'He is fairly specific. About a place near Gisors. And my enquiries also suggest that Lady Paget has had a hand in spreading the rumour, too. Some of the whispers have come through her friends. She has access to diplomatic sources, of course.'

Charles was silent. He had not seriously suspected Serafina of spreading those rumours herself, whatever he might have implied to her, but it was a blow to discover that the damage had been done deliberately, by his own enemies and former friends. He was more responsible than he had thought for bringing disaster on Sally. It was a poor way to reward her for her courage and audacity. Then he stiffened as he reminded himself that Sally—the Sally he had known—did not exist.

'What are you intending to do about it?'

Charles looked up with a start. 'What's that? I'm not quite sure. There's little enough I can do about Barros. And Louisa Paget is finished anyway.'

'What about the girl—Miss Feverel?'

Charles looked at him coldly. 'I'd like to know what makes you think it is any business of yours what I do about Miss Feverel.'

Mr Ashleigh's cheeks were suffused with colour but he stood his ground. 'I. . . I am impressed with the lady. If she is ostracised by Society then it will be totally unjust, and you know it. . .sir.'

'What do you suggest I do?'

'Why, ask her to marry you! And if you do not, then I will. . .sir!'

'I did, and she refused me, my dear boy. You may have better luck with the lady. Why don't you try?'

Mr Ashleigh looked at Charles in amazement. 'I could have sworn. . . Thank you. I think I will.'

Charles felt a sudden surge of irritation, but he restrained himself, and said as warmly as he could, 'Good luck—and my thanks for your work, David.'

With relief he saw his visitor out and went back to his den.

Throughout the following week Charles had an opportunity to observe just how courageous Serafina Feverel could be. Society wasted no time in making their view of her quite plain. She was frequently ignored and sometimes even snubbed. Her crowd of admirers had vanished, but Mr Ashleigh was a constant friend and they attended several public events together. There was a sudden dearth of invitations to private ones. Miss Feverel was pale but perfectly composed. She responded with pleasure to those of her friends who continued to acknowledge her, and seemed not to see the rest. Charles, watching her for any sign of distress on the one hand, or any indication that she might be finding consolation with Mr Ashleigh on the other, saw nothing of either. He had heard from Lady Chilham that Serafina had written to her family and preparations were under way for her to travel to Sussex very soon. Charles could not wait for her to be gone from London. She dominated his life while she was in the same city. Once he could no longer see her, no longer feel himself obliged to keep an eye on her he might start to forget Serafina Feverel and to enjoy his own old life again.

The day before she was due to leave London he caught sight of her in Green Park. She was standing, somewhat forlornly, looking at the children playing, and he was hard put to it not to go over to her. But he remained where he was and stared away towards the Mall. When he next looked she had a companion—a man. He was bent towards her, his head close to hers. . . Serafina made a gesture of repudiation and started to walk away. The man caught her wrist and held her. Charles did not hesitate this time. He strode up to them both as swiftly as he could. 'Barros!'

Barros turned, and when he saw Charles he smiled. 'Good morning, Lord Aldworth.'

'Release Miss Feverel at once!'

Barros lifted Serafina's wrist then dropped it. 'Certainly,' he said. 'I have said all I wish to say.'

Charles glanced at Serafina. She looked composed, but he noticed that the knuckles of the fingers holding her reticule were white. 'What has he been saying to you, Serafina?'

The words tumbled out of her as if she was trying to rid herself of something loathsome. 'He said that we were both leaving London tomorrow, he and I, both in disgrace. That I had caused his downfall, and that he had taken his revenge. He asked me if I enjoyed being an outcast, and wondered why my father had not called you out for not. . .not offering to marry me.'

Charles swore, and then turned in fury on Barros and knocked him clean off his feet. When Barros tried to get up, Charles knocked him down again, and then stood over him, his fists at the ready. After a moment he said, 'I was right—you are vermin, Barros, best got rid of as soon as we can. No! Don't try to get up. Just lie there and listen to what I have to say. I have laid no official complaint against you for what you did in France. Any disgrace is of your own making. But, by God, I will pursue you to the ends of the earth if I hear that you have approached Miss Feverel or have mentioned Miss Feverel's name again. And unless you leave England today I shall arrange the sort of diplomatic incident your

ambassador will find not at all to his liking. Understand?
Now go!'

Barros scrambled to his feet, cursing in Spanish, and
hurried away. Charles said, 'I'm sorry you were subjected to that scene.'

He regarded her anxiously, but she replied calmly,
'You were very expert. Michael would have admired
your technique, I am sure. Thank you for rescuing me.
He is an unpleasant man.'

'Has he approached you before?'

'Yes, at the Home House, but I had forgotten. Other
things were on my mind. Thank you again, Lord
Aldworth.' She held out her hand.

'I'll see you back to Lady Chilham's.'

She said with decision, 'That isn't necessary. It isn't
far.'

Charles said firmly, 'You put me off escorting you
home once before. I am not being put off this time.'

He watched as she remembered the previous
occasion. A look of great sadness filled her eyes, and
she said, 'It would have been better if you had taken me
home then. You would have found out. . . Very well,
Lord Aldworth.' They moved towards Piccadilly.

At Lady Chilham's house she turned and offered him
her hand again. 'I do not expect to see you again. I leave
London early tomorrow.'

'How will you. . .? What will you do in Sussex?'

'What I always intended to do before my godmother
put ideas into my mother's head. I shall stay at Feverel
Place and study. Pray do not concern yourself about me.
I shall be quite happy. My family are so. . .so eager to
have me back, and all so loving. I am looking forward to

it. Goodbye, Lord Aldworth.' He had taken her hand but could not seem to let it go.

'You are not going to marry Ashleigh?'

She had been smiling, but now her expression grew cold. 'That is not your concern. But I did tell you, I believe, in what circumstances I should consider marriage. They are most unlikely to occur. Now I must go.' She drew her hand firmly out of his and vanished into the house.

Charles walked back to Berkeley Square with a curious pain in his chest for which he could not account. At last he would be free of her presence—this woman who had plagued him for so long—and now all he wanted to do was to hurry back and beg her not to go. Ridiculous! Some exercise was called for. He went to the stables and demanded his horse. But, though the gallop through the fields to the west of Hyde Park was invigorating, it did nothing to alleviate the pain.

CHAPTER FIFTEEN

LORD ALDWORTH was not finding it as easy as he had hoped to enjoy his life now that Serafina Feverel had left London. He started to consider quite seriously whether to ask for another mission which would take him out of England—but not to France. Meanwhile he found little solace in the amusements usually associated with gentlemen seeking distraction.

Some time after Serafina's departure he arrived home surprisingly early after a very dull evening gambling at White's to find that his grandmother was still up. When she invited him to partake of a glass of wine with her he accepted with alacrity. Her French common sense was what was needed to dispel his gloom. That, and several glasses of her excellent wine, perhaps.

'So,' she said, 'having turned you down, the little Feverel girl has gone to Sussex. She's a fool, but she's gallant, that one.'

'She's not the fool she made herself out to be, Grand-mère. Far from it,' said Charles with feeling.

'I think she has been foolish beyond measure recently. If you mean that when you first met her Miss Feverel deliberately hid her undoubted intelligence behind a façade of stupidity, you are right, of course. But then, I was never deceived by her. Not for long, at any rate.'

Charles was in the act of sitting down, but this startled him so much that he stood up again. 'You knew?'

'I observed, Charles. Which is more than you ever did. And I was interested in the chit. Which is more than you ever were.'

'Do you mean to say,' said Charles, his temper rising, 'that you and Miss Feverel plotted against me together?'

'Don't take that tone with me! You deserved it. It wouldn't have been hard for you to see what Serafina Feverel was really like if you had taken the trouble. She was clever about it, but not clever enough to deceive someone who really paid her any attention. Sit down. I don't like staring up at you. Help yourself to some wine first.'

Charles slumped back and gazed into the ruby tones of the wine in his glass as he thought about what his grandmother had just said. It was true. Before Christmas he had been so fascinated by Louisa Paget that he had not taken much notice of meek little Miss Feverel. Sally had said as much, too. The thought of Sally caused him the sharp, familiar pang. But, he reminded himself, Sally was Serafina. Serafina had in fact warned him herself. He gave an exasperated sigh. Even now he found it difficult not to think of Sally and Serafina as two separate people.

'What is it, Charles?'

'Why did you help her? Miss Feverel?'

'She was absolutely right for you—or so I thought at the time. The marriage you had planned—I know I suggested it originally, but that was out of desperation. I wanted you married. But it would have been completely unworthy of you, Charles. Just as Miss Feverel's planned match was unworthy of her. You each wanted something which, if it had gone as you intended, would have ruined you both.'

'She said she thought me arrogant and selfish.'

'I know. She said as much to me soon after I met her. And you were. Conceited, too.'

'Ha! If I ever was, Miss Feverel has cured me.'

Lady Aldworth bent forward. 'Then why did you ruin her? Because you wanted to teach her a lesson in return? If so, that was really unworthy—despicable, even.'

'That was the last thing I wanted, Grand-mère! I did my best to protect her. . . I didn't know where those rumours came from. I even suspected Serafina Feverel of starting them herself.'

'Why in heaven's name would she do that?'

'To force me into marrying her.'

'You can hardly still believe that to be so. She has refused you—indeed, left London.'

'I know. And I now know who was responsible, as well. But you may believe me when I say I never intended Sally. . . Serafina any harm. Those damned names!'

'Names? What are you talking about? Has Miss Feverel two names?'

Charles gave his grandmother a twisted smile. 'You don't know the half of it, Grand-mère.'

'Then tell me the whole story. We have time.'

'I suppose it really began when I came back unexpectedly from Vienna after Christmas. . .'

Time passed, and the candles burned low and were renewed, but the Dowager still sat listening as Charles unfolded the tale of Sally and Serafina. She quite often laughed out loud at the girl's audacity as he went on, and Charles suddenly found himself laughing with her. He began to enjoy it, even to feel admiration at the skill with which Serafina had played one part against the other, how she had manipulated her characters. And, what was more, he began to realise how many clues there had been to what she was doing, if only he had thought enough of Serafina to notice them. But thoughts of Sally had so dominated him that Serafina had remained a dim shadow, a pale imitation of her sister.

When he came to the story of his capture, and Sally's impulsive and desperate journey to France, his grandmother grew quiet. She chuckled once or twice as he described how Sally had bewitched Juan and Luis, but then grew serious again, interrupting him to exclaim, 'But she was magnificent! What courage! What enterprise! She did all this for you?'

He nodded. Somehow in all the drama that had followed he had lost sight of the real heroism Sally—no, Serafina!—had displayed on that boat in Dieppe. In his feeling of humiliation later he had even resented the fact that he owed her so much. Charles began to feel ashamed—he had been much less than just to this girl.

'Go on, go on,' said his grandmother impatiently. He realised that he had fallen silent, and resumed his narrative.

The impossibility of sending Serafina back, the decision to take her to Paris and the subsequent wanderings through the leafy lanes of the Vexin—these were touched on, but how could he convey the magic of that journey, even had he wished? Sally's spirit, her gift of listening, her laughter—all Serafina's of course. When he came to the point at which he had asked Serafina to pretend to be Serafina, he thought his grandmother would choke, she laughed so much. His own lips twitched, and he remembered how Serafina had laughed—if only they could have shared the joke then! But she had afterwards cried as if her heart would break.

Serafina's triumph at the embassy ball was already known to Lady Aldworth. She sat there with a satisfied smile on her face and said, 'I knew it! She's the very one for you!'

There was a sudden silence. 'She won't have me, Grand-mère.'

'You must have been remarkably maladroit when you asked her, Charles. What? This girl goes through all these perils for you, shows you her devotion in a thousand different ways, and then you believe her when she says she won't marry you? Of course she will!'

'I have hurt her too badly. You don't know. . .'

'Tell me.'

Charles reluctantly described the scene in the small parlour at Feverel Place. His grandmother's face grew more and more disapproving and she was finally so shocked that she said, 'What made you behave like that to a girl who had done so much for you, and who loved you?'

'She said she loved me. But how could I believe her? If she loved me so much why didn't she tell me about herself sooner?'

'When?'

'Why not at the beginning?'

'You would have dismissed her as a possible bride immediately. I never knew anything about Sally, of course, but I myself didn't tell you that Miss Feverel was clever for exactly the same reason. No, Charles, she wanted to make a good match and that would have destroyed it. Her reasons at that time were no more or less honourable than your own, and equally hard-headed. She didn't love you then.'

'Then why didn't she tell me later—in France?'

'It would have been better if she had, certainly. But how could she be sure that you would not reject her out of hand—as you rejected her when she did finally tell you—and leave her to fend for herself? Or worse, force her to travel with you all those miles in mutual antipathy?' She paused to let this sink in. 'Then later, once you reached Paris, you yourself suggested the double deceit of Sally pretending to be Serafina. I suppose by then she had decided to wait till you got home before provoking what was always bound to be a very awkward situation.'

Charles stared at her. This was a point of view he had never considered.

His grandmother looked at him shrewdly, then went on, 'But why are we conducting this inquest? Do you honestly believe she lied when she said she loved you?'

'I don't know. . . I didn't know what to think. And then when I saw her in London. . .'

He went on to describe his subsequent behaviour in London and Lady Aldworth exclaimed, 'I am no longer surprised that she refused you! I would have myself! But you are not normally so cruel, Charles. Why did you treat Miss Feverel like this?'

Charles got up and offered his grandmother some wine, then poured a glass for himself. He drank deep, then said, 'I thought at the time I was justified. But I now think I really wanted to hurt her. I thought she had been laughing at me all the time we had known each other, and I wanted to make her hurt as much as I was hurting. Not very noble, was it? And certainly not the action of a gentleman.' He drank again. Lady Aldworth watched him, a troubled frown on her face. This was a Charles she had never before seen. The Charles she knew was handsome, debonair, light-hearted except in his work, confident in his attraction for women, and, it had to be admitted, somewhat ruthless. His commitment to his career was a redeeming feature, but though she had felt that somewhere there was a different Charles, one capable of devotion, almost the only evidence she had ever seen of it was the love he bore her, his grandmother. Now she *was* seeing that Charles, but he was deeply unhappy.

'What are you going to do, my dear?' she said gently.

'What can I do? Tell me!' He suddenly raised his head and she was shocked at the look in his eyes. She hastened to comfort him.

'You must go to see her.'

'I can't!'

'You must! Go down to Blanchards. From what you tell me the house is comfortable, but much still needs to be done outside. See to that, and wait for the moment. Then, when you think you are ready, call on her.' She leaned foward and put a wrinkled hand on his knee. 'You have offered her settlements and an establishment. If that is all you still have to offer, she may refuse you again, Charles. You will have to think of something else she might want.'

Charles delayed only long enough to put one or two urgent affairs in order before going down to Sussex. His grandmother saw him the night before he went and embraced him warmly.

'You will be successful, Charles. I can feel it in my

bones. And then you and Serafina will live at Aldworth, and I shall see my great-grandsons there at last. Good luck, my darling.' When he reached the door she said, 'And when you are down at Blanchards make sure it will be absolutely ready for your stepmother and the rest! It's time we were rid of the screech-owl, too. We shall want some peace and privacy at Aldworth!'

Blanchards looked much the same. One or two of the trees were turning, but it was still high summer. He had seen the agent in London, and work was in hand on the gardens and fields round the house. The travelling coach was still in the coach-house. He roamed about the house restlessly. It was too soon to go to see Serafina, but there was nothing else he wished to do. He made up his mind to go for a ride.

Up on the downs there was a fresh breeze. He rode to the top and gazed down on the English Channel—Beachy Head to the left, Newhaven down below him on the right. How had Sally found the courage to board that boat, going off into the unknown?

'Hello!'

He turned round. Rafe and Michael were behind him, each on a sturdy pony. Michael was looking embarrassed.

'Hello, Rafe! Michael.'

Michael flushed and said brusquely, 'Good afternoon, Lord Aldworth. Come, Rafe!'

'No wait! Don't go—I'd like to talk,' Charles said.

'I'm sorry—we have to get back——'

'That's a whopper! We've got all afternoon,' said Rafe. 'And I want to ask Lord Aldworth about those villains. The ones that gave Sally a black eye. Have they been punished for their dastardly deeds? She's not been the same since, you know.'

'Oh, come on, Rafe! You talk too much. Lord Aldworth can't possibly be interested in gossip about us.'

'I assure you I am. What is this about your sister? She isn't ill, is she?'

'She's perfectly well, thank you,' said Michael, scrupulously polite. 'It's just that she's a bit quieter than she used to be.'

'It's Mr Ashleigh. She's always quieter when he's been here.'

'Hold your jaw, Rafe!' said Michael fiercely.

'Does Mr Ashleigh often visit her?'

Michael's lips were firmly shut. He was obviously not going to say any more. Fortunately Rafe was less discreet.

'He's been twice. And Sally cried a lot after he had gone. I don't think he ought to come any more.'

At this Michael grew even redder and said gruffly, 'I don't think you ought to listen to what a little boy tells you about his family, Lord Aldworth. It's cheating, a bit. Anyway, I. . .we thought you didn't care about her any more. And now it really is time we went.' He gave a little nod and caught Rafe's bridle.

'Will you tell your sister that you have met me here?'

'No,' said Michael briefly. 'And nor will Rafe unless he wants a thrashing.' Then, amid angry protests from his brother, he firmly led the ponies away.

Their departure left Charles in a thoughtful mood. So David Ashleigh had taken him at his word! He supposed it was to be expected—Serafina and David had much in common, though he would have said that David was a little staid for Sally's more exuberant moments. But perhaps she no longer had those? The boys had said that she was quieter. Perhaps she and Ashleigh were even better suited than he had thought? And the boy had said that Serafina was always upset when Ashleigh left. Charles set his horse off at a gallop—it appeared that he had come down to Sussex not a moment too soon. . .

At Feverel Place Serafina was sitting in her favourite place on a stool by her mother. Her father was away at a conference and the three Feverel ladies were having a comfortable, non-intellectual chat, such as Mr Feverel deplored.

'I hear that Hartley Pennyworth is married.'

'Yes—to Lizzie Beaminster, of all people,' said Mrs Feverel. 'It seems to be working. Lizzie is hardly a match for Mrs Pennyworth senior, but she makes no attempt to compete.'

'You should see Hartley, Serafina!' cried Angelica. 'He's getting fatter by the minute, and his air of complacency. . .!'

'Good luck to him. I knew Lizzie Beaminster was the one for him.'

'And what about you, Serafina? Mr Ashleigh seems very eager. He is a pleasant young man, and very knowledgeable.'

'I like him,' said Angelica eagerly. 'He's quite good-looking, though not as handsome as——' she stopped.

'Lord Aldworth.' Serafina finished the sentence for her. 'No, he isn't.'

Mrs Feverel and Angelica spoke together. 'Did you know that Miss Twitch——?'

'Papa says that the rainfall this year——'

Serafina smiled and said, 'You are both darlings. But you should stop trying to cosset me. And I wish you would abandon these attempts to marry me off, and realise that I intend to be the best maiden aunt the Feverel family has ever seen. All I shall need is lots of nieces and nephews! So, Angy, as a first step, let's start training you for your introduction to Society. That's something I can do to perfection—I can even deal with an ambassador's ball. Why, perhaps I could give classes in the neighbourhood, with a recommendation—"as seen in Paris"!'

'One of the family working for a living is enough, Serafina. Though Gabriel seems to be enjoying his stint as librarian at Arundel. I think he will be quite sad when he goes back to Oxford in October. But what a relief that his debts are being paid off—slowly, but still. . .' Mrs Feverel paused. 'But can you imagine what the neighbourhood would say if Sally Feverel were to set up as an arbiter of good behaviour? Mrs Pennyworth senior would have apoplexy.' The three Feverel ladies burst into laughter.

When Michael and Rafe came in from their ride it was clear that Rafe was big with news—news which Michael was determined to suppress.

'What is it, Rafe?' asked Serafina with a smile.

'Oh, it's nothing,' said Michael. 'Don't encourage him, Sally.'

'It is, it is!' cried Rafe excitedly. 'But Michael says I'm not to tell you.'

'That's not very fair, Mick—you know how impossible it is to keep Rafe from telling everything he knows. Aren't you being a trifle unkind?'

Michael gave a sigh, and with a stern look at Rafe he said, 'It's only that Blanchards is occupied again.'

Serafina lost a little of her colour. 'Is it being let, then?'

'No, it's him!' shouted Rafe, skipping out of Michael's reach. 'Lord Aldworth! And I wanted to ask him about the emeralds and those men. But Michael wouldn't let me. What's the matter, Sally?' His voice faltered, and he turned to his mother. 'Why is Sally looking like that?'

Michael advanced on Rafe with a menacing air, took his brother by the ear, and dragged him out of the room. Mrs Feverel put a hand on her daughter's shoulder.

'It's all right, truly!' said Serafina. 'Angy, do go out and stop Mick doing whatever he's threatening to do to Rafe. He's only a little boy—he doesn't know how to keep secrets. Tell Mick I sent you.' Angelica went out and Serafina let out her breath in a shuddering sigh.

'Serafina——'

'Pray don't worry, Mama. I. . .was stupid. It was a shock. I'm perfectly all right now. Really.'

There were sounds of argument outside the door. Rafe burst in and ran to Serafina, hiding his head in her skirt. 'I didn't mean to upset you,' he sobbed. 'I didn't know you'd look like that. I'm sorry, Sally.'

'What nonsense you're talking, Rafe. Look like what? See, I'm quite my usual self, and to prove it I'm going to tickle you any minute now!'

As far as the family was concerned, Serafina remained her normal composed self for the rest of that day. She was quiet, but then she very often was nowadays. But in fact the tension within her increased by the hour. Charles was once again quite near—near enough to call at any moment if he chose. Why had he come to

Sussex—was it merely to see that the work on Blanchards was finished? Surely he could have done that through his agent? Her heart raced as she thought that he might have come down to see her. . . But the day passed without a sign of Lord Aldworth. She spent the night that followed lying awake, wondering, hoping, despairing. The pain in her heart might have dulled during the weeks since their parting, but it had never gone away. Poor David Ashleigh's visits to Sussex were merely a reminder of Charles and what she had lost, and each time he left the pain was worse for a while until it dulled again. She fell asleep towards dawn, and when she woke there were tears on her cheeks.

Her case was not helped by the anxious looks directed at her over the breakfast-table. The family had been a wonderful support to her since her return from London, but sometimes their concern oppressed her. She announced that she would spend the day in the library, preparing some notes for her father, and, reassured by her air of calm, they left her to do as she wished.

She spent the first part of the morning on her notes without, in fact, achieving very much. But then, when the sun got higher, she decided she would work outside. She gathered up her book and notepad, and a couple of apples from the kitchen, put them into a bag together with a small cushion, and went out into the garden. But the sunshine and fresh air enticed her further, and she wandered down the drive as far as the old oak. Here she stopped. It was here that the Sally-Serafina saga had started all those months ago. . . Her mind skittered away from the memory like a frightened animal, and it was suddenly difficult to breathe. She would think of something else. The tree had always been a favourite

place for her. She had hidden here so many times to
escape the attentions of Hartley Pennyworth. She
smiled—he wouldn't be calling again. Poor Lizzie
Beaminster!

As she looked up through the leaves she could see
glimpses of the branch which had been her refuge then.
It was tempting. . . No one would know, no one would
find her. And she could see if. . .if anyone came up the
drive. In two minutes Serafina was safely ensconced
with her apples and her work, her back comfortably
cushioned against the trunk, her legs stretched out along
the branch. She worked for a while, but the sun was
warm, even among the leaves, and Serafina's sleepless
night caught up with her. Her eyes gradually shut, and
she dozed.

Charles had woken that same morning with a feeling of
excitement and dread. Today he would visit Feverel
Place. Serafina was at home, he knew that. Perhaps she
would agree at least to see him, to give him an
opportunity to tell her how he regretted what he had
done in the past. Then, later, when he had visited her
once or twice more, he might be able to overcome her
prejudice against him, convince her that he had
changed. . . But what about Ashleigh? Perhaps Serafina
was already experiencing with him that—what had she
called it?—that 'unity of spirit', without which she
would not marry. His blood ran cold at the thought. He
must see her.

He rode along the lanes, so engrossed in considering
what he was going to say that he had reached the
beginning of the drive which led to Feverel Place before
he realised. Here he reined in. This was the oak tree out

of which Sally had fallen all those months ago. She had knocked him flat then and, he thought whimsically, he had never truly been his own master since. One thing was certain. If by some miracle Serafina Feverel did agree to be his wife, he would never be wholly his own master ever again. Nor did he wish to be. Marriage to Serafina would be like nothing he had ever envisaged — more exciting, more unpredictable, more all-consuming. Certainly nothing like the contract he had twice offered her. His brows drew together. Would she forgive him?

An apple dropped out of the tree and rolled towards him. An apple? In an oak tree? He peered up through the foliage and had a tantalising glimpse of a figure perched on a branch some way up. Its legs were stretched out along the branch and it was leaning comfortably against the trunk of the tree. He dismounted and moved nearer.

'Sally!'

The figure gave a start and leaned over to look down. Another apple dropped down, followed by a book. 'Oh! It's you! Who told you I was here?'

'I found you for myself, Sally-Serafina.'

'Why are you here?'

Charles looked up at the face framed in the leaves — perhaps a little thinner than it had been, perhaps a touch paler, but infinitely dear, incomparably lovely, the embodiment of everything he now desired. The carefully prepared speeches were forgotten. 'I love you,' he said simply. 'I couldn't keep away.'

A delicate flush appeared on Serafina's face. 'Oh!' she said softly. There was a short pause, then her eyes began to sparkle. 'Is that all?'

'I want you to marry me.'

'To bear your heirs while you live your own life?'

'Certainly!' It was his turn to smile as Serafina looked a little disconcerted. Then he added, 'But my life will be your life too, my heart. One life—together.'

'Oh, Charles!' Serafina stared down at him, smiling mistily, an expression of wonder and delight on her face.

They gazed at one another wordlessly, then Charles said, 'Er. . .this is very difficult. Shall I come up to you, or will you come down to me? It's very awkward proposing when I can hardly see you.'

'I'll come down. Oh, Charles!' Serafina started to climb down, but as soon as she was within reach Charles caught her and lifted her down the rest of the way. He didn't release her, but held her close.

'Sally?'

Serafina flung her arms round his neck and pulled his head down to hers. 'Serafina wanted to do this so often, Charles, but she never dared.' She kissed him, and in that kiss was all the deep commitment of Serafina, all the exuberance of Sally.

He laughed unsteadily. 'I never thought you'd forgive me. . .'

'Shh! It's forgotten. We both made mistakes. But that's all over. Now it's just Charles and. . .and who? Sally or Serafina—which do you want?'

'My darling, I love them both! I can't live without either! But neither of you has yet said that you'll marry me.'

'Then you may have us both, Charles,' said Serafina, with a generous wave of the hand. 'Sally for weekdays and Serafina for best. We'll both marry you.' They kissed again, but when Charles would have released her Serafina said, 'No, wait! That one was for Serafina. Now you have to kiss Sally.'

'How about Cherubina?' murmured Charles after a minute or two.

'Cherubina?'

'Wasn't there a Cherubina? Or was that just Sally's real name? I've forgotten, but it doesn't matter—I'll kiss her too.'

Laughing and murmuring to one another, they passed an ecstatic few minutes before Serafina said, 'My goodness, what would Mrs Pennyworth say? Such behaviour! And I was just thinking of setting up to be an arbiter of propriety, too! Allow me to tell you, Lord Aldworth, that you have a shockingly deleterious effect on my behaviour.'

They started walking up the drive. They had not gone far when they were greeted by shouts from Rafe, who came hurtling down from the house and nearly knocked them over. 'Sally! Sally! You're with him! I knew it would be all right.' He did a kind of war-dance round them both, then said, 'Race you up the tree, Sally!' and raced off to the oak tree, where he hopped about impatiently.

Serafina looked enquiringly at Charles, who grinned and nodded. With a whoop of sheer delight, Sally picked up her skirts and chased off after Rafe.

GET 4 BOOKS AND A MYSTERY GIFT

FREE

Return the coupon below and we'll send you 4 Legacy of Love novels absolutely FREE! We'll even pay the postage and packing for you.

We're making you this offer to introduce you to the benefits of Reader Service: FREE home delivery of brand-new Legacy of Love novels, at least a month before they are available in the shops, FREE gifts and a monthly Newsletter packed with information.

Accepting these FREE books places you under no obligation to buy, you may cancel at any time, even after receiving just your free shipment. Simply complete the coupon below and send it to:

HARLEQUIN MILLS & BOON, **FREEPOST**, PO BOX 70, CROYDON CR9 9EL.

NO STAMP NEEDED

Yes, please send me 4 Legacy of Love novels and a mystery gift as explained above. Please also reserve a subscription for me. If I decide to subscribe I shall receive 4 superb new titles every month for just £10.00* postage and packing free. I understand that I am under no obligation whatsoever. I may cancel or suspend my subscription at any time simply by writing to you, but the free books and gift will be mine to keep in any case.
I am over 18 years of age.

1EP5M

Ms/Mrs/Miss/Mr _____

Address _____

_____

_____ Postcode _____